TANGO

DARK WATERS
BOOK 4

J.L. DRAKE

TANGO
DARK WATER SERIES

Cover & Interior Design by Spellbinding Design

Editing by Lori Whitwam

CAST OF CHARACTERS

- **Daniel:** Cole's father, first generation Blackstone. Married to **Sue,** Cole's mother.
- **Edison:** Cole's grandfather. Married to **Meg,** Cole's grandmother.
- **Abigail "Abby":** Mark's adopted mother, Cole's childhood nanny, house aide. Sister to **June.**
- **Dr. Reid Roberts:** House psychologist. Dating Abby.
- **General Frank Brandon:** Blackstone contact for the Army. First generation Blackstone member.
- **Zack:** First generation Blackstone member.

FAMILIES

- **Cole:** Owner of the Shadows safe house. Leader of the Blackstone special ops team. Married to **Savannah**. They have two kids, **Olivia** and **Easton**.
- **John:** Blackstone member. Married to **Sloane.**
- **Mike:** Blackstone member. Married to **Catalina.** Daughter **Gabriella.**
- **Keith:** Member of Blackstone. Married to **Lexi.** They have two kids, **Brandon and Reagan.**
- **Mark:** Blackstone member. Married to **Mia.** They have a set of twins, **Liam** and **Ethan,** and a daughter **Tabby.**
- **Paul:** Blackstone member. Deceased.
- **Dell:** North Rock member. Dusk Safehouse in North Carolina.

- **Davie:** North Rock member. Dusk Safehouse in North Carolina.
- **Steve Chamness:** North Rock member. Dusk Safehouse in North Carolina.
- **Denton Barlow:** The American. Deceased.

ANIMALS

- **Goats:** Friendly reminders of home.
- **Chickens:** Annoying and always in the way.
- **Scoot:** A-hole house cat.
- **Butters:** Mark and Mia's Husky.
- **Tripper:** John and Sloane's German shepherd.

To anyone who chose to do that right thing, no matter the cost.

ONE

ERIC

"P aul?" Frank repeated, and I squeezed my eyes shut and cursed. Everything was heading south so quickly I could barely keep up. "What's happening?"

"The subject…" The words were like a ball of acid in my throat that slowly dripped down into my chest and burned. "The subject is down—" A cry ripped through me. "Jesus, Frank," my voice quivered, "Lexi's dead."

Silence.

Frank made a sound, and I knew it had hit him, then he cleared his throat and was back to business.

"Have you been compromised?" His normal voice commanded and helped ground me.

"Yes."

"Pull the pin, take nothing. Get out. You know where to go. And Paul…"

"Yeah?"

"No man left behind. You'll be met. Do whatever's necessary to get both of you out."

"Roger that." The line went dead.

I glanced at my phone for a moment then shoved it back into my pocket as I desperately tried to clear my head. I needed a way out. I needed to blend in with the locals, and that wouldn't be easy with Lexi. I knew there would be police everywhere after the convoy was attacked.

I bent down and scooped Lexi's limp body into my arms and cradled her close to my chest. I raced down the street in the opposite direction from the one Alejandro had taken. Once I got to the end of the alleyway, I risked a quick look around the corner but quickly whirled back around, slamming my back to the wall. Two police cars crawled by with their lights flashing.

"Stay off the streets," one yelled in broken English over a speaker. "Go inside. It is not safe for you."

I inched forward, shifting Lexi in my arms, and saw a crowd of young people who looked like tourists, standing in front of the nightclub trying to catch a peek at what was going on. Clearly, the sound of bullets in the distance didn't get through their drunken revelry. Blood from Lexi's stomach wound made my hands slippery, and I fought to hold her tight against me. This wasn't going to work. If one person saw the blood, they'd scream. I sat her against a wall behind a trash bin and peeled off my bloody dress shirt, then whisked out into the busy street. A vendor was preparing to close, and I quickly caught the door as he went to shut it.

"Please," I said in Spanish, "I need a jacket, or a sweater, a shirt, just something. My friend got sick all over me and I need something clean." When the man shook his head, I fished out a bill. "This for anything you've got." He turned to a shelf and tugged out a t-shirt and a ratty old blanket. He grabbed the bill and tossed me the stuff then yelled at me to get out. I was happy to oblige.

Keeping my head low as I pulled the shirt over my head, I hurried back to where I'd left Lexi and gently pulled her arms through the sleeves of my suit jacket and fumbled my way through the buttons. I pushed the ratty blanket inside the jacket to try to camouflage the blood.

"I'm so sorry, Lexi." I tucked her hair behind her ear and fought the nausea that wanted to come up. Suddenly, Keith's face flashed in front of me, and I heaved over to the side and purged what I had in my stomach. Mostly liquor. More sirens could be heard, and I knew I needed to move. The city wasn't that big.

Chatter from the crowd in the street had me gather up Lexi again. The group of partiers were loud and obviously had had a lot to drink, which would serve my purpose well. Some had their phones out recording a patrol car that was stopped a few blocks down. Others carried tequila or beer bottles as they milled about. The officers were placing barricades to block off a street. Fuck me, the entire city was going to be locked down. If I didn't get out of here soon, I'd be stuck.

I quickly darted across the pavement and joined the tequila-soaked crowd. Lexi's arm dangled, and I quickly tucked it up with a comment to a couple girls about my drunk woman.

"Any idea what's happening?" I stepped closer as I used their bodies to hide me from the police. I had to concentrate hard to fit in and not let my mind go dark.

"No," one girl looked at me, clearly half in the bag, "but there's police everywhere."

"Do you guys know where the blue hotel is?" I played dumb. "My girl's had way too much to drink."

"No, sorry, I don't." One girl quickly shut me down, but the other pulled out her phone.

"Do you remember the name of it? I could look it up for you."

"I feel like an ass, but no, I don't." I tried to look like a dumb tourist and shrugged with a sloppy smile. I hoped I looked like I'd had a few too many myself.

"Shit, bro, was that gunshots?" One tuned in, and I hoped to hell they didn't start to freak out or run.

Another police car came by and slowed as they went by us. I tilted Lexi's body like I was placing her down on her feet when one guy glared at me.

"Dude, she's too wasted to walk, just carry her ass home." Then the guy turned and wrapped an arm around his girl's shoulders.

"That's what he's trying to do." The girl shoved the guy's arm away.

I scanned the street ahead, and the guy must have caught my uneasiness.

"Take your problems somewhere else dude." I didn't like the look he gave me, and I backed off. His other friends seemed to be picking up on the uneasy vibe. Great, just what I needed right now, a scene. I swallowed hard as I felt Lexi's blood soaking into my t-shirt. I didn't dare look down and give them a reason to follow my gaze.

"I mean no harm. I'll ask a local for help." I stepped back. Just then I spotted Filippo as he raced around a corner and more police lights lit up the building in front of us. They were closing in. It was now or never.

"Let's bolt. This shit is getting nuts," one guy called to his friends, and they all started to walk away.

Normally, I was more resourceful, but given that my head was stuck in a loop, and my brother's dead wife was in my arms, I found it impossible to get a clear thought.

I whirled around and ducked under an awning to get out of sight.

"Eric." I couldn't miss that smooth, whiskey, billionaire voice. "My friend, you look like you could use a hand." Damn. I wondered how long he'd been watching. "You look like shit," he added. Grim's eyes darted to Lexi in my arms then back up to me. The tattooed cross just below the corner of his eye twitched. It was obvious he knew shit was going down.

"Grim—" I started to speak, but he shook his head

and pressed the button on a key fob. I saw the lights flash on a car. Then he stuck his fob into my jeans pocket, as both my hands were locked around Lexi's body.

"Black Lincoln across the street." He turned his back and walked inside the building without even so much as a hesitation.

I didn't miss a beat either and bolted in the direction of the car. Shouts came from down the street, and I worked quickly. Carefully, I lay Lexi on the back seat, jumped in the front, and, against all my instincts, eased slowly onto the street, thankful the windows were tinted as black as night.

I watched as two police cars rolled up to the building Grim went in, and officers raced inside. I let out a heavy breath and glanced back at Lexi. I knew I just saved the both of us in very different ways.

I drove to the outskirts of town, constantly watching my mirrors. I needed to pick up the pace. It wouldn't be long before the entire Cartel would realize Lexi and I were nowhere to be found and would be on our trail. I wondered how Castillo would take the news that he'd been working with a former Blackstone agent for over a decade. There was a part of me that wished I could have been a witness to that moment. I'd have liked to have watched as his reputation was ripped away from his nasty hands and watched how others turned their backs on him.

The sun was just up when I pulled into a gas station. I looked around at Lexi. She was as pale as paper, and I reached back and gently brushed my hand down her arm.

Once again, I apologized for not being able to keep my promise to her.

I turned the engine off and pulled the blood-soaked blanket out of the suit jacket and folded it over Lexi as though she slept then stepped out of the car and took a quick scan of the place. A chicken truck was parked in front of me. *Perfect.* I pulled out my phone, cleared the call log to Frank, and tossed it in among the clucking hens.

Years ago, before I left for Mexico, Frank had given me some advice. Find myself a safe place to hide what I might need in case I ever needed to flee. I thanked him internally as I went inside.

The owner of the gas station barely looked at me as he dropped a ring of keys on the dusty old counter. I headed without comment toward the back stockroom and unlocked the door. I'd chosen this place for a good reason. Most people would take one look at the place and want to get in and out as fast as possible. The old guy and I had made an agreement years back, and I had a fancy safe installed under the floorboards that could only be opened with my fingerprint.

After the door was locked behind me. I grabbed a book bag that was slung on a chair and emptied out the contents on the floor. Very aware I'd left Lexi out in the car, I tried to hurry. A sweatshirt hung on a hook nearby, and I pulled it on over my t-shirt. It was small, but it would do. I glanced around. I wanted to be careful not to leave anything behind that could connect me to the old man outside, and that included fingerprints. I ran my stained fingers under the rusty tap and did my best to wash the tacky blood away. My fingernails were a dead giveaway, though, and showed I was deep into something bad. I grabbed a rag and made sure to wipe everything I touched.

I strained to listen in case there was anyone around. Satisfied, I pushed the deep freeze over a few feet, then used the heel of my shoe to jimmy a floorboard to loosen the old nails. I flipped open my pocketknife and popped the nails free. The safe was exactly how I'd left it. I thumbed at the protective flap that hid the screen and placed my middle finger against it. It scanned my print, and a satisfying click vibrated under my finger. With a sigh of relief, I reached inside and pulled out four passports and four stacks of cash that went with each passport's country. I was even happier when I removed the weapon and two magazines of ammunition. I took out the burner phone. I knew it was already programmed with a single number. Underneath that was a small, square, black box.

I stuffed everything into the bag, tucked the gun into my waistband, and pushed the freezer back in place. I quickly wiped everything with the damp, greasy rag. I hoped it was enough.

Slowly, I opened the door a crack and looked around. The place was quiet. I made eye contact with the owner as I walked through the office, and he gave me a slight nod that the coast was clear.

"*Gracias.*" I grabbed a power bar, a battery, and a couple bottles of water and placed some money on the counter along with the keys he'd given me. "I'll send my last payment next month. Stay safe."

"You too, *mi amigo.*" He tucked the money in his shirt pocket and went back to watching his game.

I got back in the car after a quick scan of the area and headed north toward Nueva. The power bar and water helped clear my head, and now I just needed to make sure I got Lexi into the right hands before anything else happened.

"Jesus, if the Cartel got their hands on you…" I muttered like she could hear me. "They're ruthless creatures. It wouldn't matter you're already gone." I shuddered at the thought and was even more determined to get her body home or die trying.

I rolled the window down, and the cool air brushed my face. I rubbed my temples to relieve the headache that had settled behind my eyes and let my mind drift into a memory.

Everything hurt, and I wanted to stay in my black bliss, but faint voices forced me to the surface…
"Paul, I need you to open your eyes." Two Franks stood over me, but soon they morphed into one as my eyes focused. I was in a room with gray walls. "We don't have much time, Paul. I need you to tell me if you can understand what I'm saying. Who's Cole married to?"

"Savannah. One child, Olivia." I choked on the sandpaper in my throat.

"Good."

A memory surfaced. "Who the fuck shot me?"

"We're not sure." He looked at his watch then over my head. "Lift the bed so he can sit up." The head of the bed started to rise, and I winced at the pain. Fuck, that hurt.

"Where am I?"

"Well, that depends on your next answer." He snatched a water from someone in the room and handed it to me. I tossed the straw and poured the cool water down my aching throat. "Paul, as of right now, your brothers think you're dead. Technically, you did flatline in the chopper on the way back."

I lowered the cup, confused, and studied Frank with narrowed eyes.

"Hear me out." He held up his hands. "There was a witness in the Cartel who told Castillo that you were dead. He said he saw it with his own eyes. The news spread like wildfire, and we're hearing chatter that one of our guys died, but they don't know for sure exactly who was killed. We can play this in two ways. You come back from the dead and join your brothers, or you fight from the inside and protect your family as a ghost agent."

"Jesus," I huffed.

"Look, Paul," Frank sat on the side of the bed, "I get it's a lot, but truth be told, you're the one agent who *doesn't have much for a blood family, no real ties to anything. You're the one guy who—other than Blackstone, of course—no one knows much about."*

"I see. And what about John?" Blackstone were my brothers, but John was on a different level. He and I were one and the same. *"You think he's going to agree to me doing this?"*

"He'll never know. He can't know." Frank put a hand on my arm, but I pulled it back and glared at him.

"I know what this means, Paul. I would never have wished this on you, on anyone, but it's happened, and when you consider how this could work, how valuable you could be…" He shrugged. *"So, maybe if you grew a beard, tattooed some shit on your arms. Well, I'd handle the rest."*

"What about the informants you have there now?"

"They're good, but nothing like you could be. You're business smart, a leader, but most of all you know how they operate. I need someone in Rosarito I trust, someone who can handle Castillo. Things are unraveling fast there, and we need someone like you there to feed us intel." He looked at his phone. *"These opportunities don't happen often, and I know it's a lot to digest. We only have a small window to play this right."* The pain I felt wasn't just from the bullet wound; it radiated through my core as my mind spun.

"Blackstone needs this."

"How can I lie to them?"

"It's a necessary lie, Paul, and in fairness, you did die. We were just able to bring you back. But this is a lie to protect them. You'll be protecting them, just from the other side."

"If," I paused, shocked I was even considering this, "I do this, I want to be already established. My name needs to already mean something within the Cartel world. Can you do that?" I didn't wait for an answer and went on. "I also want a house with soldiers, and I need to know I have constant communication with you when I need it. Regular check-ins." I shifted. I could remember hearing the horror stories about other agents who had switched to ghost agents and had lost themselves mentally in those positions.

"I've already thought that out. You'd be Denton Barlow's cousin. As for everything else, I'll handle it. It'll be done." He held out a hand, and one of the armed men in the room handed him a small black box. "Do we have a deal?"

I'd do anything for Blackstone and Shadows. He was right. I had no real family. My sister was much older and had her own life struggles, and my aunt who raised me when my parents bounced would survive. No one would really care enough to come looking for me. I tried not to think of John and all the memories we had together. How we talked about our future families and how we were brothers 'til the end.

"Deal." What the hell was I thinking?

"These," he set the box next to me, "are going to be given to the team because what Cole went through. We thought it was time you all had some kind of tracker." He explained how the watch worked. "I removed the battery from yours, but you are and will always be a Blackstone member, so I had this one made for you. This, your passports, money, and a weapon should be stored somewhere safe outside of town. If you ever get compromised, all you need is a watch battery, and once it's powered up, the tracker will send a signal to us and we'll find you. If you get caught, pull the pin and swallow it. That way, we can still track you even if the watch is taken."

"Okay." I couldn't believe I was doing this. I hated to know I was going to bring my brothers at Shadows such pain, but if I could make a difference to protect them, I would make the sacrifice.

"Your country thanks you." Frank shook my hand.

A bump in the road jolted me back to the present, and I shook my head clear. Ten fucking years I'd lived with and as the enemy, but Frank had kept his word and checked in with me every single month. If I hadn't had that, I was sure I'd never have survived at all, certainly not as long as I did.

I eyed the small black box, then thumbed it open and pulled the sleek black watch from its case. I pressed my palm hard against the wheel and used my knife to pop the back off, then ripped the battery package open with my teeth. Despite my large hands, I was able to drop it in place and saw the mini contraption come to life. I spotted the little pin in the strap, but only because I knew where to look.

Nice job, Logan.

Once I was a mile from the safehouse, I used the one number that was programmed into the burner phone. I turned it on, shocked that the friggin' thing even worked, and waited for them to answer.

"Are you here?" It was a male.

"I'm a mile out, in a borrowed car, and I'm not sure—"

He cut me off. "Stay put. We'll come to you."

Though I didn't have the exact address to the safehouse, I did have a point of contact that would have called them once I made it there. We were close to the San Ysidro port of entry between Tijuana and San Diego, and that meant we were in heavy Cartel land.

It didn't take them long to find me. They had their weapons drawn as they exited their car. Two men opened the back door and carefully lifted Lexi's body out as three men covered me.

"What's your code and number?" the one in charge asked.

"Fox One. 135241494."

The man repeated the information into his radio. "Confirmed. Let's go." They formed around me, and we rushed to the Land Rover.

I watched as the others drove off in a different direction with Lexi and we headed for the border.

"Major," the leader turned in his seat, "we've got no time to go to the safehouse. We have orders to cross you now." He looked at my dress shoes and pants then at my sweatshirt. "Shit."

Yeah, I looked like I was the one just kidnapped.

TWO

"You seem off," Moore side-eyed me as we prepared for a round of interviews for our new team, "like your head isn't in the game."

"I didn't sleep well last night."

"Have you," Moore lowered his voice as we passed by the meal hall at Camp Green, "spoken to Ivy?"

"No." I wavered in my step. "She slept in her room last night."

"No, she didn't." He shook his head. "But Abigail said she was fine when I asked this morning."

"You asked?"

"When have I not had your six, on and off the field?"

"True." I pushed the door open between two hallways. "Where'd she sleep, then?"

"She wouldn't say, just that she's okay. I waited around

to see if I could spot her, but given we left at the ass crack of dawn…"

"Yeah, well, I wanted to see how well these guys work in the morning. But thanks for that."

"Hooah, brother."

Twenty minutes later, we were in a room with three physically drained Dark Water recruits. Ray stopped at the door and looked in. He was the one who oversaw Camp Green and was a former Blackstone agent under Cole's father. He gave me a nod, and I nodded back. I really appreciated his help with the recruits. I put my attention back on the three men.

One of them was Tommy Gear.

"Sir," he sat straighter when we did the one-on-one interviews first, "I listened to what Dr. Knight said, and I took the time to understand exactly what I wanted out of life and if I can leave my family. My decision wasn't taken lightly, nor should it be, and no matter how many times I talked myself out of not doing this, my heart wouldn't let me. I was made to be a part of this team. I feel it deep inside, and I want the chance to prove it to you."

"I'm glad you did that. It shows a lot about your character, Gear." I had a good feeling about him.

"I assure you that my sister and mother have lots of help, and they both understood I needed to live for me now and not be on hold."

There was something to be said for that, but there was still a part of me that wondered if he'd be better suited for the team at Dusk rather than Dark Water. That way, when he got leave, he'd be closer to home.

"Okay," I nodded and looked at his file, "let's finish with this interview and see how you do with the group one."

"I'm ready." He smiled, and I knew he was.

I'd taken a page from Ivy's playbook and after we asked all the prepared questions, I went deeper into their minds on their group interview.

I really liked that Steven Lee was smart and quick on his feet. Chris Perez was funny and resourceful. Perez was the smallest of the bunch, and I knew that could be an advantage in the field. Gear answered our questions slower the second time round, he put more thought in his answers. I could tell he'd gone away and really thought about what it might mean to join Dark Water. He impressed me a lot, but even better, he won over Moore. Perhaps I was wrong about Gear. I now believed he was what we were looking for.

"At ease." I closed their files and watched as they sagged into their seats and smiled, pleased the group interviews were over. "We're going to step outside. Hang tight." We removed ourselves from the room and went into another room farther down the hall. We didn't have a window to watch them, but we did have a live camera feed. This was an exercise to see how they interacted now they weren't trying to impress us or each other.

"I've never wanted something so bad in my life." Lee rubbed his crewcut with a huff. They were all exhausted but hadn't let it show, even to each other, until they were finished and somewhat alone.

"We all know how badass Blackstone is, and now there's a new team that's gonna work right alongside of 'em," Perez grinned. "And we're being considered? This is next level shit." The guys in the room all gave a *hooah*.

"I like them," Moore said quietly next to me. "I think we have something good here."

"Agreed." I kept my eyes on Gear.

Perez reached over and offered Gear a hand. "I know we were introduced, but I'm Chris Perez. I respect your answers about your family, by the way. I think it's cool you included them in your decision. I only have a half-sister, and she's eleven years younger, so we aren't that close."

"Thanks. Tommy Gear." Gear took Perez's hand and gave it a shake. "It's mostly because my sister's in a wheel-chair, so I know my mom needs a lot of help. When I told her about the position I was being offered and that I might give up the idea to try out for this team because of my sister, she smacked some sense into me real fast. Said it was about time I started living for me."

I glanced at Moore, and he felt it, too. Gear *was* the right kind of man we wanted for our team.

"That's impressive." Lee held his hand out to Gear. "I'm Steven Lee, "and I'm sorry for your sister."

"She's living her best life, and she's super tough. She'll be okay." Gear smiled for the first time.

I turned off the camera, and Moore and I went back

into the room to spend a little more time with our possible new team.

———

We were almost back at the house when Moore got a text message that made his face fall.

"Wow," he huffed and texted something back.

"Are you gonna keep me in suspense?" I stopped at the first check-in and rolled down my window to give a face ID.

"Guess who asked to be transferred to Camp Green?" Moore sipped his coffee. "Dustin."

"Dustin?" *What?*

"Yeah. And with his rank and at his age? That would only mean one thing."

"Wants distance from Hill and Rivera." I shook my head. "I wonder if that means Hill's slipping even more."

"My guess would be yes." He held up his ID with mine at the second checkpoint.

"What the hell?" I caught sight of a flashy gold pendant when it slipped out from under his shirt. Moore said nothing as he tucked his ID into his bag. "Are you wearing Gadar?" I reached over, but he slapped my hand away with a laugh. "Don't act like you don't have some."

"I mean I do, but I don't wear it." Shit, I still had a ton of Gadar gold left from Afghanistan. We sometimes used it to buy off the Taliban in sticky situations. It looked real but was actually just cheap stuff imported from India. It had saved our necks a few times.

"It's a memory piece." He patted his chest then rolled his eyes at my smirk.

"You look like a pimp," I said, deadpan. "You look like the inside of Flavor Flav's mouth. You look like LL Cool J's gangster cousin twice removed."

"Are you done?"

"No, I've got more." I laughed, and he punched me in the shoulder. We used to make so much fun of the young Taliban men who liked to flash around their Gadar jewelry. They thought they were such hot shit, but we all knew that fake gold only cost pennies.

"Before we go in, I wanna ask you for a favor." I slowed the car as two soldiers walked by. They held up a hand, and we both waved.

"Sure, shoot." Moore tucked his phone in his pocket and gave me his full attention.

"When I'm gone, keep an eye on Ivy, will ya? Have her six when she's in town or off somewhere whenever you can. I need to know you're with her when I'm over there."

"We already have a date, so that won't be a problem." He grinned, and I eyed him. "We both agreed that we're the most important people in your life, so we need to get to know one another better."

"Oh." I tilted my head at him and pondered if that was a good idea or not. "Just be careful, buddy. She can get inside your head without you even knowing it."

He laughed. "Excellent. So many stories and only five days to share them all."

"Remember story time works both ways," I shot back, "but thanks. I need to know she's okay." I tapped the wheel and thought again.

"Are you second guessing going?"

"No," I answered truthfully. "You and I both know I need to do this."

"Yeah, we do, but does she? You need to make it right with Ivy before you leave. Going over there with any kind of shit messing up your head is a recipe for disaster."

"I know." Huh. I suddenly realized that was one of the reasons I kept my family at arm's length.

Once we parked, Doc Roberts met us at the door.

"Good morning, gentlemen." He nursed a steamy cup of coffee. "Ty, Savannah says you're looking for some hypnotherapy before you leave for Afghanistan?"

"I am, yes. Would you have any time for that?"

"Good plan," Moore commented. "I know a lot of guys who find it helpful."

"Yes, it's becoming more and more popular." The doctor smiled at Moore. "I have time now, actually, Ty. Shall we?" I handed Moore my files and followed Doc to his office.

I took a seat on the couch, feeling a bit anxious about what I was about to do. The idea of allowing someone to dig around in my subconscious made me uneasy, but I trusted the doc. After all, it was my idea. Hypnotherapy had been recommended to me more than once by guys I'd served with. Some found it useful when preparing for life after service, and others found it helped to clear their heads before a posting.

"Before we get started, I want to know how you're feeling today in three words." Doc's voice was calm and low. I nodded and went with the truth.

"Nervous, excited, disconnected."

"Interesting use of words today." He scribbled on his tablet. "Let's start with the first one. What are you nervous about?"

"I'm partly nervous about this trip to Afghanistan, which is odd, because normally I can't get there soon enough."

"All right." He made a note of my answer. "Why do you think you're nervous this time?"

"Because of…" I trailed off when I remembered who I was speaking to. Ivy's uncle.

"Hmm," he gave me a knowing smile, "you know."

"I found out recently."

"Then you should also know that when I'm in here, I'm your doctor. I leave all feelings for my family outside that door. I've done that for years and will continue to until I leave this profession."

One thing I was sure of about Doc Roberts was that he didn't lie. He was honest to a fault, and right now I needed that.

"Okay, I'm worried that if I leave, Ivy will think I'm choosing my own personal issues over her. She seemed upset when I talked to her about it."

"Dr. Knight is an educated woman. This certainly wouldn't be the first time she's dealt with couples having to separate because of a mission. She's often done couple's therapy to help spouses who are upset the other has chosen to return to war." He seemed to think for a moment. "I'm not saying she's not upset, but I can promise you it's not because she thinks you are choosing it over her."

"Good to know." I shifted on the cushion.

"You mentioned you were excited. Tell me about that."

"I spent eight years in Afghanistan. I wanted to be there more than here in the States. I admit I love the idea of going back and living that life again, even if it's only for forty-eight hours."

"Good. Use that excitement when you go over there. That kind of controlled excitement is what you need to focus and get your job done."

"Agreed." I ran a hand through my hair while my chest tightened. "I've just never felt quite like this before. Like there's a disconnect."

"Okay, let's talk about the disconnect. Elaborate for me."

I couldn't explain what I felt about that word. It was so tangled up in my head. My emotions were all over the place.

"I'm not sure I can."

"Well, how do you feel inside when you think of that word?"

"Twisted and bent around something, like I can breathe but it hurts to." I started to tap deeper into my feelings. "I hate the idea of hurting Ivy, but I need to go over there and figure this shit out for not only Brown's family but for me. I have no idea what I'm looking for or what I can bring back as evidence, but I need to try. I know if I don't, I can't move on. And if I can't move on, I'll lose her." I looked over at him. "I can't lose her, Doc."

He nodded slightly but didn't say a word, so I went on.

"I have two parents, and all they want to do is spend time with me. My sister and my niece moved here with my parents in hopes I'd give them a bit of my time, but I just can't do that. So, I avoid them." I inhaled sharply.

"But yet, this gorgeous, incredibly smart, funny, strong woman comes into my life, and suddenly everything changes. When she's near me, I start to care about things I never did before. She makes me think about everything I do. Even about my family. She's good for me, good for my soul. But I think I broke her last night when I told her I was leaving. I literally spun her off her axis. What does that say about me?"

"That you care that you hurt someone you care about."

"Who I love," I blurted, and my gaze snapped up to his.

"And there's your answer." He smiled warmly. "You're disconnected from yourself because you don't want to hurt or lose the woman you love."

"Shit." I leaned back, baffled by my confession. "What the hell do I do, Doc?"

"Tell her how you feel." He closed his tablet. "Once you do, everything will smooth out inside."

"If it doesn't?"

"Well, that's a risk you're just going to have to take."

"I don't like those kinds of risks, Doc."

"No one does," he chuckled, "but that's life." My heartbeat sped up, and I tried to think about what I should do. "May I offer some advice from someone who has worked in this field longer than I care to share?"

"Please." I gestured for him to go on.

"You need a clear head going over there, and that's why you came to me for help, correct?" I nodded. "A clear head starts with a clear conscience. A clear conscience will be yours if you start with a young woman whose heart is just as vulnerable as yours. Tell her how you feel so if the unthinkable happens over there, you left Ivy with the knowledge she was loved. Who doesn't want to know they are loved by someone?"

He was right. If I could give her anything in this world, it should be my love. She deserved that, at the very least. Everything inside me went calm, and I knew what I needed to do.

"I won't lie, I'm terrified to even say those words. I'm afraid of that kind of commitment. I'm not sure if I'd be any good at it."

"You never know 'til you try." He smoothed his tie and stood, and I followed.

"I think I'll skip that hypnosis."

He smiled then moved to open the door and walked with me down the hall. "I'll be here if you reconsider."

"Thanks, Doc."

"No, Ty," he placed a hand on my shoulder, "thank you." My brows pinched, confused on what he meant, but then I realized we weren't in his office anymore and he was her uncle once again. "You're good for her, too."

"I think I needed to hear that."

I smiled as I headed for the kitchen. As I walked past Cole, I caught him staring hard at his phone like he was trying to figure something out.

"Everything okay, Logan?"

"What the hell is that?" he muttered to himself. He obviously hadn't even heard what I said, so I moved on and reached for the coffee pot.

"Hey, Savi." I poured myself a coffee and followed her gaze toward Cole. "Have you seen Ivy?"

"No, but I know Keith has."

"Where's Keith?"

"With Ivy." She, too, seemed a million miles away.

"So, Keith is with Ivy, but you don't know where Ivy is?"

"Sure, I'll get the cook to make that," she murmured. I moved to stand next to her and watched her watch her husband.

"What is going on?"

"A new tracker apparently popped up on his radar."

"Which means?" I prompted.

"All team Blackstone have trackers in their watches." She stopped and thought about her words. "There's a tiny pin embedded in the strap. It tracks their whereabouts when they're in the field. They can turn it off when they're on leave and whatnot. It's not like they're used to keep tabs on them that way." She spoke quickly when I gave her a look. "They got them after Cole was…" She shook her head as if the memory hurt. "Anyway, there are six active trackers as of an hour ago."

"I don't follow."

"Blackstone has five members."

"Where's the sixth tracker pinging from?"

"Mexico."

"Could it be?" I didn't want to say it, but I knew we both thought about Lexi.

"No, it's impossible. Only five watches were ever made under Frank's orders. They were given out by Cole himself to each member of the Blackstone team."

"What does Cole think?"

"That's the million-dollar question." She stepped back and covered her face, as stressed as Cole seemed to be. "Don't share what I told you with anyone yet. Cole needs to think. We don't need any false hope right now."

"I promise I won't."

THREE

"You can't hide in here forever, you know," Keith called as he stepped into the belly of the chopper. He sat down next to me and handed me a travel mug filled with hot coffee.

"I'm not hiding. I'm just sorting out my thoughts."

He nodded behind his own mug. "Now, that's something I can relate to."

"How are you holding up?" I hoped to move the attention off me.

"No," he shook his head and peered at me, "this moment is about you, not me."

"Professionally, I'm okay, thanks." I sighed. "But personally, I feel like a balloon that just had its strings cut and now I'm slipping away."

"That's normal. I've heard the wives say that kind of thing before when we're about to go off on a mission."

"You see, I know that." I sniffed. "That's my field. I sit in front of people or couples and coach them through the panic of a spouse leaving. But…" I sighed heavily.

"But you've never been the one experiencing the feeling."

"Guess I'm really not good at being on the receiving end." I shook my head.

"No one is," he admitted, and for a half a second, I saw his mask slip. "Savi is someone great to talk to about this stuff."

"I can't. I shouldn't even be here talking to you about this. Here I am, terrified about Ty leaving, when all of you are dealing with the biggest thing Blackstone and Shadows have ever faced. I feel terrible about it. I can't be that person."

"Why are your feelings less important than others'?"

"I'm supposed to be the rock for you all. Not hiding out in a freezing chopper feeling sorry for myself."

"All right, so let's get you through this so you can go back to being the rock again." He patted my back.

I was relieved he saw that it was what I wanted, not to mention needed.

He cleared his throat and thought for a second. "I'm going to be honest with you for a minute." He squeezed my arm and sat up straight. "Look, Blackstone is thick as a brotherhood can be, which means we feel and experience everything together. One feels pain, we all feel pain, if you know what I mean. You know Lopez was in the room with me during one of my sessions with you. We have nothing to hide from one another. I've been on the front lines when Logan, Lopez," he counted on his fingers, "Irons, and John all realized they'd found the one they loved and wanted to marry. What does that tell you?"

"You've been in love four times?" I joked.

"No," he chuckled, "but it means I've experienced four different ways people can fall in love. Make that five because they were all there for me when I chose, too."

"That's a pretty cool way of looking at it, actually."

"It is." He held up a finger. "You know what else it means?" I shook my head. "It means I've gotten pretty good at spotting love, too."

I opened and closed my mouth. I wanted to deny it, but the truth was he was right. The night Ty came into my room and stayed with me, I'd felt something shift inside. He'd held me and never asked for anything in return. Sex could have happened then, but it didn't. He wanted to be there for me, and that was it. It meant the world to me. I knew I wanted to ignore that feeling because I felt his heart was in Afghanistan.

"Dr. Keith does have a good ring to it." I sidestepped the truth and fumbled with my hands for a moment. "I'm scared."

"You don't think all of us weren't? Being vulnerable sucks." He chuckled sadly into his mug. "But running from love won't get you anywhere, trust me."

"What does it feel like?"

"Incomplete."

"How do you feel now, given your situation, I mean?" He eyed me hard, and I winced. "Sorry, it's a habit. You don't have to answer that."

We sat in silence listening to the wind blow through the cracks in the building. Both of us just enjoyed each other's company in that moment. We didn't want to face the world just yet.

"Truth," he said just above a whisper, "I've put my emotions on pause. Not sure what that says about me, but it's the only way I'm surviving this."

"It means you're human." I pulled the blanket tighter around me.

"Come on." He jumped up and offered me a hand. "It's about twenty-one degrees out, and we're expecting snow. We don't need our doctor getting sick on us. Besides, I know Ty's back from Camp Green, and I'm sure he's looking for you." He helped me down from the chopper then opened the door of the hanger for me. We were met with a freezing wind. "Brrrr, let's hurry."

"He was at Camp Green already today?" I looked at my watch and saw it was only ten thirty in the morning.

"He and Moore were gone by zero-four-hundred."

"Why so early?" I hurried along beside him.

"When you're interviewing for possible teammates, you need to ask them the hardest questions when they're tired and the easiest when they're not." He smiled and took my arm. "Ty arranged for Ray, the guy who runs Camp Green, to get someone to take the candidates and do drills most of the night. They had maybe forty-five minutes of sleep before they were called to the interview room."

"I've heard of that before. I think Frank mentioned it at one point."

"Most likely. It's pretty common. It's just another way to weed out the weak."

Something made a strange sound in his pocket, and he pulled out a small radio.

"Repeat." He spoke with a strong tone that was all business.

"It's Frank. Come to the house." Just as he put the radio away, we stepped into the clearing and saw everyone gathered outside on the front porch.

"What's going on?" Blackstone and the wives were all huddled together, and I felt something colder than the wind pass through me.

"My guess," he cleared his throat, "they found out something."

His face fell as we grew closer. Ty's intense stare found mine.

"Keith," Frank stepped forward, and the rest stayed in a horseshoe formation, "I heard from one of my informants."

"Save me the formality and lay it out," Keith grunted, and I scanned the wives' faces and could tell Frank hadn't shared the news with any of them. Cole was the only one who knew, as his pale face was like stone, and he moved forward and anchored an arm around Savi.

"The informant was transporting Lexi when they got ambushed early this morning." Frank paused to take a strangled breath. "I'm sorry to say she was shot and died shortly after."

The entire group went still, like a painting of pain, their expressions frozen. Then as the words sank in and their brains absorbed the blow, they began to react. Catalina was the first to turn into Mike's chest with a sob, Mia and Savannah reached out and linked hands, while Sloane covered her mouth, her eyes wide as tears streamed down her face. Then one by one each Blackstone member put a hand on each other's shoulder and pulled Keith into their core. As his body went slack, they held him up and moved as one into the house. The howl that ripped from his throat would forever be embedded in my memory.

Frank stepped back and whispered quietly to Ty and Moore, while I stood and watched and realized that history was made this day. The Cartel had won this battle. There was now a crack in the Blackstone armor.

I felt the hot tears slip down my frozen cheeks. I hadn't known Lexi well, but that didn't mean my heart didn't break for her and for the rest of them. A sudden thought of the kids pushed through, and my insides went to jelly as I thought of poor Brandon and Reagan and how they no longer had a mother. The ripple affect it would have on their lives would forever change them. I knew it would intensify the fear they'd have when their father left for a mission, and the blame Brandon carried that he was somehow responsible for his mother leaving would be worse than ever because he'd never had a chance to speak to her.

In that moment, I vowed I would do whatever it took to help them all get through this.

"Ivy," my uncle was suddenly at my side, "are you all right?"

"It's not me you should be asking." I gave him a sad look, and he nodded.

"Let's all get inside out of the cold," Abigail called. "We'll need a warm drink." We followed her into the house. Then Abby, June, Sue, and I headed toward the kitchen.

I thanked my uncle then veered off to my room for a shower and some alone time. I felt they all needed privacy. The hot water began to thaw my body, and I let my tears flow with it down the drain. I would have felt funny crying with the others. What right did I have crying over someone I barely knew? Deep down, I suddenly felt like an outsider, but one with a job to do.

I cried for Keith and for the children and for Lexi, enough to ease the knot in my stomach. Then I felt the unresolved nerves of Ty's upcoming trip to Afghanistan bubble to the surface. I leaned in and pressed my forehead to the tile and focused on my breathing. The last thing I needed was a panic attack.

In and out. In, slowly, and out, slowly.

I reached for the handle and turned off the water and stepped out. I dried myself then used the hum of the hairdryer to calm my thoughts and get my head on straight. I dabbed a light layer of makeup over my face to try to hide the evidence of my full-out sob fest. Then, dressed, I gave myself a pep talk and headed back downstairs, ready to be strong for those who needed it.

Daniel gave me a hug without saying anything. He kissed the top of my head and whisked off to wherever he was heading. Daniel was great that way; less was sometimes more.

"Tea?" Abby asked as I entered the kitchen. She dried her damp cheeks then tucked her handkerchief in the sleeve of her shirt. She was obviously trying hard to keep it together. These women were incredibly strong, and it was admirable.

"Maybe something stronger?" June opened the liquor cabinet and set a bottle of gin in front of me.

"I'm sorry, Sue." I covered her hand with mine. "I wish I had something better to say at this time, but I don't."

"Sadly, dear," her red eyes blinked more tears, "I think there was a part of all of us that half expected that call. Sometimes you just know."

"We should all just be thankful she went fast, and not have the unthinkable happen." Abby swallowed hard. "I just couldn't imagine what they might have done to her. That poor man in there, if he'd had to see anything more than just her casket." She covered her mouth with her hand.

"I know," I said and rested my hand on Abby's. Then Sue took her hand and placed it over mine. With that small gesture, I did feel I was part of all this and took some comfort from it.

"If there's any light at all in this terrible thing, it's that."

June placed four gin and tonics on the counter in front of us then held one up.

"To Lexi. May you finally find peace, and may we get the answers we need to allow our men to serve out justice to all those awful people who did this." We clicked our glasses and took a sip of what was apparently a triple shot of gin.

"Ivy?" Ty said from behind me, and I turned on the stool. "Can I speak with you?"

"Of course." I dried my cheeks again as I followed him down the stairs into one of the conference rooms.

He closed the door behind me and frosted the glass on the doors. He pulled out a seat and waited for me to join him, then turned off the lights and turned on the laptop.

"I know we need to talk, and I'm sorry I disappeared."

"Ivy," he moved in front of me and clicked a button, "just hear me out first." A map appeared on the wall behind him. "First, take this." He handed me a twenty-dollar bill. "This is me asking for a session with you."

"Why?"

"Because this needs to stay between us, and if there's money involved you can't legally share, correct?"

"Yes, that's correct." He nodded once and went back to what he was showing me.

"I want you to know I've never shared any part of a mission with a civilian, until now." I went still, unsure exactly what he planned to share with me. "I asked for permission and am laying myself on the line to share this with you. I need you to see I know every step of my mission inside and out. I'm not reckless, Ivy, but this is something I must do, not just for me, but for us."

I nodded, unable to speak. Today was emotional enough as it was.

"I leave for Washington in a few days, where I'll be briefed and provided with everything I need. Then, the next day, I leave with another team. They have a whole other mission. The seven of us will be dropped here," he pointed on the map, "and travel by foot across here." He dragged his finger farther along. "At this point, I'll branch off on my own, and head east until I get to this town." I pressed both hands against the table to steady them as my stomach plummeted. I needed to stay calm because I knew how important this was to him. He double tapped the clicker and zoomed in on the map, and using a marker, he circled the town. "This house here is where Brown was killed." His face fell for a moment, but he kept going. "After forty-eight hours, I'll meet the other team here," he drew an X outside the town limits, "and from here I return to Washington, and then from there I come home to you."

I nodded and tried to blink the tears back. I knew what it must have taken for him to share something like this, and I also knew he had to be struggling to let me in this much.

"I have a question." I could barely get the words to form on my tongue. "What if you don't find anything. Then what?"

"Then I know I've done everything I could, and I can cross Afghanistan off my list of places I need to dig." He tossed the clicker on the table and pulled out the chair next to me. He pulled me to him and tucked my knees between his and took my hands. "Ivy, I know this is scary, but you have my promise that I wouldn't even dream of doing this if I didn't feel a hundred percent sure about all of it."

"I know." More tears fell. "I'm just so scared that something will happen to you."

"I feel the same way about you." He used his fingers to dry my cheeks.

"Why are you worried about me? I'm in a safehouse."

"I'm worried because this is the first time in my life I've loved someone." He held my gaze as my eyes widened. "I hate the idea of leaving you, and now I'm even more terrified given what's happened to—" He shook his head. "It's one thing for them to hunt us. Soldier to soldier we can handle, but to go after our wives or girlfriends, that's—"

"Ty," my voice was soft as a delicious warmth spread through me, "I'm terrified because I'm in love with you, too."

He scooped me up and sat me on his waist to straddle

him then moved his hands to my face on each side. "You love me?"

"I do love you." His silly, teary-eyed grin made me lower my lips to his, and we sealed our truths. There was a part of me that felt terribly guilty for sharing a moment like this at such a time, but Lexi's passing had given us the push we needed.

He rested his forehead against mine. "She loves me," he whispered.

"I do."

After our stolen moment, we walked together back to the others. The sadness simply simmered in the room. Cole had his face stuck in his phone, and Frank steadily watched his screen as well. Abby and June hovered. They were so alike, and they needed to do things for the others, anything to make sure everyone had whatever they might need. Mike, John, and Mark sat quietly with Keith, who still looked completely checked out. None of them spoke or did more than glance at us, and Ty went to join them.

"Ivy," my uncle appeared, "may I have a word?"

"Of course." We stepped outside the door.

"I don't think we should attempt to speak with anyone today about how they're feeling. We need to just let everyone digest this terrible news."

"That's my thought, too. I just want to make sure they know I'm around in case they need me."

"Good idea." He gave me a tight smile. "I'll do the same."

"I wanted to talk to you, too." I took his arm, and we walked toward his office.

"What is it?" he asked as he closed the door.

"I know none of this is my business, but I can't help but notice a change in Frank. Is everything okay? Is the house in some kind of danger? I feel there's more going on than what we've been told."

"You always were quick to pick up on a vibe." He chuckled sadly. His face scrunched up as though he contemplated what he could share. "It's the informant, the one who tried to get Lexi out. Now he's been compromised and is on his way here to stay."

"Oh, I see." I shook my head. "The fact that this person didn't succeed in getting Lexi out," I thought of all the ways it could go wrong, "it might be very upsetting for Keith to have him here."

His face fell, and he sank into his chair with a sigh. "This conversation never happened." His tone changed and sent a cold prickle up my back. I had a sudden feeling another storm was heading our way.

"Uncle," I pressed my hands into his desk and leaned over, "is Blackstone about to get another hit?" I needed to know what I was in for, what they were in for. When he held my stare, I got my answer. "How bad is it?"

"It's unlike anything we've ever dealt with."

"When is this situation going to happen?"

"That depends."

"On?"

"What happens with the Cartels at the border."

"And if things go wrong?"

"Then we never, ever speak of this again. I mean it, Ivy. This is some classified red-tape level stuff."

"I understand." I felt my blood pressure rise.

"That includes sharing with Beckett."

"Why would I share this with Beckett?"

"I know how close you two have become, and sometimes things can slip."

I folded my arms and tried to read his face. "What do you know?" He didn't give anything away, but I still rolled my eyes because I knew he was a vault when he wanted to be. I slowly lowered into the seat and felt the heaviness that hung in the air. "My heart breaks for the house," I admitted.

"Mine, too." He pulled off his glasses and pinched the bridge of his nose. "It's strange, you know." He settled back in his chair. "Though Lexi was making progress the first few years at Shadows, I think her postpartum really set things on the wrong course for her. I know she fought it and tried hard to do what she knew she should. But sadly, I think all of us knew she'd be the one to get into trouble. If anyone would. She meant well but was reckless by default."

He stood and looked out the window for a moment. "I believe when you start to see the men for their sessions and they open up to you, you'll find they all knew this might be the outcome. She was on a dangerous road and had gone well past the time of being rescued, even with the help of the undercover informant."

"She must have been so scared knowing the chances of ever coming home were slim to none." I bit down on my bottom lip as I thought.

"Perhaps she knew it was hopeless. The wives here are well trained on what to say and how to act if they ever got captured. It's why this place isn't for everyone. It's sad, but it's reality, and it needs to be this way. What happened with Lexi is exactly why. Lord knows what she went through, though."

"Do you think she gave them any information on the house?"

"I don't." He shook his head. "We'd already know if she had. The way the Cartels work, if they had gotten any information, it would've spread like wildfire, and we would have been stormed days ago."

"That's a terrifying thought." I shuddered and rubbed my arms at a sudden chill. My uncle looked at me in sympathy.

"The house is due for another safety drill, especially given the nature of what's happened. If it makes you feel any better, there's a bunker below the house and a tunnel that leads to the other side of the mountain. The Logans thought of everything when they built this place, and over the years, they've added to stay current as the threats increase."

"That helps a bit. Thanks." I rubbed my eyes. "I know

this is probably the worst question I could ask right now, but when will the kids be brought home?"

"Brandon and Reagan will be returning with Olivia tonight. The rest of the children will be told at Dusk."

"Is that fair?" I blinked in shock. "Won't the children need their parents at a time like this?"

"Normally, I'd say yes, but given the situation with the informant coming here, and the possible fallout, we felt it was best for the parents of the younger ones to leave them where they are for a bit. The guys especially will have a lot to get through these next few days. The children will only bring extra stress." I highly disagreed with that. Even though it wasn't my place, I did make a mental note to run my concerns by Cole myself.

"Do you know who the informant is?"

"No." He looked me straight in the eye, and I knew he told the truth. "I believe only Frank does." His gaze shifted suddenly, and I felt something.

"But you have a possible idea of who it could be?"

"I might have." He nodded.

"And if it's who you think it is, how badly will this affect the house?"

"I honestly, don't know the answer to that. I wish I did, since it would help me to prepare."

"Jeez," I huffed and got to my feet, "I need to walk or something. Clear my head so I can be all theirs when they need me."

"That's a good idea."

"I'll see you in a bit," I mumbled as I headed for the door.

"Ivy?" He stopped me. "For the record, I think he's great for you." He gave me a small smile, and I knew he was just trying to help, which I did appreciate.

"Thanks. I think so, too."

FOUR

"There's been more and more Cartel presence at the border in the last six months. Rumor has it they're moving in on Guzmán, El Chapo's son." One of the soldiers handed me a Gap polo, and I looked at him like he was nuts. "Remember, *you* might be dead, dude, but," he looked at my new passport, "Chad Johnson, age thirty-one from Jacksonville, Florida, wears Gap and boat shoes with dress pants and Maui Jim sunglasses." He gave me a brief grin, then his face fell back into its previous grim expression. The current situation was far from humorous, and chances were high we'd never make it through in one piece. The guy popped a piece of pink gum in his mouth and chewed loudly, and I allowed myself a quick smile. I couldn't help but think how Mark would love this moment. People like us had to see the humor when we could.

"Thanks." I snatched the sunglasses from him and pushed them into place on my face. I cringed when I caught myself in the window of the SUV. I'd burn this shit if I ever got safely over the border.

"Look," the soldier moved in front of me, "I'm not gonna give you a rundown of how this'll go down. You already know, but if we get stopped by anyone else but the border patrol, we're all fucked."

"Understood—" I turned as two SUVs drove fast, straight into the parking lot, and men in suits hopped out. "Company. Yours?"

"I don't work with suits." The soldier's hand flexed on his rifle.

"Major Paul?" A man approached me and flashed a badge. He removed his Ray Bans. "Cooper Collins, FBI." He nodded sharply. "At ease." He looked at the tense soldiers with me. "I got wind of your situation and thought we could be of some assistance."

"That's convenient," I muttered.

"General Frank called in a favor this morning." He settled my thoughts, and one of his men handed the lead soldier a phone. "The border's crawling with Cartel. You'd be spotted in minutes once you're in the lineup. We've made the calls to CBP, and we're cleared to take you through, but you won't ride in comfort." He chuckled.

"What's the catch?" I glanced at the soldier next to

me. I didn't care to learn their names, and they didn't offer them. It was better that way.

"You're not the one who called in the favor," Collins shot back.

"It's okay, you're cleared to go with them if you want." The soldier handed the phone back. "That was General Frank confirming it." I wanted to speak to Frank myself, but I knew the clock was ticking.

"I appreciate your time." I fist bumped both soldiers. "Be safe."

Collins walked back and opened the trunk for me to get inside. "Sorry about this, but if you want to live…" He shrugged and pointed at the tiny space I had to fold myself into.

"I've been in worse places." I chuckled and grabbed the bag that held my things and tugged it with me into the small space.

"Just in case, are you armed?" Collins eyes my bag. I wanted to lie, but I knew I was getting a favor. I reached inside my bag and handed him my weapon. My stomach sank as Collins slammed the flooring back down and closed the trunk. There was no turning back.

I was entirely too large to hide in such a small spot, but I shifted about until I felt somewhat comfortable.

A small sliver of light made its way through the metal just above my eye level, and if I stretched my neck, I could see the material of one of the agents' suits. I concentrated on taking slower breaths so I could listen to their conversation.

"Yes, we have him. We released the other two men. I'll call when we're through." Collins paused to listen. "I understand. He's in good hands."

I closed my eyes and tried to think of something else. Lexi popped up in my head, and because I was alone and no one could see me, I let the tears fall. I was sure by now Frank had shared the news about her death with Keith and the others. I couldn't imagine how the house took it. Lexi had shared that she and Keith had kids.

In my conversations with Frank for the first few years, I'd avoided asking about my brothers at Blackstone, and I never wanted to know about their families. It hurt too much. But over time, when I caught myself slipping, Frank seemed to know and would speak of them. He knew it was what I needed not to lose myself completely. I had become good at turning sides of my head off. One side was Eric Noah, the rising Cartel member, and the other was Major Paul, a well-respected Blackstone member. I needed to remember that to keep me grounded and sane. I knew if I forgot who I really was, then my time of ever having a real family was over.

My parents had never really wanted me as a kid. I always figured I was a late life oops, and once I became a teen, I was left to be raised by my aunt. I had a sister who was much older than I was, but she had her own set of problems and didn't want the bother of a much-younger sibling. We lost touch. When I joined the military, I met John, and in time his family took me in. Then when we joined Blackstone and became part of Shadows, those were the best of times. For the first time in my life, I felt loved and accepted for who I was. No undercover job or Cartel life could ever take that from me.

So, Frank knew what I needed, when I needed it, and would let slip the smallest things about their lives. It gave me my reason for staying in Mexico, a steady reminder of why I'd made the decision to give up everything. I needed to do it for my brothers. I'd had to become one of *them*.

The struggle that played out in my head now was how they would accept me back. I wondered how the guys thought about me after all these years. Was I thought about in a quiet moment then forgotten? What of my sweet Olivia? I'd loved being Uncle Paul for baby Olivia, but now I'd just be a stranger. I knew she'd been too young when I left to have any memory of me now, and that was a whole different kind of hurt. I thought of my best friend, my brother. But it was too overpowering to think of John either. I pushed it all away.

"Just keep moving." Collins' voice pulled me from my thoughts, and I tuned in to my surroundings again. "Don't give them a reason to watch us. Just keep one hand on the wheel, look relaxed. They'll watch the little movements you do." He seemed to be coaching the driver.

Fuck me, is this the driver's first time crossing the friggin' border?

"So many fuckin' criminals, and all in one spot," the guy next to him muttered. "Man, we're seriously outnumbered." He leaned forward, and I caught a glimpse outside the window as a border patrol agent walked by.

"If you called this in," the driver nearly whispered, "why is BP watching us?"

"It's their job. Relax." Collins' voice oozed confidence. "If they didn't give us a good once-over, the Cartel would catch it."

"Be sure to stay all the way over to the left," Collins instructed the driver. "If not, we'll have to get out and do this shit all over again. Okay, now all the way over to the right."

"Here's my SENTRI pass." The seat above me flexed as the agent in the back seat leaned forward and must have handed Collins his fast pass. "It's only a," I heard his finger tap on his phone screen, "six-and-a-half-minute wait."

Thank fuck.

Slowly, the car crawled forward, and every moment was painful. I was sure the driver was going to shake right out of his skin.

"Fuck," the agent in the back seat cursed, "just roll your window down and buy something, anything."

"I'll take two." Collin tried not to sound too annoyed. "Just give me both. *Gracias.*" I heard plastic rattle, and something was tossed in the back after the window rolled up.

"Shit," I couldn't tell who spoke, "we've got eyes, there and there."

It killed me I couldn't see. I already had allowed my head to slip back to Rosarito, and I was stressed over what mayhem might be happening back there, and now this added on top of things had my nerves completely on edge.

"That guy's got his phone out!" The driver's voice was high.

"He's just calling something in." Collins was calm, unlike the driver. "Just show our passes, passports, and permits. Answer the questions like we practiced."

"Good evening," the border patrol agent said loud and clear. "How long were you in Mexico?"

"Seven days."

Seven days? What the hell was the FBI doing in Mexico for that long?

"Purpose of the stay?"

"Trip with some old friends." There was a pause.

"Anything, fruits, nuts, cash amounts I should know about inside the vehicle?"

Shit. That wasn't a standard question for an agent, not worded like that.

"No, sir."

"Good. Then you won't mind pulling over there, so we can be sure of that."

"Sure." The driver slowly veered off to the right and came to a stop.

"Stay silent," the back seat agent muttered and tapped lightly on the floor. "I can feel them watching us."

"Unlock your doors," a border agent ordered, and the sound echoed in my ears. Nothing was right about what was happening. If they truly had called it in to CBP, we should have been waved through after they showed their documents.

The trunk lid went up, and I prepared myself for a fight. I had no idea where it would land me, but I wasn't going to be put into the hands of any authority on this side of the border. Things were moved around, and voices could be heard outside. Dogs barked, and the smell of exhaust filled the air.

Sunlight broke through the seams of the carpet above me, and I knew they were close to discovering the hiding place. My heart pounded in my chest, sweat broke out all over, and I forced myself not to adjust my position and give myself away.

I could feel something and knew it was someone's hands tugging at the edge of the carpet above me. I knew once that was lifted, it wouldn't be long before they found the seam in the metal floor. I held my breath.

Fuck. Here we go!

"Agent Collins," someone called, and the sounds above me stopped, "forgive the delay. I see the order to let you pass didn't make it down here."

Slowly, my muscles relaxed, and I allowed myself a slow breath. My fists uncurled and flattened out. I'd been ready to swing regardless of the consequences.

"I was surprised by the holdup." Collins' voice sounded calm. "I trust this won't happen again?" Another pause.

"No, it won't. You've got my word on that." The man's voice seemed nervous.

Who the hell was this Collins guy? He obviously had pull.

"Excellent. How are the kids doing? And how's Ruth? Is she still baking her pies for the fundraisers?"

"Yes, sir, she is, and my kids are doing well. Thank you for asking. Now, I'll let you get on with your drive."

"That's real nice to hear. You carry on with your day as well." Collins' smooth voice oozed confidence. "I'll see you again soon." This time I thought I heard a hint, almost a threat in his tone.

If that wasn't a shift in power, I didn't know what was. I wondered how well Frank knew Collins, because everything inside told me he had a lot of pull here, and that meant money and lots of it. He had to be a guy who got his hands dirty. These guys didn't cower easily, but it was obvious he instilled fear.

The vehicle started, and we were on our way. The vibe in the vehicle was different. No one spoke, and I could only hear the engine. I pushed a finger up through the hole in the carpet to widen the gap a bit to let in a little more light.

I thought again about the whole border incident and let it go 'round and 'round in my head. I decided I just couldn't deal with it right now. Shady FBI agents who smuggled people across the border, that was for a different day.

I took a slow, deep breath in through my nose and out through my mouth and tried to let the stress of it all leave my body so I could focus on what I might have to face next. I knew I had to reach out to Chili and find out what he knew.

I began to lose the feeling in my arms, and my back started to seriously cramp up, so I was very happy when I felt the car slow then stop. I felt the trunk as it was lifted, then I blinked up at a gloomy sky. It was a wonderful sight.

"Welcome to San Diego." Agent Collins smirked as he helped me out of the vehicle. Then he opened the car door, and I managed to slip into the back seat. We continued our drive north. "I figured you'd want to get out of there." He pointed to the floor.

"Yeah, no kidding." I unfolded and awkwardly rubbed my now tingling arms and legs. "Got any water?" My mouth was like sand.

"We do." He reached into a cooler between us and handed me a bottle. "Hungry?"

"No." I opened the back of my throat and downed the entire bottle of water, and he handed me another. "How far out are we from the hotel?"

"Forty-five." Collins looked at the GPS. "Just enough time for you to explain why you were worth Frank calling in this favor."

"That," I crumpled the empty bottle between my hands, "is for Frank to explain. I do want to thank you for your help, though." I took another swig.

"You can thank me by answering my question," he pushed.

"You have your orders, Agent Collins, and I have mine. There's nothing more to be said."

"Fine." He reluctantly let the topic go.

My head started to thump, and I closed my eyes and leaned back. I allowed myself a moment to soak up the realization that I'd made it this far with my head still attached. I took a quick peek at Collins. His eyes were shut as well. I studied him a moment then closed mine again.

I must have slipped off to sleep. The sound of a phone as it vibrated in a cup holder pulled me out of my groggy state. Carefully, I opened my eyes a slit and focused in on Collins' phone screen.

GG: Did you cross yet?

Collins: Slight trouble at border. We're through now.

GG: Now what?

Collins: Now we drop off package. I'll be in touch.

I closed my eyes again and wondered who the hell GG was. The only GG I could come up with was Grim Gates, and I'd bet good money it sure as shit wasn't Grim talking to a damn FBI agent.

A short time later, we were at The Hilton Embassy Suites. I caught a glimpse of the four of us as we walked by a full-length mirror in the lobby. Three men who screamed government with their suits, shoes, and sunglasses, and me looking like I stepped out of a Gap photoshoot. I hoped I didn't look like I just got picked up at a local bar and was looking for a good time with these guys. Or maybe people would think I was the star of a boy band, and these were my bodyguards. That almost brought a smile to my face. Oh, God. I figured I must be losing it. Thank hell no one knew me here anymore.

"Here's your key." The guy behind the desk eyed me up and down, and I gave him a smirk. "Would you like an extra cot?"

"One is fine." My smile widened.

"Sure." He grinned. "Everything has been handled, Mr. Johnson. I hope you enjoy your stay at the Embassy Suites."

"Thanks." I snagged the key from him as my humor evaporated. I was suddenly exhausted. I only hoped the suitcase Frank had arranged for me had some aspirin in it. Collins hung up from his phone call.

"This is where we part ways."

"Again," I shook his hand, "thanks for your help."

"If you ever need any help in the future, don't hesitate to call." He handed me his card.

When I flipped it over there was a number scribbled on the back. I nodded my thanks again then turned away. I wanted nothing more than a shower and to be left alone to think.

"Oh, by the way," Agent Collins called, and I looked back, "be sure to say hello to John Black for me." I squinted at him, unsure why he'd single out John. "Take care, Mr. Johnson," he called as the elevator doors closed. I was more than happy to shed the FBI from my six, especially when I wasn't even sure they'd really had my six.

I opened the door to my hotel room, locked it behind me, tossed the suitcase on the bed, and opened it. A cell phone was on top with a note stuck to it.

Call me – Frank.

"You good?" he offered as a greeting.

"Ask me again when I'm farther away from the border."

"Fair enough."

"Lexi?"'

"Her body's on its way to the North Dakota morgue. Look," I heard a door close, "the phone's untraceable, but make all your calls then ditch it before you board the plane. Debrief, get your head on straight, and let's finish what we need to do."

"Roger that."

"And Paul?"

"Yeah?"

"Glad you're coming home. It's time." He hung up, and I was left with mixed feelings on the word *home*.

My shower felt good, but my military clothes felt better. It had been over a decade since I'd worn fatigues, boots, and a black t-shirt. After I'd shaved and shortened my hair, I checked out the rest of what Frank had sent. I pulled out a Shadows duffle bag. He'd known I'd want to travel with that instead of a suitcase. I silently allowed myself a moment as I shook it out and held it up.

I sat down on the side of the bed, closed my eyes, and slipped away, remembering that time.

"Eric! Eric!" My shoulder was smacked from behind, and I turned with a raised fist. "If we're going to do this, you need to know your fucking name!" Ángel was annoyed at me again. "It's been three days since you got here, amigo. *If you don't know your name, how can you do your job? One slip, and you're dead." He rubbed his forehead. "Now, say it again."*

"I'm Eric Noah from Austin, Texas. I'm forty-two and have been working in Mexico for the past fifteen years."

"And?"

"Look, I don't care if I'm supposed to be his fucking cousin. You can't pay me enough to wear that cowboy hat or those ridiculous cobra boots. They looked stupid on Denton, and they'll look even worse on me." I pushed the hat away again when he shoved it at me. "No. Eric Noah is his own person. He's not gonna dress like a freakin' billboard for both countries."

"Fine." He tossed the white hat. "Tell me about your family."

"I've got none."

"No, you have a brother—"

I cut him off. "Less is easier to remember. I know Frank asked you to help me, and I know you're doing

*your job, but the only way this whole thing will work
is if I have some say in creating my own world."
"Fine." He pulled out a Jarritos soda from the fridge
and handed it to me. "Have you met the priest yet?"
"No."
"Let's do that now, then." We stepped outside, and he
snickered at the heat. "If it helps, you'll never get used
to it."
He was right.*

A knock at the hotel door jolted me back to the present and I grabbed a metal coat hanger and untwisted it quickly. I wound it around my fist, then inched close to the door.

"Who is it?" I called.

"Room service."

"I didn't order any room service."

"I know, but a Frank Washington did." I lowered my fist and opened the door a crack. I kept my boot against it as I swept my gaze over his shoulder and down the hall.

All clear. I rolled my eyes at Frank's not so subtle alias.

"Ah," the man sensed my mood, "why don't I just leave it here, and you can wheel it inside your room."

"Good plan." I waited until he left then quickly pulled the cart into my room. I locked the door and wedged a chair under the handle. I tried to shake off the feeling of unease about being in a hotel room by myself with no real weapon.

I had to focus minute by minute. If I looked too far

ahead my mind would spin out. The smell of steak found me, and suddenly I felt starved.

I ate the meal and drank the beer that came with it. I glanced at the bar fridge and wished I could have another, but I knew it wouldn't be a good idea. I couldn't afford to alter my head in any way. I didn't bother to wheel the cart back out; they'd get it when I left in the morning.

I picked up the laptop Frank had sent and put it on the table. I opened it and logged in to the server for my house in Rosarito. I needed to download my files. Even though I'd installed safeguards, I knew I couldn't risk my videos, audios, and emails might end up in someone else's hands. While the files downloaded, I checked the live camera feeds around and inside the house.

The entire perimeter crawled with Castillo's men. I tapped another camera and brought up the living room feed and inched closer to the screen. Alejandro paced the floor. He was obviously pent-up and tugged at his hair. He kept looking out the window, then would look at his phone and began to pace again. Who was he waiting for?

I grabbed a water glass and moved to the couch, then pulled out the phone. I dialed the number by heart and waited for it to connect.

"Chili," he answered.

"You alone?"

"Jesus," he hissed. "Just a sec. Let me." I heard him walking then everything went quiet. "What the hell happened?"

"What do you know?"

"Just that you got ambushed and you and the girl are missing."

"Did Frank call you?"

"He did, but I couldn't answer. Castillo came by."

What? That made me nervous.

"When?"

"Early this morning, like six thirty."

Huh. "What'd he want?"

"He wanted to know if I heard from you." There was a sudden lightness to his voice. "I got to get in his face and demand my money back. That felt damn good."

"I bet." I chuckled darkly. "How'd he take it?"

"He backed down only because he could tell I had no idea what was going on."

"Good."

"Eric, what happened?"

"We got ambushed."

"By who?"

"No idea. I'm still not ruling out Castillo."

"Smart."

"We got away, but then she was shot. I barely got out alive myself."

"What? Is the girl dead?"

"Yeah." I hung my head and rubbed my neck. "Look, Chili, things got messy. Alejandro heard me calling in to headquarters. I'm watching him on the feed now. He knows who I really—" I saw Filippo rush through the front door of the house, and Alejandro dragged him into my office.

"Eric?"

"One sec." I tapped the screen to the office camera and turned up the volume.

"Where the fuck have you been?" Ale screamed in his face.

"Can you hear this?" I asked Chili.

"Yeah. Is that Filippo?"

"He just showed up. He's with Ale." I went quiet so we could hear their conversation.

"Look, man," Filippo sounded scared, "I just managed to get my ass back here after being shot at all night. Where's Eric?"

"I need to tell you something, something big—"

"Should we be here, in his fucking office? What if he comes home? What if there's cameras?"

"He's not, and he's too paranoid to put cameras in here." He pushed Filippo into a seat and sat on the table to stare at him.

"We are in big-ass fucking trouble!" Ale shouted. "Like strip us naked, jam needles into our mouths, saw off our heads fucking trouble!"

"What are you talkin' about?" Filippo started to catch Ale's mood.

"The girl's dead, the deal's off, and worst of all, Eric's working with fucking Blackstone!" I watched as Filippo's eyes bulged out of his head. "Yeah, I walked up on him while he was talking to someone, used the same call signs as Blackstone does. Shit, maybe he is Blackstone. When he saw me behind him, it was written all over his face. He knew I caught him."

"What'd you do?" Filippo was in shock.

"I," he stumbled, "well, I ran. What else could I do? What if the feds suddenly showed up?"

"Coward," I muttered and heard Chili huff.

"We need to tell Castillo!" Filippo jumped up, and I saw Ale slam him back down.

"And how will that look? That our boss is an under-cover fuckin' agent. We'd be tortured for information we don't even have!" he screamed. "No, this shit stays right here. Not a single person can know." He gave Filippo a hard tap on the face. "Which means if Castillo walks through this door right now, all we know is our boss and that bitch are missing. We haven't seen either of 'em. Got it?"

"Got it," Filippo agreed.

"Jesus. Chili, can you believe that?" I muted the feed and spoke into the phone. "They're scared to tell Castillo. He doesn't know."

FIVE

"How're they doing, do ya think?" I asked quietly as I rested my chin on Ivy's shoulder. We watched Keith and the kids as they sat on the couch at the other end of the room and stared out the window at the snowfall. "I mean all things considered, of course."

I slipped an arm around her waist as she sipped her coffee, and she used her free arm to cover mine.

"They're numb." Her emotion was thick on her words. "He told them last night, and they slept there together. They woke a bit ago, but they haven't moved. They cry, they stare, they cry some more. It's utterly heartbreaking to watch."

"Has Doc Roberts tried to talk to them yet?" I knew

Ivy was giving them their space, but I wasn't sure if Doc would use the same approach.

"I don't think so. Abby said he hasn't been around—"

"Shit." Mark's curse made us both move toward the kitchen. The place was a mess. He had flour in his hair, and an egg and some milk dripped from the counter. He had on an apron, which I assumed was Abby's, that hung loosely from his hips where it provided no protection whatsoever for his clothes.

"What are you doing?" Ivy moved a cutting board that had begun to smoke from the open flame on the stove.

He scowled at her. "I'm trying to make cookies. Savi gave me the kids' favorite chocolate chip cookie recipe, but she failed to mention how many damn steps there are. Who uses a blender when making cookies, anyway?"

Ivy leaned over and looked at the recipe. "You only blend the oats."

"I saw that, but I got egg on me, the flour bowl knocked over and puffed a white cloud in my face, then I knocked the milk over." He closed his eyes. "I can make a bomb with fewer ingredients than this." He dabbed at the counter with a dish towel. "Apparently, I'm about to be taken down by cookies." I grinned and thought about the last time I'd tried to bake anything. I nearly burnt down Mom's kitchen. I knew my place, and it sure wasn't the kitchen.

"Hey," Ivy placed a hand on his shoulder, "you're trying to do something nice. Why don't I help you?"

"Really?" He looked worn out but then narrowed his eyes on her. "What's the catch?"

"There's no catch," she swatted him, "but if Abby sees this kitchen, she just might ban you for life."

"Okay." He ran his eggy hands through his hair and put two new stripes of white through it. The egg made it stand straight up. Ivy fought a smile as she encouraged him to start washing the dishes while she began to look the recipe over.

"I'd ask what's happening here," Olivia took the stool next to me, "but one look at Uncle Mark and all my questions have been answered." Her eyes were puffy and her cheeks were red, but her sarcasm was right where it needed to be.

Ivy chuckled lightly. "Good morning. Your Uncle Mark is trying to make something special for Brandon and Reagan."

"Well, you know what they say," she sighed, "it's the thought that counts."

"Watch your six, little Logan." Mark snickered over his shoulder while I hid my smile.

"How was your trip home, Olivia?" Ivy stepped in.

"It was hard to leave the other kids when we all knew something happened. Reagan wouldn't let my hand go the whole way home." Her lip trembled a little.

"And B?" Mark asked as he dried his hands. Ivy handed her two eggs to break into the bowl she set in front of the little girl. She mindlessly went to work, which I thought was Ivy's intention.

"You know B, he's Uncle Keith Junior." She shrugged. "He hardly talked and listened to music the whole way back. I just let him be. When we got home, he gave me a long hug then he went to where they were meeting in Dad's office." She swiped at her eyes. "Mom found me in my room and told me what happened."

Ivy handed her the chocolate chips to pour in and stir. "And how are you holding up?"

"I'm okay. I figured it out when Dad hugged me when we got home. He does this extra-large bear hug thing, you know." She paused. "They're my favorite." She glanced at Ivy and got teary-eyed. "I'm just sad for a different reason."

"Grief can hit you in different ways, sweetie." Ivy handed her a spoon of cookie dough to eat. "Some people get mad, some get sad, some are happy. There's no right way to mourn someone."

"It's different than that." She cleared her throat and looked away. She seemed almost ashamed to speak.

Ivy studied her for a second, then a light dawned in her eyes, as if she understood. Mark and I were totally lost.

"That's normal too." Ivy leaned her forearms on the island and lowered herself to Olivia's eye level. "That's being scared. Scared is on that list."

"I know my mom was kidnapped years ago." Olivia spoke quietly. "I've heard people talk about it lots of times, and I mostly figured out what happened. I just can't help thinking what if...it was my mom." She started to cry, and Mark tossed the spoon he was holding into the sink and raced to Olivia. He pulled her off the stool, and she buried her face in his shoulder.

"Truth," he said into her hair as tears leaked down his face, "there was a moment I thought the same thing." She sobbed even harder, and I had to blink a few times to stop my own emotion from bubbling over. "The difference is your momma would never leave this house, leave your dad, leave your brother, leave you, or any of us. Your mom and dad are in a whole different place than Uncle Keith and Aunt Lexi were. You understand that, right?" He held her tight as she continued to sob.

Savannah ran into the kitchen with Cole on her heels. They must have heard her crying. Olivia looked up at the sound and swung herself into her mother's arms then pulled her father in close.

"She's scared about the what-ifs," Ivy explained. "If it was Savi." Cole's face fell.

Mark leaned in and kissed Olivia's head then turned back to washing the dishes.

"I think we could use a little family time." Cole began to usher them out of the room but not before he stopped and looked at Mark. "Hey." Mark slowly turned to look at him, and I saw something pass between the two. Mark nodded.

Ivy put the tray in the oven and set the timer.

They worked in silence, so I stepped into the other room. Brandon and Reagan still held on to their father like a lifeline. Moore caught my eye as he came in through the dining room and held up his phone and a finger to show he'd be right over. The smell of cookies filled the room, and I felt my appetite kick in and moved back to the kitchen.

"Ivy," Mark said over his shoulder, "do you believe that things happen for a reason?"

"Only when I can make sense of it," she admitted as she pulled the tray from the oven and set it on the cooling rack. I had to agree with her. There were way too many things that were wrong in this world to believe in something like that. "Why do you ask?"

"I just can't help but think you were brought here to help us get through all this."

"Well, if I wasn't, Doc Roberts is here." Classic Ivy. Whenever any praise came her way, she shared some of it with others.

"Roberts is great, but you," he paused, "you're somethin' special. Cole was right to fight for you."

"Fight?"

"Yeah. Frank wanted you back to work directly with Eagle Eye, but Cole wasn't going to let you go without a fight. Keith spoke on your behalf, too."

"Really?" Her face lit up.

"Even Ty did." He shrugged at me. I guessed some secrets were meant to be shared.

"I didn't know that happened." She eyed me. "I must say that's really nice to hear."

"Thanks." He put some cookies on a plate. "I'm going to go see if they want some."

"You're welcome," Mark responded to their thanks. It was nice to see the kids perk up and take a cookie each. Mark took a seat next to Keith and began to speak quietly.

The Blackstone way of understanding each other was my goal for my team. I couldn't have asked for better mentors than these guys.

"So, you spoke on my behalf?" Ivy broke a cookie in half and popped a piece in my mouth. I pulled her to me.

"Did you really think I was going to let you leave?"

"I just didn't know Frank was considering pulling me for his team."

"He brought it up to Cole the other day while Keith and I were in the room. We gave him our feelings on it."

"Yeah, and what were your feelings, exactly?" She nibbled on the cookie.

"That you leaving wasn't an option both for professional and personal reasons." I slipped my hand in her hair. "That the house needed you as much as I did."

"That was a pretty big admission."

"You're worth it." I gently brushed over her lips then stepped back. "I need to go meet with Frank. I'll find you later?"

"Okay." She checked her watch. "I've got to find John in fifteen, anyway."

I raced toward the stairs and heard Reagan's laugh and found myself smiling. Mark was extra at times, but he loved this house with all his heart, and his humor was just what they needed.

Frank had the conference room ready to go by the time I joined him and Cole for another run-through of my mission to Afghanistan. We went through everything step by step, minute by minute. We researched local weather, chopper conditions, but when we got to the part about the town, Frank paused.

"What's wrong?"

"There's new satellite footage that shows a sudden increase in Taliban presence there." He clicked the remote, and it showed a lot of activity in the town.

"Shit." I couldn't believe what I was seeing. I knew they were there, but this seemed to show they were looking for something. "Any idea what's going on?"

"I have my suspicions."

"Which are?"

"I hate to say it, but I wonder if they've been tipped off about you going back. Maybe not you specifically, but a word about a U.S. soldier going back there would set things in motion fast."

"No way." I shook my head. "Even Hill wouldn't be that stupid to tip off the Taliban. They've been the enemy we've fought for years."

"I'm just saying a sudden increased presence of that enemy would be a good way to have you change your mind about going back there." Frank shrugged.

"If I may," Cole got up, "I've seen firsthand what a fellow soldier is capable of. How someone can turn and work with the enemy." Frank shifted uncomfortably. "Hill seems to be unravelling, and he's probably desperate. It's obvious he's hiding something, and if he did tip off the men he spent the last how many years trying to kill," he made a face, "in my experience that means you must be close to finding the truth, my friend. And whether that means the evidence is over there or here, it just might have him in panic mode."

We all looked up as Keith walked by the door with John close behind. They both looked wrung out. Cole pushed the door open and called out, but they didn't hear him and kept walking.

"Logan," I felt the heaviness of the house flow through the open conference room door, "I'm fine with this new development about the Taliban, but be straight with me. Should I be leaving Shadows? I know I'm new and didn't know Lexi, but we're a team, and I don't want anyone thinking my situation trumps Keith. Because it doesn't." Keith suddenly materialized in the doorway.

"Life can't stop because another's has, Beckett." He swallowed hard. "Besides, I'm ready to shed some blood, so go do what you gotta do and get back here, so we can leave for the south. But we're not leaving without you." He gave me a tight nod and left.

"I think you have your answer." Cole nodded with a grim face.

After that, we finished the rest of the mission review then closed up for the day. When Cole mentioned the idea of training on the mountain, Frank advised against it.

"I need you to gather Blackstone in the entryway." He looked at me. "That includes you and Moore."

"Yes, sir."

Frank hurried off toward Doc Roberts' office.

"What's going on?" I asked Cole, whose face was unreadable.

"I have no idea."

I quickly called Moore and met him outside in the driveway. He looked at his phone as he approached.

"Everything okay? You seem to have something going on." I pointed at his phone.

"Yeah." He tucked the phone away. "It's Jay. He called twice but then didn't pick up when I called back. It's odd, that's all. We've been trying to hook up."

Jay, Rowe, and Beam had all gone to work for the Redstone police after we got back from Afghanistan. Redstone had been in desperate need of officers, and when we got back, the three of them had followed Frank's suggestion and applied to work there. They'd all been happily hired on the spot.

"I want in on that. I'd like to see Jay. Try to make it for when I get back?" At the sound of Frank's voice, we both turned.

"What's going on?" Moore asked Mike as we got close.

"Lexi's body arrived in North Dakota." His face was grim. "We're doing this as a family."

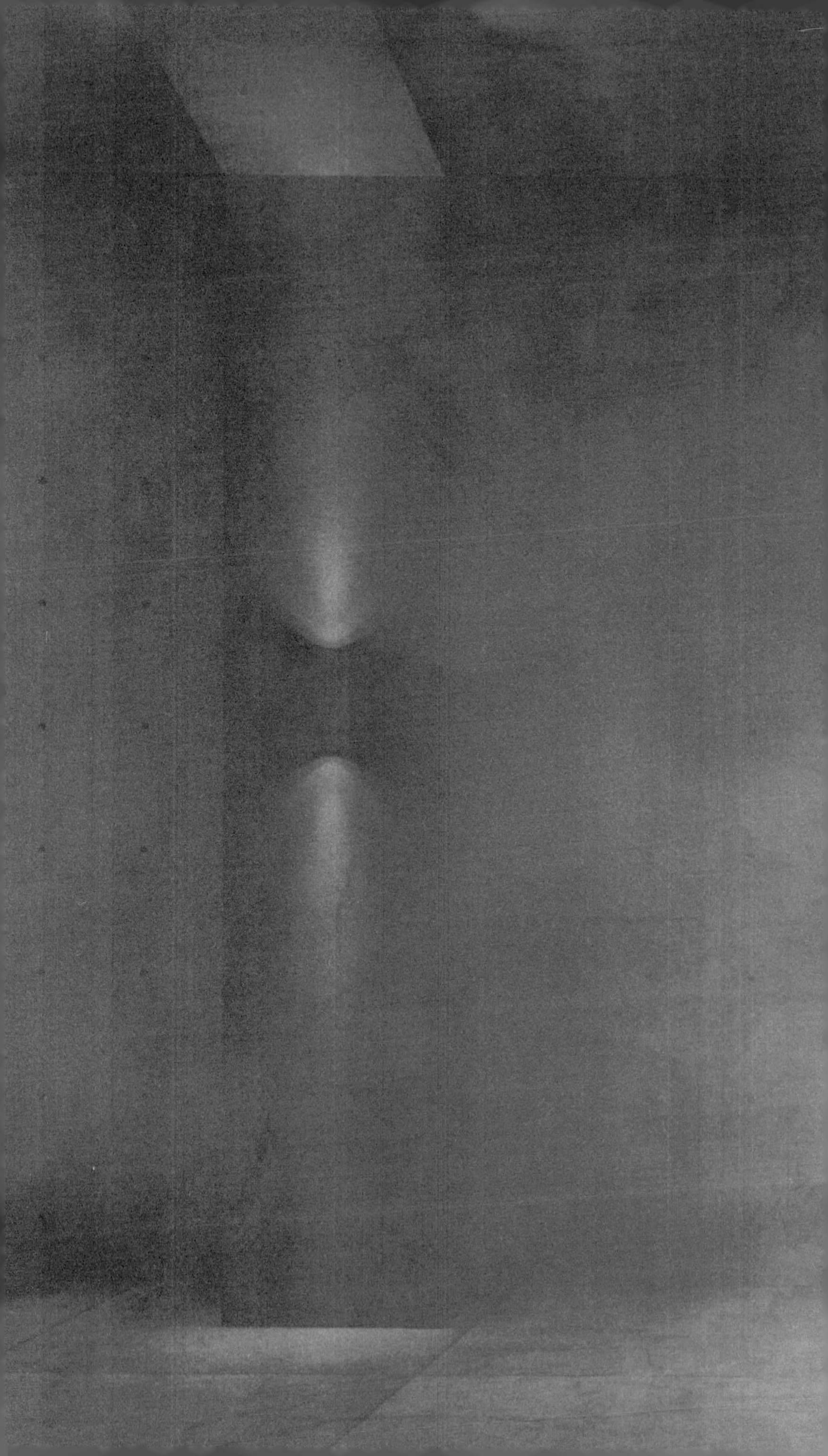

Special Mission Unit Debriefing
Location: United States
Coordinates: Classified

MAJOR PAUL

Also known as Eric Noah
Undercover Mexican Cartel Member

My head felt like it had been opened and dissected piece by piece, with no part left untouched. I was asked a hundred and one questions one way and a hundred and one questions another way. I knew what they were doing, and I understood the importance of it, but it didn't mean it hadn't taken a tiny part of me away.

I'd seen three psychologists and still had one more to go. I had no idea at that point if I'd even passed any of their tests, but if that was what it took to get me home, I'd do it.

"B-13?" One of the men stood in the doorway and had used the only name he'd been given for me. "Right this way."

I followed him for the fourth time down the long dark hallway. I wondered if they'd ever thought to install a couple of windows in this place. Three stripes of colored tape on the floor led you in the direction you needed to go, but there was barely enough light to make them out. When I arrived, I was given a letter, a number, and a color. That was the only thing anyone knew about me. That was how classified this place was.

"When that light turns green, you head inside." The guy's voice was monotone. "When you're finished, you head out the other door and wait for me to come get you." I nodded and took a seat on the now familiar cold metal chair and rubbed my fingers against my thumbs. I heard the light click over to green, and I took a deep breath, stood, and opened the door.

Holy shit.

We both mirrored each other's shocked faces. Sure, I knew this moment had to come at some point, but I wasn't prepared for it.

"*Major Paul?*" he stuttered then pointed to a chair like a robot, but his face was flushed with emotion.

"Doc Roberts." His name felt good to say, and I exhaled with ten years of secrets weighing heavily on my chest. "You look good."

"And you look…*alive?*" He shook his head in disbelief then removed his glasses and blinked a few times as he tried to regain his composure.

"I believe this is the first time I've seen you lost for words." I chuckled, more out of nerves than anything.

"Well, it's not every day you find out that one of your own is back in the flesh." He pushed his glasses back on and grinned.

"How's John?" I blurted without a thought.

"Oh, my. Well, let's jump right into it so we can get you out of here."

"I'd really like that." I nodded for him to begin, not realizing how much my brother had been on my mind.

Like a wire brush to the gums, I answered the same painful questions as before about where my loyalty lay and if I was fit to be back with the team fighting the ones I'd just lived among. I was sure he added a few other questions that he just wanted to know.

"You can relax now." He closed the file. "You did well."

"I hope the other psychologists felt the same way."

"They did," he reassured me. "I glanced at their results just before I came to meet you. They all gave the green light for B-13 to return to duty." He smiled.

"Really?" I couldn't fight the relief that spread through me, but it was quickly replaced with nerves.

"Yes, Paul, it's time to go home." He clapped me on the back and made a gleeful sound.

"Yes, home," I repeated, letting some of my defenses fall. He smiled and waved me to follow.

———

"Anything to drink, sir?" the flight attendant asked as she handed me a hot towel. Thankfully, I'd been on a private plane once before with Castillo. The experience hadn't been enough to prepare me for this, but at least I didn't look around all round-eyed. I managed to take it in stride.

"Whiskey sour, please," I said from habit. "I mean, make that a beer. IPA if you have it."

"Of course." She hurried off, and I leaned back in the soft leather seat. I figured Frank would bring me home via coach or in the belly of a cargo plane, but to my utter discomfort, I was going home on a private jet. I felt self-conscious and nervous that whoever picked me up would think I wasn't the same old Paul if I arrived in this fancy machine.

Dr. Roberts sat across from me, nose in a book, but a few times I caught his eyes go to the window. He didn't say much, but in fairness, neither did I. There were so many unanswered questions still between us, and I knew they needed to be addressed. I figured he must have decided to wait until we were with the others so I wouldn't have to tell everything twice. At least I hoped that was the case.

When the flight attendant returned with my beer, I nearly drank the entire thing in one swallow.

"Another?" She smiled.

"No, thank you." I handed her back the glass and let the alcohol tame a little of my anxiety. I looked at Doc. "I don't drink like that normally. Must be nerves."

"And here I was thinking I'd be ordering a double scotch on the rocks." He chuckled. "Please don't take my silence as judgement, Paul. I'm merely processing what's to come."

"I think that's become my new insecurity," I confessed.

"I don't blame you. I find myself questioning why Frank didn't warn me about who I was sent to bring home. Perhaps he wanted you to have a little practice run of what you might expect," he sat back, "because they'll all be thrown by your sudden, ah, resurrection. It took them time to accept and deal with your death. It's a lot to understand and process. Humans are surprisingly good at adapting, and things will all be okay, but in time. Everything takes time." He smiled encouragement.

"I know that, and I totally get it." I nodded. "And I can imagine this isn't a good time what with Lexi and—" I stumbled over her name and swallowed back my own emotion, and he studied my face and nodded.

"I think it just might be a good time." He looked

thoughtful. "They're mourning Lexi, yes, and they'll be thrown to see who brought her home, but I think it just might be a good time."

"Right." I knew I sounded doubtful and turned to look out the window just as the wheels touched down. We taxied to a private hanger, and I craned my neck and saw the two SUVs open their doors. My heart nearly plummeted.

My brothers.

"Let them have a moment with Lexi, then when you're ready, come out." Doc undid his seatbelt and paused. "Remember, shock, anger, disbelief, acceptance, but most of all, time. Remember you're the one who brought her back to them."

"Thanks, Doc."

The door opened, and he walked down the stairs. I watched the dark wood coffin as it was removed from the plane's belly. I knew it was just a temporary thing. She'd already been cremated and was resting in an urn inside. Frank thought the first glance should be of a coffin, something about how the brain processes things.

A huge lump formed in my throat as Cole walked with Keith toward the coffin. He put an arm around him as my brother broke. A few moments later, Cole stepped back, and I could see him gather himself while the others came forward to touch the coffin and give their support to Keith. Each muttered something as they stood there. I didn't lip read out of respect.

The doc looked toward my window and I knew it was

time. How I willed my feet to move was beyond my understanding, but it was now or never.

I fixed my ball cap as I came into view of the door, snagged my duffle bag, and stood at the top of the steps. I kept my head down until I was on the ground then lifted it. The first set of eyes I found were John's.

His face drew back as he took me in, his eyes wide. Then he turned white. The others looked over at him as he froze, took a step back, and put a hand to his mouth. Then John slowly began to move toward me. He stepped past Mike and Mark, his eyes in a squint to try to get a better look at me. No one else moved as he took the last three steps and stopped in front of me.

My jaw ticked and my heart bounced around in my chest as our eyes locked. Recognition dawned and affirmed.

"Son of a bitch," he hissed then he swung and punched me right in the jaw. I held my ground and didn't waver as the pain turned to fire and brought tears to my eyes as I tried to hold his stare. His eyes went red and glossy, then he reached forward and pulled me hard into a hug. "Paul?" he whispered, and I dropped my bag and wrapped my arms around him.

"It's me," I choked out. "It's really fucking me."

One by one, each of the guys took their turn to greet me in some way. Little was said. They were all trying to figure it out, but we all knew it wasn't the time. A couple of other guys I didn't know held back.

Frank waved them forward and quickly introduced

me after he saw me glance at them. "This is Ty Beckett, the leader of our newest team, and Kit Moore, his second." I gave a quick nod, and they both did the same.

I knew there'd be things that had changed while I was away, but a new team sure wasn't something I expected. I'd have to get my head around that one, and that was okay. I just needed to get through this.

"Paul?" Keith, who had been through hell and back, stumbled to make sense of what was happening. "You're supposed to be dead." He looked at Cole. "Please tell me you didn't know."

"I knew nothing." Cole glared at Frank, who shook his head. "But my guess would be that you were Frank's informant in Mexico?"

"Yes." I watched as everyone absorbed that.

"Which means," Cole shot another death glare at Frank, "you and Lexi were in a heap of shit."

"He still is," Frank corrected. "Look, I know there's a lot we need to talk about, but everything will be explained in time. We need to get back to Shadows."

"Yes." Cole nodded and put his arm around Keith's shoulders. "Let's get our girl home."

That was all that needed to be said, and we walked together beside Lexi's coffin to the SUVs, and then Keith carefully lifted the urn from the satin cushion inside the coffin and set it gently in the back.

SEVEN

IVY

"Hey," Savannah knocked softly on my office door, "got a minute?"

"Always." I pulled off my computer glasses and waved her to a comfy chair then sat across from her. Scoot yawned at the interruption to his nap.

"Don't complain, kitty." I gave him a quick ear scratch. "These are our people, remember."

"Don't even bother asking how I'm feeling because I have no idea." She chuckled heavily as she kicked off her heels and pulled her feet up to get more comfortable. "Doc Roberts would ask for three words, and I'd say sad, tired, and relieved." I let her run with her thoughts. "Then

I'd probably cringe at the words I chose because it'd be horrible to be relieved that someone's dead."

She stopped a moment and looked at me, but when I didn't reply, she bit her lip then continued. "But I am relieved, it's like we were all stuck. No one could move forward or backward. Every day was filled with the same dread, every phone call, every text, and our stomachs would tighten. What if it was her? What if it was about her?" She covered her face with a groan. "Then my poor Liv had a breakdown. She was so scared it would happen to me, and," tears flowed down her cheeks, "call me terrible, but I just need to laugh or scream or something. Oh, Ivy, this house has been through so much over the years, and it's all so heavy. Will it ever end?" She let out a short breath and gave a little hiccup. "Don't answer that. We knew this was a possibility when we married these guys, but trafficking a wife? What's next? Our kids?" She squeezed her eyes shut like that thought made her ill. "Sorry, that was dark." Then she just sat back as if exhausted, but her face showed she'd finally gotten what she wanted off her chest.

I stood and tapped my lips while I pondered what she really needed. I walked over to my desk I pulled out a notepad.

"I don't like pills." She shook her head.

"This isn't for pills." I ripped the paper off the top. "This," I moved back to the couch, "is to be taken in the evening only, and can be used as much as needed." I handed it to her, and her face lit up.

"Girls' night out?" She raised a brow. "I think this is the best prescription I've ever gotten."

"I completely understand how you've been feeling, Savannah. And you know, sometimes the best way to break free from that heavy feeling is to completely change what you've been doing. Maybe, after the funeral, we can plan a night. We all need to burn off the darkness that's hung over us."

"Yeah, I like that idea." She caught a tear as it slipped out. "We can have a drink for her." She smiled.

"That's a nice thing to do." I squeezed her hand. "What happened sucked." I knew she needed to hear it real. "It's friggin' devastating that Lexi lost her life and the kids are without a mother, but she knew the risks and still chose to be reckless. I'm not blaming her because no one deserves to have their life taken from them, but choices have consequences."

"I think that's why I'm so wound," she huffed. "All of this could have been avoided!"

"Yes, it could have. Lexi was suffering mentally and needed help. She couldn't change who she was, no matter how hard she tried. Some just can't or won't accept help. And sadly, we can't change what happened. We just need to mourn, then process and learn from what happened and hope the future brings Keith and the kids some happiness again."

"I'm scared for B and Reagan."

"Don't be." I shook my head. "You need to worry about yourself, your kids, and Cole. Let me worry about the rest. I know you're a fixer, but don't carry that on your shoulders, or you'll burn out. I don't have the emotional connection you had with Lexi, so it's easier for me to help the others. It's why I'm here."

"Okay." She pulled at the sleeve of her sweater as she thought.

"How are the rest of the wives? I haven't seen much of Catalina."

"Mia and Sloane are feeling like me. Cat is taking it the hardest, but all things considered, she's hanging in there."

"Is it worth me seeking her out yet?"

"Honestly, I wouldn't. I think this," she held up the prescription, "is the best way to deal with her. It's a wonderful idea."

"I appreciate the insight."

I tapped my finger on the couch and chewed the inside of my cheek as I contemplated the secret that I'd learned that morning.

"What?" She sensed my hesitation.

"I just might have overheard something this morning that might cheer you up a little."

"Oh, my God," her face brightened, "is it something on Mark? Because I always feel better when I can take him down." I laughed. I loved this house more and more every day. "Wait, are you it?"

I chuckled. "No, I got Ty with that one."

"Ha! I wish I was there for that."

"No, this is about June and a *sext* I accidently stumbled across."

"Oh, my God. This is like Christmas for me." Savi sat up straight with a smile as she prepared herself for the news. "Okay, so tell me, do you know who she's been dating?"

"If that's what you want to call dating, sure." I laughed loudly.

"Well, spill it!"

"They're back!" June shouted through the house. We both jumped up and hurried out of the office. There'd be time to pick this up later.

The SUVs pulled in one behind the other, and the doors opened. The guys' heads hung heavy, and they moved slowly. Keith was stopped by someone I couldn't see. I squinted through the snow flurries but couldn't get a good look. Whoever it was placed a hand on his shoulder, spoke a few words, and then stepped back as Keith disappeared around the SUV. A moment later, he returned holding a dark green urn.

"Who's that?" I asked Olivia when she appeared by my side with a book hugged to her chest. The fact she didn't recognize him made me more curious as to who our guest was.

"Probably one of Uncle Frank's team. Eagle Eye. But not sure." She shrugged then made a funny little noise when Ty made a rush toward the front door of the house. "What's with Ty?"

"I'm not sure." The rest of the guys started toward the

house, and the wives all gathered in the entryway to greet them.

"I'm not sure I'm ready for this," Cat whispered loudly enough for me to hear. She reached for Brandon as he came up the stairs from playing Xbox. She kissed his head, but he didn't react, just stood there with his face blank. We watched as Keith carefully shifted the urn from one hand to the other. My uncle held Reagan in his arms, and she had a death grip on his neck. Her eyes were puffy from crying, and her sniff made my insides hurt. Those poor kids. What a confusing time for them.

"Wait, who is that?" Abby stepped out on the porch to get a better look at the mystery man. I leaned forward to see, as Cole moved closer to Savi.

Why does he look so familiar? Just then, Ty came up and made a beeline for me.

A scream from Abby made us all freeze as the guy looked up and moved toward her.

"Abby?" Savi flew to her side and then followed her line of sight to a man about John's age with a duffle bag at his feet. "It can't be!" Her knees buckled, and Cole wrapped an arm around her, holding her close.

"Hey, Sav," he smiled widely, "I missed ya."

Reagan reached for her father when he got close enough, and June quickly whisked the urn out of sight. She curled into Keith while Brandon stood next to Olivia.

"It's okay," Keith assured Brandon with a hand to the top of the head. Sue grew pale and stepped into the other room, most likely just needing a moment.

Ty drew me protectively to his side. It wasn't a show of ownership. It was more that he was nervous, which quickly put me on alert.

"Apparently, Major Paul has returned from the dead," Ty whispered into my hair. "It's been a strange day, to say the least."

Oh, the picture, the one the guys always touched. Now I knew why he looked familiar. "Just when I thought the house couldn't take any more blows." I sighed and tucked myself closer to absorb his warmth. I needed some comfort as I scrambled to figure out just what effect this latest news would have on everyone.

"If this doesn't fuck us up more, I don't know what will." Mark slapped Paul's shoulder with a classic Mark grin as he gave us all a look. "Wait, what am I smelling? Is that pie?"

"It's kind of amazing how he processes shit." Frank shook his head. "Come on, Paul. Why don't we come inside, and you can share some of your story."

"Or all of it," June chimed in next to him.

"We have a lot to go over, and we have to prep for this afternoon, so not too many questions," Frank warned.

"Ah, before we start," Paul held up a hand, "Frank and Cole, can I just have three minutes of your time?"

"We can do that." Cole jerked his head toward his office. John began to follow, but Paul looked at him and he stopped. "I promise I'll be quick." His face was unreadable, but John nodded then turned and began to walk toward the others in the living room. I had heard that

John and Paul had been very close before he'd supposedly died. They obviously had a connection, as he didn't question Paul.

Olivia grabbed her mother's hand, and they walked together to join the others. I had noticed Olivia seemed to need to touch her mother more lately. I tucked that information away.

Keith came in and gathered Brandon with a one-arm bear hug, then they sat down. I saw Abigail and June go over to them. I knew they would know just how to soothe the grieving family.

Ty kept me locked in place, then once everyone had moved on, he pulled me down the hallway and into my office.

"Are you all right?" I asked after he closed the door and took my hand again. "Did something come up with Hill?"

"I'm struggling," he admitted, "with this Paul guy. I don't want to be, but I am."

"Okay." I kept my mouth closed.

"My head's all," he waved his free hand around, "twisted up."

"Okay."

"Apparently, he died, but lived, and became some undercover informant working for the damn enemy."

"Wow, okay." I felt like I was in a damn novel.

"Okay?" He looked at me strangely.

"I'm treading carefully here, Ty. I'm merely listening."

"What does that mean?"

"I know how you get if I become too supportive. You'll say I'm being Dr. Knight, so I'm just listening to what you have to say instead."

"How I get?" His face pulled back in defense.

"Are you looking for a fight?" I pulled my hand from his and rested it on my hips. "If you need that, fine. Just let me know because I'm still digesting the last bit of news you shared with me." Yup, I was still processing the news he was leaving me for Taliban country.

"Fuck!" He closed his eyes and took a deep breath. "I'm sorry." I could see he was. "I don't deal well with things that bother me like this. Okay," he breathed through his nose, "I'm going to try to do this right. Why am I so twisted up inside that one of their fallen has suddenly returned?"

"Do you want me, or my doctor take on this?" I wanted to be clear on how to answer him.

"Give me your doctor take." I saw his mask slip. This was hard for him, but I wasn't going to hold back because that wasn't who I was.

"From what you've just told me, and your past, I'd say you don't trust him. You still view him as the enemy."

"Yeah, that's exactly it." He nodded quickly. "I look at him and see a snake in the grass. How do we know he hasn't flipped? He fooled the Cartel for ten fucking years. How do we know he wasn't sent here to do the same?"

"Well, that's something you'll have to figure out on your own."

"That's your advice?" he griped.

"Yes, it is. I can't change your mind. I haven't experienced what you have. What I would suggest is to tread very carefully. To everyone else, he's someone special." I hurried for the door, as I wanted to hear the story from Paul himself. "Remember, very few have walked through that door, so the fact that he's here means he's been deeply examined by top-notch psychologists. If he got cleared, then his head must be screwed on straight." He looked away, as he knew I was right.

"Ivy," he called as I opened the door, "for now, can you just keep your distance from him?"

"No." Because I knew I wouldn't. I held up a hand to stop his protest. "But I will keep my guard up. I promise. Come on. Let's go down and hear what he has to say. It's important to me to be in on all this firsthand."

As we settled on one of the open couches, Paul returned with Frank and Cole. I reached for Ty's hand and tried my best to ground him. Paul sat on the brick at the base of the fireplace and let out a long breath. Everyone impatiently waited to hear his story.

"If I may?" Mia spoke first, to my surprise. "I wanted to ask you to start at the hospital."

"Sure." Paul brushed his thumb over his lips as Mia continued.

"I saw you die for a second time on that table, Paul. It's something I've carried with me for years. I also remember Frank came in with some others, and I was asked to leave and go share the terrible news of your death with the others." She shot her father a nasty look.

"It was—"

"No," she cut Frank off, "I'll deal with you later. Right now I want to hear it from Paul." Frank cleared his throat, and I thought he might lash out at her, but instead he just swallowed back her comment and stayed quiet. Smart man.

"I did die," Paul cut in. "That wasn't a lie. Frank told me his team began to work on me and managed to get a heartbeat. Once they did, he realized the opportunity." He glanced at Frank. "Then I guess I was taken to some other room away from you all. When I woke up, I was in so much pain. I didn't know what end was up. Then I was given a choice, an opportunity to help and protect all of you. Just from a different side."

"Jesus, I had no idea," Cole muttered as he side-hugged Savannah. "For the record, up until this very moment, I was in the dark, too." Again, a few sets of angry, hurt eyes moved to where Frank stood.

"Then what?" John broke the silence.

"I listened to what Frank had to say. I began to understand what it might mean to have someone on the other side. He made me see how valuable I could be. I didn't have any blood relatives to leave behind, and Frank knew that, too. It wasn't an easy decision, but it was one I had to make quickly. I hardly remember agreeing to it. I just knew that if I could help in some way, it would be worth taking the chance." He paused and bit down on his knuckle, clearly trying to control his emotions.

"So, you just became a member of the Cartel?" Mike blurted. "Just like that." He snapped his fingers.

"Not just like that, but I stepped into an already moving operation. Frank had it all set up. I just needed money, knowledge, the right mindset, and a solid backstory—"

Cat jumped in and fired off a question. "Which was?" Paul's reaction to her was subtle but obvious as he glanced toward Keith and his dazed children.

"Maybe we can visit that another day." He directed his eyes back to Cat.

"Agreed. Just stick to basics for now," Frank added with a *no room for argument* tone.

"Um," Paul tried to find his place, "my job was to take charge of the tunnel from San Diego through Rosarito. Which was run by Martin Castillo." I felt the mood in the room shift.

"The man who took Lexi," Keith confirmed.

"Come on, kids, I think it's time for some ice cream." Doc held out a hand toward Reagan, and Abigail threw him a relieved look. Reagan stood, and he swept her into his arms. Brandon got to his feet and folded his arms, and Olivia went to stand next to him. Their expressions were set, and it was obvious they were going to stand their ground. Doc looked at Keith and then Cole, but neither said a word, so he took Reagan into the kitchen. I was pleased that she was too tired to care about leaving every-one. The older children relaxed. I felt they needed to be included. It was a difficult subject, but they weren't your average kids. Paul hesitated but then continued his story.

"Yes, but he had help. Long story short, Rosa Coppola owed Castillo for reasons that would take a while to explain. She and her right-hand man, Tieri, were running from Elio Capri for a different reason." Ty looked at Keith, and they shared a quick moment. "Castillo found Rosa and Tieri and nabbed both of them. Rosa was desperate and, again, a long story, made a deal with Castillo to give him Lexi. Through a series of events, Tieri, through sheer coincidence, had found out where she was through her old friends the Almas Perdidas. Tieri was the one who led Castillo to her, yes, but I want to be clear here. It was Castillo who ordered her to be taken."

"Holy Christ." Keith sank back into his chair, and Savannah quickly joined him. Brandon put a hand on his father's shoulder.

I spoke up. "This is a lot. Should we stop?" I could tell this was hard for Paul, and his story was certainly complicated.

"Just a little more," Mark urged gently. "What role did you play in all this?"

"Okay, um," he rubbed his head to help sort out his thoughts, "normally, I'd get the girls when they came through the tunnel, keep them at my house until things were safe, then sell them to my buyer." I noticed he didn't give a name. "Once the money cleared, my buyer would hand the girls to another set of people, and they'd return them safely to the U.S. It was one big loop, tunnel, me, buyer, sent back to the U.S."

Sue addressed the elephant in the room. "The glaringly obvious omission is who is responsible for grabbing those young people in the first place."

"That's the part we need to stop, but at least I played a part to get them back. Especially Lexi. I really tried." Paul directed a painful look at Keith. Brandon glared at Paul, and he turned away.

The room was quiet as they absorbed the information.

"Thank you, Paul." Sue placed a hand on Daniel's arm, and he nodded and stood with her. "I think it's safe to say we are unbelievably happy you're here, and now we have the gift of time to learn all the details. But right now, we have a loved one to lay to rest."

Everyone went their separate ways, and I went to my room to prepare.

I was almost changed and ready to leave. Ty tapped on the door and opened it. He leaned his hip against the doorframe and folded his arms over his broad chest. His muscular body filled the space. A lot of emotion could be felt throughout the house, and some I secretly kept hidden because I didn't want to let the others know I was terrified of Ty leaving tomorrow. I forced the nerves aside and started to button up the last few pearls on my blouse. He pushed away from the door and stood behind me in the mirror and took over. His big hands were gentle as they moved upward. Once he was finished, he buried his face in my neck and breathed in deeply.

"You okay?" I tried to keep my own voice normal, but I knew the truth of how I felt was written all over my face right now that I was with only him.

"I will be when…" He stopped himself.

"If you get b-back?" I stumbled over the words and caught his gaze in the long mirror.

"When," he corrected and placed a soft kiss below my ear. "When I get back."

I closed my eyes and willed myself to live in the moment even if it was just a few seconds.

"Come on. I don't want to be late." I started for the door, and he caught up to me and slowed my near run with his hand. He put his arm around me, and we walked silently together.

Abby found us as we walked together up the mountain. The well-cleared path we followed was one the guys often used to get to training.

"Ty, why don't you go up with Keith, while I borrow Ivy for a moment." She smiled. Ty looked at me for a moment then nodded at her and did what she said. Abby always had the best intentions.

"I thought I should give you a little history lesson. I know you can do your job better if you know all the ins and outs of the house."

"I'd like that. Thanks." I looped my arm around hers to help her over an icy patch. Daniel had offered to drive anyone who wanted one, but most had declined. I think the walk was what many needed.

"Given the nature of our enemy, Lexi was cremated,"

she began. "Grandpa Edison Logan, years back, put in place some rules on how core members of the Shadows family should be handled after death. Burying a body in the town or even on our land isn't something we do. If the Cartel were ever to find out the location of the safehouse," she gave me a terrified look, "they might do some truly heinous things. So, because of their violent nature toward the living," she hesitated, "and the dead, we choose to cremate."

"That's smart."

"Yes, Edison was a smart man. He wasn't the type of person to leave anything to chance. He thought everything through. We hold a funeral up on the top of the mountain and release the ashes over the side so the body becomes part of the land again. There's a spot at the base of the mountain that has a beautiful view of the lake and the sunset. There are markers there for both Edison and Meg Logan. Lexi will have her own marker next to them. That way those who love them have a place to visit."

John quickly walked by. He reached out and squeezed Abby's arm as he did. Once again, I was impressed by the power of family in this house. It was staggering.

"I'm glad to hear there's a place for those who care to go and visit. That will be healthy for the kids, too. It doesn't always have to be a grave. Personally, I like this idea better."

"It's a little less formal," she replied, "like the tree and picture we have for Paul."

We gathered on the chilly mountaintop. It had

snowed the night before and made the trip up the side of the mountain trickier than we expected it to be. Everyone was there, though, and some had obviously put in the time to make it work. There were even a few folding chairs for the kids, Sue, and the aunts. I noticed Reagan was glued to her father's side while Olivia stayed close to Brandon.

"You good?" Frank asked as I stood slightly away from the others. I wanted to give them their space to grieve.

"As good as I can be on a day like this. I just want to be here in case someone needs support."

"Just being here is support enough." Frank tucked his hands in his pockets. "Thank you for being here to help everyone navigate through this, Ivy. I know Doc Roberts appreciates the help." I looked up at him and saw how much this entire situation weighed on him.

"When are you going to come see me?" I raised an eyebrow.

"Funny." He tried to smile, but it didn't work.

"I wasn't kidding."

"I know." He closed his eyes for a moment. "This wasn't supposed to happen. We had everything in place, then somehow, we lost control just like that." He snapped his fingers silently. "Now, here we are."

"What is it that you always say? *Adapt, and readapt.*"

"Now you choose to listen to me?" He tried to joke.

"Truth?" I turned my back to the others and faced the opposite side of the mountain. "Maybe Lexi leaving was a sign it was time for Paul to return. She knew her reckless-ness came with consequences. It was no secret the odds weren't in her favor. Maybe it's life's way of balancing out the scales again." He knew I wasn't wishing Lexi harm, just trying to find a way to say there was something posi-tive that came from what she'd done.

"You're a mind reader now." His face told me every-thing I needed to know. He was pissed at Lexi's actions, and I didn't blame him. The ripple effect of her actions had been selfish.

We both turned and tuned in when everyone went quiet.

Daniel hosted the service and kept it short. He welcomed others to come up and say a few words. Cole stepped forward when the others hesitated.

"Lexi was a free spirit who lived her life the way she wanted. There's something to be said for that. She may not be here physically, but she lives in the two of you." He pointed at Brandon and Reagan. "Never forget that."

Mike went next, then Savannah, and Catalina followed. It was lovely. Short and sweet was the way everyone needed it to be. Just a chance to say goodbye.

"Brandon and Reagan, would you like to come up here with your dad and help release the ashes?" Daniel handed the urn to Keith and Brandon. They both knelt to Reagan's level, removed the top, and set her free.

As the ashes poured from the jar, I closed my eyes and tried to picture Lexi being set free. She danced in the wind, sparkling and glittering as she became one with the mountains. I hoped the others were able to see it as I had. I felt the sense of relief from those who stood around me that at least this difficult part was over.

EIGHT

The funeral was short. No one went on too long, but it was long enough. It was simple and respectful. The kids were emotionally exhausted when we got back to the house, and they were all passed out in the entertainment room by six thirty. Daniel lit the firepit, and some of us gravitated down there to talk without worry we'd wake the kids.

The fire burned hot and bright, and I was glad because light snow continued to fall throughout the evening, and although Ivy would never admit it to anyone, she looked frozen. I tucked a blanket around her legs and draped my arm over the back of her chair. I just started to enjoy myself. I loved sitting there by the fire with Ivy. The snow looked nice, and just being with the guys and their families as they slowly made their peace with Lexi's loss made me feel part of them. Then *he* sat down across from me. I immediately tensed up. I didn't fully trust Paul yet, and neither did Moore. I saw him pull his legs back when Paul sat down. He was on edge around him, too, or maybe he was getting vibes from me. I had to consider that, as we still hadn't had a chance to talk things out. I nodded to myself as I thought again how great it was to know Moore had my back no matter what.

Regardless of my feelings, I knew the house needed time to recover. They needed to laugh, have a few beers, and talk it out. They all had pain to shed, and I couldn't think of a better way to do it.

"It was a beautiful service, a nice way to send her off." Savannah was the first to break the silence. "Cold, crisp air and a fresh layer of snow. A Shadows recipe at its finest."

"Agreed." Cole squeezed her hand. "Cat, I really like what you said about the kids not being alone because we're all here for them. That was a good reminder."

"They needed to know none of us are alone."

"A bit windy." Mike changed things up.

"Yeah, it's always windy up there. I just kept worryin' it was gonna change direction when they were sprinkling her ashes," Mark blurted. We all went silent and looked over at Keith, who erupted in a full-out belly laugh. Relieved, we all joined in, and we laughed until our sides hurt.

"I'm so glad I'm not the only one who thought that."

Keith laughed harder. "That would so be something Lexi'd do."

"It would, wouldn't it?" Doc Roberts shook his head. "Good lord, that young woman was always pulling something on you guys."

As the dark humor emerged and grew, I got the feeling from listening to the comments around me that it was just the type of thing Lexi would have liked. No tears, just inappropriate laughter, and a bit of fun.

"Remember when she stuck the Furby in your underwear drawer, Mark?" Mike laughed to the point of tears. "And you jumped so hard you tripped over Liam's truck and went flying?"

"I don't remember that," Paul blurted, and the laughter dissolved instantly.

Mike tried to be kind. "It was last year. Sorry, man."

"No, it's okay." He waved him off. "Sounds like it was fun."

"Must be strange being back," I cut in and knew my tone was a bit sharp. Maybe even more than I intended. "Do you ever find your head slippin' back?" He held my gaze for a moment, and for a brief second I felt bad for my wording. I couldn't help it. He'd lived with the enemy for over a decade, and I didn't know him to start with.

"No," he cleared his throat, "I had my ways to keep my head on straight."

"Oh, how?"

"Ty," Ivy looked at me, worried I was about to cross a line I couldn't come back from.

Cole, to my surprise, stepped in. "It's okay. We all have questions, and we can't expect Beckett or Moore to feel like we do about Paul. We've got history with him." He turned back to me. "To you and Moore, he's a stranger, but to us he was and is still family."

"I appreciate that," Paul answered but kept his focus on me. "I don't know a lot of informants, but from what I know, they often shut themselves off from the life they left behind. I chose to do the opposite." He ran his hands over his thighs to warm them.

"That doesn't really answer my question." I couldn't seem to stop myself.

"Back off, will ya, Ty?" Mike huffed, but Paul held up a hand.

"Look, I never asked for what happened to me." He looked around at everyone as he spoke. "Blackstone gave me the life I always wanted. I'd never had a real life before I came here. I cared so much for this place and these guys that part of my agreement with Frank was that I never wanted to forget. I insisted on monthly ten-minute calls with him just so I could hear about my brothers' lives. I needed to stay grounded and focused, and that worked for me."

"You had calls at your house?" Moore asked as he declined a phone call on his own phone.

"No, of course not. Frank set it up with a local priest. I'd go to church, and he'd let me use his office. My guys figured I used the church to clear my head. I guess in a way I did."

"And you trusted this priest?"

"I trusted Frank." He glanced over at Frank, who stood back from the rest of us. "Besides, everyone has a price, Moore. I'm sure you experienced that over in Afghanistan."

"We did." Moore glanced at me, and I felt Ivy flinch. Clearly, Frank had given Paul a rundown on us and our history.

"I hear you're goin' back tomorrow on a turnaround mission. Hope you find what you're lookin' for." I shot Frank a pissed look, and he shrugged. Nothing seemed to faze him. I knew everyone was aware I was leaving, but to tell the new guy… I was more than pissed.

"I need a refill." Ivy hopped up and headed toward the house.

Savannah flipped her cup over to show it was empty and stood. "Wait, Ivy, I need one, too." She threw me a look, and I appreciated Savannah so much in that moment.

"Okay," Cole held up his hands, knowing where this was headed, "clearly there's tension and shit needs to come out. But tonight isn't the—"

Keith interrupted him. "I have a lot of questions." He sat forward in his seat, and Cole backed off. "I'd like to start with you." He swung around to glare at Frank. "For tonight, we set our ranks aside. Man to man. Can we do that?"

"Fine." Frank tilted his head, ready for the storm that brewed.

"Cole?"

"Agreed." He gave a tight nod and looked at all of us, who also agreed.

"Frank, I've trusted you with my life. We all have, but I can't believe you knew Paul had my wife in his custody all that time and you never told me."

"You know I can't share an informant's information. You know—"

"The only thing I know, Frank, is that I could have spoken to my wife one last time before those savages drilled a hole in her stomach."

"I had no idea that things would go the way they did."

"And I get that, but you took that moment from me. We are and aren't part of the U.S. military. It depends on who's asking, but we've bent the rules before. We've crossed over lines in all walks of life to get what we needed done. I just don't know why you couldn't've crossed that one for me."

The only sound that could be heard was the snap of the fire as we waited for Frank to speak. He looked stricken.

"I just couldn't risk it." His face fell for a moment. Then he looked around as if to see who was listening. "She made a conscious decision to step out on her protection, Keith. Lexi knew the consequences. We did everything in our power to protect her. We all did. I wanted to bring her home. You know that. Paul did his job and did it well. It took a lot for him to take on what he did. To risk blowing his cover just wasn't something I was willing to do."

"On that note—" Paul tried to jump in.

"Not yet, brother. I'm not done, but you're next." I could see Keith tried hard to curb his anger. "He was doing his job well?" Keith said each word slowly as his voice rose. Cole was right. Emotions were entirely too raw, but maybe this needed to happen. I just hoped it didn't cause any damage. I took a quick glance at Moore as he watched the two men intently.

"You have no idea what that man has done for all of you!" Frank yelled, his voice full of pent-up anger. He stood, his fists balled tight, and Keith matched his stance.

"Easy, boys. Leave 'em be," Cole said as Paul and Mike stood. Cole shook his head and motioned for them to sit down.

"Mike," Frank looked over, "do you think Plan B at the border happened without Paul? Who do you think made sure there were no other casualties when you needed an escape?" Mike's face dropped, and he looked at Paul.

Cole shot a look at his father, who seemed to be processing that news as well. Clearly, Frank had kept that a secret all these years.

"And John," Frank continued, "who do you think was crazy enough to let you jump on the back of their semi-truck at the gas station when you and Brick were under heavy fire?"

"Holy shit," John covered his mouth, "I looked right at you."

"And showed me your American patch." Paul nodded like he remembered it well.

"How did I not know it was you?"

"You were kind of running for your life and dodging bullets. You might have had your mind elsewhere."

"Well, I appreciate the lift." John smirked and shook his head like he couldn't believe it and waved for Frank to go on.

"And Ty," Frank whirled to look at me, "who pulled you backward when the explosion went off in the house?" He pointed at Paul, and I stared in disbelief. Shit, that was crazy to wrap my head around.

"He's been running alongside all of you this entire time. Look, I'm sorry for what happened to Lexi, Keith." Frank stepped closer to him. "My God, man, she was one of the family. You have no idea how sorry I am, but I did this for all of you." When Keith drew in a deep breath, Frank sighed heavily. "Be pissed, toss your shit at me, but I was only trying to do my job. I tried to make a change from the inside out, and up until what happened with Lexi, it was working."

"It's still working," Paul added. "Give me a few days and I'll prove it."

The pent-up anger seemed to die down some after the air cleared a little more between them. I was still unsure how to feel. I guessed it would take some time for me.

My head was shot after that. I must have glanced at Ivy's window a hundred times that night. I wanted to go to her so badly, but I also knew I needed to be a part of this. The ups and downs of Shadows were what had formed them into such a tight-knit group. Me and Moore being there was necessary if we wanted to be part of the family. I rubbed my eyes and forced my brain to focus. Things seemed to settle a bit more. Paul and Frank began to talk quietly. John stood and began to talk to Keith and Mark.

"Beckett," Cole called over the light chatter of the others, "you ship out at ten-hundred. Go be with your girl."

"Fuck me." Keith turned and slapped a hand to his face. "I'm sorry, Ty, I—"

"It's only a forty-eight-hour trip. Don't be sorry." I slapped his shoulder as I stood. "I feel shitty on the timing of it."

"All I ask is you come home with something."

"That's the plan." I glanced at Moore, who had his phone to his ear then threw out a few curse words.

"You good?"

"Yeah, just still playing phone tag with Jay."

"Doesn't he leave a message?"

"All he said is he needs to talk. We keep missing each other, but he doesn't want to leave a message." He shrugged it off. "So, I let it go."

"Speaking of tag," Mark piped up, and I rolled my eyes.

"Good night, all." I threw a wave over my head, and they all murmured back their good nights as I headed for the house.

I found the living room empty, and Savannah caught me at the stairs.

"She's in your room." She smiled warmly.

I rushed up the stairs and into my room where I was hit with the smell of something sweet. I followed the trail and found the huge bathtub was filled to the top with bubbles.

"Gosh!" She jumped as she came out of my closet. Her silk robe drifted open at her quick movement and exposed her bare breasts. "You just took three lives off of me." I let out an animal grunt in response. My gaze traveled down her hardened nipples, the luscious curves of her breasts, to her smooth stomach, to her waxed V. "You look…" *Untamable.* "Interested." She purred, and I kicked the door shut. I reached back and tore my t-shirt off then tossed it on the floor.

"I was just about to go for a soak." Her smile grew as she saw I had other plans. In three steps, I scooped her up and urged her legs around me.

I exhaled slowly as she nearly brought me to my knees. I felt the heat from between her legs against my stomach and marched her to the wall. As I pressed her against it, I looked up at the face of the woman who held my delicate heart hostage in her hand.

"I'm sorry I couldn't come up sooner." *I really was.*

"Your brothers needed you." Her voice let me know she understood. She turned her head, so her hair fell to the side, and my nostrils instantly flared at the scent of her floral shampoo. She rubbed my shoulders as her warm eyes drew me into her spell. *God, it felt good.*

"I never wanted to fall in love," I confessed, "and now that I have, I'm terrified I'll lose it."

"Well," she massaged my neck a little more as she thought, "I think we both want this, so we'll just have to make it work. Scared or not." Her face slipped slightly, and I knew tomorrow's departure weighed on her. It weighed on us both. "You know," she flexed her legs, "the wonderful part of being in love is the sex just keeps getting better and better."

I grabbed her chin and dove in for a kiss. She instantly parted her lips and let me in. We needed to shed the tension we both felt with the loss of Lexi, with the arrival of the new guest, and especially with my trip. We needed time to reconnect. Tonight, was about us.

I wound my fingers through her hair and held her tight. She rocked her hips, needing friction between her legs, and I smiled, loving the feeling. When she gasped for air, I moved to her neck, along her collarbone, and across her shoulder. My mind clouded but became clear all at once. I craved everything about this woman. Not just for the sex. It was everything. She was the whole package. I deepened my kiss with the sudden realization that my father was right. When you were really in love, it consumed all of you.

"What is it?" She felt my moment.

"Nothing." I grabbed her hands and lifted her arms

above her head then used my hips to hold her in place. "Mm, defenseless," I teased.

"Whatever will you do with my body?" She played along.

"Everything." I tossed her on the bed, and a moment later, after I tore off my clothes, I was back between her thighs.

I nudged between her slick folds and teased her opening.

"Oh, okay." A wicked smile broke over her lips, as she knew I had control. My hands once again pulled hers above her head, holding her secure.

"What are you gonna do?" I teased her lips with mine.

"I'm going to top from the bottom." Her eyes twinkled with fun. I gently pulled back to dive straight inside, and as I did, she used my hands to move herself up on the bed, allowing only the tip to go inside her. She laughed, very pleased with herself.

"Look at you." I grinned and nipped at her nipple, loving how fun we both could be in bed. "What else you got?"

"Mmm." She suddenly tried to flip me with her body weight in an effort to throw me on my back so she could gain the advantage. I didn't budge. "Mark taught me that move." She laughed when she caught my expression. "Clearly not when we were naked." She giggled. "You know what I mean."

"If you want to learn some moves, come to me." I kissed her neck.

"Will you teach them to me naked?"

"I'll teach you one now. Ready?" She nodded, and I thrust deep inside of her, and she gasped. "This is called mine." I grinned, and she rolled her eyes at my lame joke, but whatever. I was where I wanted to be.

I stopped then and rested my weight on my forearms and stared deep into her eyes. We'd always had hot sex, but tonight I wanted her to see I could offer her more. She stilled under me and seemed to wait.

Never in my imagination could I ever have pictured myself being this vulnerable, until I met this woman. She brought out something in me I never knew I had inside. I felt tenderness, and the fact that I was about to leave her the next day made me suddenly want to show her this side of me. She deserved it. I wanted to express it.

"Do you believe you were meant for me?" I wasn't looking for an answer, really. I just wanted to say what I felt. "Because I think in some way I wished for you, and you came true." I brushed her hair with my fingers. "I've never known someone as gorgeous as you are on the outside to be the same on the inside." She blinked a few times as if my words caught her off guard. "To think that your heart wants me, a man who ran from affection his whole life. It kind of makes me want to prove to you that I'm worthy of it." I started to move my hips and made love to her slowly. She wiggled her arms free and took my head in her hands to show me the pleasure I gave her.

"I've never wanted someone as much as I want you." I

sealed my lips over hers and kissed her deeply. With every thrust, I felt both of us pledge our love as we fell harder and harder for one another. I broke free of her kiss and lapped at her neck as I reached back and hiked her leg over my waist. The change in angle made her breath heighten.

"I can't get enough of you, Ivy," I panted in her ear. "I can't get deep enough. I want all of you."

"You have all of me," she cried as she climbed her way toward her bliss. My stomach coiled, and I knew I was close. I didn't want to come. I wanted to spend the entire night like this, deep inside without an end date.

She moaned a warning. "Ty…"

"I'm about to come, too," I grunted and thrust harder because I couldn't control it anymore. "Remember me like this inside you when I'm gone and that you're mine forever." She came undone, and her spasms sent me right after her. We shot off hard then slowly floated back down together. As she fought for breath, I pulled her limp body off the bed and carried her to the waiting bubble bath.

"Watch your step." She was like Jell-O as I climbed in with her in my arms. I lay back in the delicious warmth and pulled her against my chest.

"You should get some sleep." She turned her head to study the clock. "You leave in a few."

"And leave this?" I kissed the side of her neck. "I'll sleep on the flight to Washington."

"Just be careful, okay?" she whispered, and I held her

tighter. "Because I don't want to do this with anyone else." She craned her neck to look at me, but I couldn't think of anything else to say. I felt her take my hand, then she sighed and settled back against me.

I promise.

NINE

PAUL

Formally Eric Noah

"Okay," Keith rubbed his head as he tried to process what I attempted to explain, "so, what you're saying is they haven't gone to your house and done a sweep for bugs, or turned your power off and ransacked the place? They've done nothing."

"No, they'd have no reason to. At least not yet. My buyer got hold of Castillo and told him I'd made contact after what happened. He said I was gonna call today to confirm where I was and what happened."

"They have that much trust in you?" He eyed me, and I could hear murmurs from the other guys in the room.

"Yes, Keith, they do." I gave him a direct look back. "Well, up to a point they do." I glanced at Cole and decided to show them something. "Let me prove it to you." I reached for Cole's laptop. "May I?" He nodded. I logged into my account and flashed the live feed of my house up on their big screen.

"Wow," Cole got up and moved closer to the screen, "the picture's incredible."

"I need to see everything, to catch the small things," I explained.

"So, that's your place?" He pointed at the screen.

"Yes. I installed cameras in every room, and so far, no one's discovered them." I tapped a button and moved the screens around. "Outside, garage, kitchen, living room, dining room, basement." Keith's expression changed, and I mentally kicked myself for being so careless. I switched to a different room and quickly addressed him. "Keith, I don't mean to be heartless. You've got my word I'll walk you through everything that happened there with Lexi and then some, but let me get through this first. Okay?"

"Fine," he muttered.

"Hang on." Cole, who'd been studying the screen-shots, pointed to one, and as I turned, his eyes burned into me. "That photo!" He leaned closer. "What the fuck is Denton Barlow doin' there, in a picture with you?"

Shit. This was exactly why Frank had told me to tread carefully with what I shared.

"He was my cover." I let out a worried breath. I knew

Denton was Cole's one weak spot, and no one blamed him for it.

"Tell me he's dead! Tell me this isn't another one of Frank's sick setups. If he lied to me on that, I'll…"

"He's very much dead," I interrupted. "We said he was my cousin and that he sent me to Rosarito to work for him. The fact that he was in prison and could only communicate a little worked in my favor. It got even better when he was killed because then I could say I was the only one who could reach him while he was in," I finger quoted, "*hiding*."

"Jesus." Cole paced, as he tried to get himself together. "Go on."

"I was able to work my way in quickly thanks to Frank. We played our scam on them and learned a lot about Denton and what he'd been planning before he went to prison."

"Which was?"

"Run his operation from Columbia."

"Anything else?" God, it was like he could see inside my head.

"Cole, some things are better left unsaid." I glanced around the room.

"I disagree." He held my stare, and I knew Frank might kill me for this, but I could never lie to my brothers.

"Let's just say he had other plans in motion to flush Savannah out." Cole's jaw ticked. "We shut it down, you guys got him killed, and anything he had in the works was quickly stamped out." I moved close to him. "There's a recorded call to Frank, of me sayin' that if I found out there was any chance at all that Savannah was at risk, I'd be on my way home on the next plane with any and all information in hand." He held my gaze a moment later, and I could see he fought against the pain that this information brought to him. I knew I'd opened old wounds with what I'd shared. Savannah was his life.

"She can never know," he growled.

"Understood." We stood in silence until Keith broke it.

"So, ten years later and my wife is taken." I could hear the pain in his voice. "There was a lot of risk there. Were you going to return home with her?" Keith's tone was low but highly charged.

I knew I had to tread lightly. I knew Keith had barely had time to process Lexi's death and my part in it. I pressed my hands into the table and took a moment to think. He deserved to hear it all, and I prepared myself for it. I could hardly blame him. I'd known it wouldn't be easy with the way things had gone down. It would take time, but these were my brothers, and I needed them to know I'd always had the family's safety at heart.

"I broke countless rules with Lexi, Keith, and I'll prove that to you, I promise. I wanted to get her back to you. You know that. When we fell into trouble, my sole purpose was to return her to you."

"And you did." Frank's voice stopped me short, and our attention flew to the door. None of us had heard him come in. "I wasn't aware we'd started our meeting yet."

"We just needed to clear a few things out of the way first," Cole jumped in. His clipped tone wasn't lost on anyone.

"I see." He looked at Moore, who sat quietly at the back. "You able to follow what's happening?"

"Yes, sir. Just soaking it all in." He quickly rejected a phone call.

"Good." Frank addressed me. "I'd like to jump in with the fact that your buyer called in this morning. Give him a call and hear what he has to say."

Mike moved the speaker phone in front of me as if to say to make the call in front of them.

"Outside," Frank ordered.

"With all due respect, Frank, I think it's time Blackstone hears it straight up."

"Paul—"

"I may not have a place on Blackstone anymore, but we need to take these fuckers down, so they need to know all." Frank bit down on the side of his lip. I knew he disagreed, but I also knew he had some trust to regain with these men. If he didn't fix things, we'd all have bigger problems in the long run. Cole turned the light outside to red so no one would bother us and locked the door to frost up the glass.

"Make the call."

Cole glanced at Keith, and I dialed the number from

memory.

"Chili," he answered.

"Hey, it's Eric." There was a pause. I figured he was making sure he distanced himself from anyone around.

"It's time to call in. Castillo's startin' to get squirrelly."

"Any indication he knows about a flip? Or that I ran with her?"

"No, and Alejandro and Filippo are still claiming you said you'd call in once it's safe."

"Good." I looked around at my team. I never once thought I'd be making a call to Chili or Castillo like this.

"Hey, ah, there's something else."

"What?" I tensed.

"Talya was looking for you." It was as if a brick hit my stomach. "Something about her and Grim. I don't know much, just that Grim is keeping his distance—"

"Just—" I didn't need this now. "Look, it's fine. Just keep the same story in play with her."

"Understood."

"Wait," something bothered me about what he'd said, "what's up with Grim?"

"No clue, but he's been quiet lately."

"Has Castillo noticed?"

"Not yet." It bothered me that I still didn't know why Grim had helped me.

"Don't give Castillo a reason to look at Grim." It was the least I could do.

"Got it."

"I'll be in touch." I hung up and caught Mike's expression. "What?"

"Nothing. We'll talk later."

Something loud pulled our focus to the cameras on the screen.

"It's him." Keith moved closer and tapped the button to enlarge the entryway. Castillo had barged inside and was yelling for Alejandro.

"I've heard nothing!" Alejandro held up his hands. "I've called everyone he worked with, spoke to the locals. Fuck, even the priest hasn't heard shit from him." I glanced at Frank, who nodded he'd check on him. "We found nothing either," Alejandro whined. "We're going through his office seeing if there's any idea where he'd go." I flexed my neck, happy I'd been careful with my files. I'd left nothing for them to find.

"If he's there," I pointed to the screen, "I'm calling. I want to watch his face when he hears it's me."

"I, for one, would love to see the show." Mark shrugged.

"Keith, you should go," Frank suddenly blurted. "If anything screws up this call to Castillo—"

"No." Keith shook his head. "I'm stayin'." He glared at Frank.

"Sorry, Keith, I have to agree." Cole put a hand on Keith's shoulder. "This is way too close to home, buddy." He tapped Keith's chest when he turned to face him. "That in there is way too raw to be here for this." In one motion, Keith spun and left.

"I'll go with him." John ran out.

Frank nodded at Cole. "Thanks."

"I didn't do it for you." Cole turned back to the screen.

Mark cleared his throat as the tension in the room rose a little higher and cracked a joke I didn't hear. No one laughed, but he scored a snicker from Moore. I was impressed with Frank; he didn't pull rank on any of them. Maybe because he knew it would only make things worse.

"He doesn't need this shit in his head right now." Cole didn't turn around as he spoke.

"Agreed." Mike added, "Get the fucker on the phone so we can all see what we're dealing with."

"Okay." I took a deep breath and dialed.

I felt my stomach tighten as the ringtone filled the room, then suddenly Castillo's arrogant voice snapped over the speaker.

"This better be good."

"It's Eric." I added exhaustion to my voice with a mix of anxiety.

"Eric?" He frantically waved at Alejandro to get out of his sight. "Where the fuck are you?"

"Where am I?" I flipped the question around. "What the hell happened? One moment I'm transporting the girl, and the next I'm being shot at and hunted across the city. Fuck me, Castillo, was that your doing?"

He looked around then dashed into my office and slammed the door. Cole switched camera views.

"What?" His fucking pitch told me everything I

needed to know. Let alone the way his hand flew to his chest like the dramatic asshole he was. I glanced at Frank and knew he'd picked up on it, too. The piece of shit was behind the ambush. "I've been working hard, trying to find out if my friend is okay, and-and you question if I was involved? Come on, Eric." I rolled my eyes at his lame attempt to lie. "We made a deal. The money was transferred." I sat up straight at his words. "All you had to do was drop off the girl."

I caught him in his own lie. "It was two in the morning. How was the money transferred?"

"*Be careful,*" Cole wrote on a whiteboard in front of him. Frank shook his head for him not to worry. *Eric* always pushed Castillo, and I knew if I didn't do it now, he'd pick up on it immediately.

"Erriic," he drawled out my name. "he was your buyer. I knew the money was good. Because if not, I'd kill you." He said it easily in a tone I knew. We were okay.

"Publicly, of course." I egged on his dark side, knowing he loved when I did that. Especially at my own cost.

"What other way is there? If you find a rat has been living inside your walls for years, you got to make a statement."

"Listen, Castillo," I stood and carried the speaker phone with me. I needed to move as I struggled to get myself into the mindset of someone who was scared. I imagined myself in hiding, in fear for my life. It was important to get this right. "Whoever it was that came after us, they were gunning for the girl."

"And did they succeed?" I watched him on the screen as he casually checked the time.

"No," I paused as Lexi's lifeless face stared up at me, "she's here with me, alive."

I saw Cole shift ever so silently in his chair and I knew as I played this last card, more questions would come.

"Let me speak to her." His voice shook with excitement. I shook my head at his image on the screen and pulled the recorder from my pocket.

"Hey," I pretended to talk to Lexi, "wake the fuck up." I hated to even pretend to speak to her like that. I pressed play, and her voice rang out in a rush.

"Get your fucking hands off me!" I closed my eyes, hating how much it hurt hearing the tone in her voice. I heard an intake of breath behind me and knew it was Keith, but I kept going.

"Take the phone." I pushed the words through my clenched teeth.

"Fuck you!"

I slipped the recorder away and tried not to look at the guys.

"Is that enough for you?"

"I want a video." *Sonofabitch.*

"After all I've been through in the past few days, tryin' to get this chick back to you, and you question me?"

"I want to post it publicly. I want everyone to know

Blackstone never got her from me. They missed their mark again!"

I played along. "I highly doubt it was Blackstone. They'd never spray bullets like that trying to save one of their own. Way too dangerous for her."

"Maybe it wasn't them, but it will be when I tell the story."

"Not everyone loves the limelight like you do, Castillo. That could backfire in several different ways," I snapped. A lazy smirk ran across his face as he sat back in my office chair and kicked his feet up on my desk.

"So, the bitch is alive. Well, that changes things." He flipped open the lid on my box of Partagas Lusitanias cigars. "Bring her to me."

"Listen, Castillo. We're safe for the moment, but we've gotta move soon, and I can't move fast. I have an idea you might like. I think we play this differently."

"You've got my attention."

"Host a dinner, invite everyone who was at the auction, including Chili. One of them wanted her dead badly enough to attack our convoy. So, let's give 'em what they want. We'll kill the bitch in front of everyone." I knew he'd like the irony since he was the one behind the attack.

"Why the sudden change of heart?"

"Because the bitch shot me. This isn't worth the money anymore. I want revenge."

Castillo leaned back in my chair and blew smoke toward the ceiling as he mulled over my idea.

"I'll be in touch."

Everyone was silent as we watched Castillo hang up. Frank moved toward the table as the guys all turned their heads toward me, and I felt the heat in my face.

"Well—" Frank started to speak, but I held up a hand to stop him as I saw Castillo dial another number.

"You failed. They're both alive. I'm giving you one more chance."

TEN

TY

There was something unsettling about not knowing the men who were about to drop with you from a chopper into a war zone. I knew my plan inside and out and was confident I could get to where I needed to go. I just didn't have Moore to watch my six, and that proved harder to accept than I expected. But he was there for Ivy, and once I remembered that, my anxiety dropped immediately. He was where I needed him most.

I leaned back and thought about the morning I left.

I couldn't sleep. I rehearsed my plan over and over from the moment I'd arrive in south central Asia. My brain drew an invisible map on the ceiling. I could envision the drop-off point, the main roads, the road

into town, and the truck that waited for me there.
I'd jump in the truck without being seen, change into
local clothing, and get dropped off near the market.
Then I'd make my way to the house where Brown
was shot. I had to be hyperaware of any Taliban who
might be watching the town. It was a longshot to
find any evidence at all, let alone get statements, and
maybe an eyewitness on video. Best case, get out
before nightfall with some type of proof in hand.
Worst case, I didn't return at all.
Ivy shifted her warm body into mine, and I kissed
her head.
We had said our goodbyes a few times without actu-
ally using words. I felt it would be best if I slipped
out quietly and didn't make it emotional.
"I promise I'll come back to you," I whispered. "It's
only forty-eight hours." I breathed in her scent and
saved it in my memory. "I love you."
Somehow, I pulled myself away and left her.

"Hey," I opened my eyes to find the team captain's face in mine, "our pickup location's been compromised." I quickly pulled out my map and drew a mental X over the old spot. He pointed. "Head here instead."

"Roger that." I studied the map and memorized the new location.

"Frank filled me in." He used short cryptic sentences, as my mission wasn't meant for the others. "I called a guy who has eyes in town, and it's crawling with roaches." He paused. "Locals are careful. Look for friendlies. They have a green stripe along the stock of their weapon." He showed me on his own. "Green stripe, not a roach."

"Got it." I held my fist up, and we bumped knuckles.

An hour later, the chopper hovered steadily as we zipped down the ropes and I prepared to head east.

"Beckett!" I barely heard my name over the noise of the chopper above us. I looked back. The captain held his hands around his mouth to project his voice. "We have orders to abort at twenty-three hundred," he yelled then tapped his wrist. "Don't make us leave without you."

"Roger that. Good luck," I called back. I slung my rucksack over my shoulders and began my long hike toward the town.

The wind blew the dust around, so I secured a rag around my nose and mouth. I fell into old habits. I scanned the mountaintops and listened for horses, gunshots off in the distance, movements on the horizon. It was almost as if I hadn't left. Almost.

When I stopped to check the time and drink some water, I fingered Halim's bracelet. I'd worn it as a reminder that Brown's death hadn't been for nothing. With the rescue of the boy, Halim, Frank was able to use his father's favor to dig deeper into the Taliban world. It allowed him a way to keep a closer eye for any indication they planned anything against America. I still couldn't help but wonder if the added stress of the boy was what pushed Brown over the edge. I may not have realized just how far gone my friend had been and had dismissed the signs because we were so close to going home. Either way, Hill had to be paid back for what he'd done, and I was here to find something—anything on him to prove it. I needed to avenge my friend. He hadn't deserved to be taken out by one of our own, and it ate at me. Hill was going down.

I kept an eye on where I stepped on the familiar terrain. Loose rock and dust were what seemed to make up this part of the country, and I could already feel the familiar scratchy throat was back. I hadn't even realized it had gone away until now. Funny how much my life had changed in the last few months. I'd missed the dry heat of Afghanistan, but now I found myself missing the cool, crisp, mountain air, the warmth of Shadows, and a certain blonde I couldn't get enough of.

The smell of exhaust found my nose, and I knew I wasn't far from town. I checked the time again and realized I was a few minutes early to meet my ride.

Afghans were a punctual people, and because this man was doing me a favor, I made sure to be early. I sought cover as I checked around near where we were to meet.

I could hear voices and saw Ahmad, my driver, was being hassled by another man. They argued in Dari as I slipped on an oversized turban and shalwar kameez tunic that concealed my camo and tucked my helmet into my pack. I stepped out and approached the two men. When Ahmad spotted me, he shook his head carefully for me not to engage, and I stepped back out of sight.

"American, you can come out now. He's gone." I

snatched up my pack and made quick work of getting in his truck. "Sorry about that, my friend." He started the engine and smiled as I quickly grabbed the window frame at the huge jerk of the vehicle as he pulled out. "Hungry?" He handed me a piece of bread. I took it to be polite, but I had no interest in eating it.

Though Ahmad was a friend of a friend of Frank's, I didn't let my guard down. One hand always stayed on my weapon as I constantly scanned the road ahead and behind.

"The Taliban visit every day now. They take what they want, then leave. Food, clothes, women, and even our…" He shook his head.

"I'm sorry to hear that." I was, but I also knew some towns had it a lot worse. We made our way through the streets as he expertly avoided the vendors, sheep, and the many stray cats that kept an eye out for any type of food. When we stopped for some kids to cross, I noticed one cat wedged in a corner, skin and bones, tongue hanging out, desperate for a scrap of something. I ripped off a piece of bread and tossed it to him. He limped over, snagged it, and pulled it back into his corner.

"You Americans." Ahmad shook his head. "See that?" He shifted his gaze to the top of a broken wall ahead of us. "They've got some of our own kids who watch for them now. Money is everything." I shielded my face as we passed by the children. "Okay, my friend," he parked the truck, and I knew exactly where we were, "are you ready?"

"I am." I placed a hand on his shoulder before we got

out and handed him a roll of bills. I knew Frank would be sure he got paid, but I knew all too well the risk he took, and I needed all the friends I could get in this place. He smiled his appreciation and tucked it away. Then we both got out.

He knocked on the door, three fast, two slow, then it was opened by a man who waved us quickly inside. I removed my boots, as was the custom, but hid them under my pack. It wasn't proper, but I knew my combat boots would stand out like a sore thumb.

I placed my hand on my chest and nodded as Ahmad introduced me. Some of the formalities were dismissed, and I assumed it was because they didn't want me to stay long. We made our way farther into the house, and I was offered a place to sit. I felt the wind get sucked right out of me as I saw the stain on the rug. Someone had tried to remove it, but I knew it was a bloodstain from Brown.

It was abnormal for woman of their culture to make eye contact, but I felt her eyes on me, and when our gazes met, she didn't look away. I recognized her, and she recognized me. If I wasn't sure just then, I was when her two daughters entered the kitchen. Here we all were right where the entire nightmare had gone down.

"I don't agree with this visit, but my sister wished to speak with you. She can be a very stubborn woman. Also, her husband." He paused. "*Inna Lillahi wa inna ilayhi raji'un*," rest in peace, "allowed her a more westernized attitude that he felt was good for her." He gave Ahmad a look and quickly changed from speaking in Dari to Pashtu. "This is too risky."

"It's all good, friend." Ahmad brushed off the brother's concern, not realizing I understood Pashtu.

It wasn't lost on me that the brother never offered his name. I understood his fear, but I also felt respect for her husband for allowing her a more modern view. That was rare here and could possibly lead her into danger if she wasn't careful. I saw her brother's nervous glance at the door and knew I had to hurry things along.

"Tea?" The woman pointed to the pot on the stove.

"Please." Dari flowed from my tongue to keep them from knowing I knew Pashtu too. I took pride in the fact I spoke their languages fluently.

We sat cross legged on the cushions, and I was careful not to show the bottoms of my feet. Even though I had socks on, it would be considered rude. The woman was dressed all in black, and the same with her thick eyeliner. She was quite pretty from what I could see of her.

"How may I address you?" I asked.

"Amina," she said quietly but directly and in English. At her tone, her brother muttered, and she shot him a glance. "My husband was a good man." She answered my unasked question. "One day, the monsters came. They wanted my oldest child." Her jaw flexed. "My husband traded places with her. We never saw him again."

"I'm sorry." The world was full of all different walks of evil.

She lifted her chin as if to push aside the pain. "What

about you? Shall I call you American?" She smiled at her comment, and I knew now was the time to stick with the truth. I needed answers.

"Beckett," I replied. I pulled my tunic aside and pulled out my dog tags. "Ty Beckett." I leaned forward and let her examine them.

"Very well, Beckett." Her accent was thick, but she nailed my name. "I heard you wanted to talk to me about what happened here."

"I do."

"My daughters still have nightmares of that day." She poured me some tea. "The Taliban are feared here, and life is very frightening every day, but the day the American soldier came into my home was a terrible thing. He pointed a gun at me and my children. Another came, then another. Three Americans came in my house, all screaming, but only two left." Her gaze flickered up to mine as she placed the tea in front of me then pointed at the bloodstain on the rug. "I was left with that and a dead soldier."

"I'm sorry for how that went down, Amina, and I'm sorry for the trauma it left with you and your girls, but—"

"You are full of sorry." She smiled, but there was annoyance behind it. "Let's leave the apologies behind us. Why are you really here?" She lifted an eyebrow as she sipped her tea. "I'm sure it isn't for the tea."

I'd planned to ask my questions, dig around, and

leave, but I could see that wasn't going to work. "You need the truth."

"Yes, that is what I ask."

I looked at her directly so she could see I was going to be honest. "The truth is the man who died on your floor was like family to me. I was his captain, and I didn't see or maybe didn't want to see the signs that he was mentally troubled until it was too late. I knew him as a kind man, a good man. The man you saw was not the man I knew. He would never have pointed a gun at an innocent family." I needed her to believe that. "When I made him see me that day, I was able to get him to lower his gun. You must have seen that?" Something passed over her face. "I had him calm. He was no longer a threat to you."

"How do you know that?"

"He was my friend," I reminded her. "He was one of my team, and when we were sent here to fight the Taliban, we all made a pact. We would keep ourselves in mental check by reciting three words. Only my team used these words, and we lived by them. It grounded us." I leaned toward her as I said them. "Whiskey, Alpha, Tango. We are together." My eyes prickled when I remembered the look on Brown's face as he repeated those words with me. "He was right there. I had him, but then…"

"The other man shot him."

"Yes." I heard the shot once again and squeezed my eyes shut as the pain washed over me.

"I think this man, he's done this before."

Her choice of words had me pull in my chin and stare at her. I nodded. "Why do you think that?"

"I've seen that look in other men before." At least she saw it, too. I glanced at Ahmad, and he held my eye. I knew I had made the right decision to come back.

"A few times, I think. Although not proven." I shifted, uneasy with the entire conversation. "I came here to find something that I could take home and use against him. He needs to pay for his crime, for all his crimes."

She reached for a sweet-looking cookie, and I watched her separate it on her plate as she thought.

"I've seen many bad men in my lifetime, Beckett. Did you know that you can see someone's soul in their eyes?" I didn't react. "When your friend had his gun to his own head, he looked over at me, and I could see he didn't want to hurt us. He was lost. I believe you are right that you had reached him. You made him see us. The man who shot him had no soul. His eyes held nothing."

"Yes." I sighed with relief that she saw so much, and that she believed me.

"As far as proof, I'm not sure how I can help you." My stomach sank. "The bad man left with his gun." I opened my mouth to speak, but she raised a brow to stop me. "But I may be able to help you in a different way." She held up a hand, palm out, then moved close to her brother and spoke quietly to him. I couldn't hear what she said. His face paled, but he seemed to accept her words. "It will take time." She turned back to me. "You must stay tonight."

I was given a pad to sleep on in the same room as her brother. I could feel his angry stare on me and knew my eyes would remain open the whole night. There was no way I'd close them even for a moment. I tuned in to the low fire that burned in the grate near the wall.

I let my head slip back to when we first arrived in this country years before.

"Say goodbye to moisture, boys," Moore squinted at the sun, "because you won't find it here."
"That's why I brought my own." Brown pulled out moisturizer and squeezed some onto his hand. "You can never be too prepared." He grinned as he rubbed it between his palms.
"Yeah, that's why you brought it." I slapped Brown's shoulder as I laughed. "Come on. I want a team meeting before we see our commander."
We made our way to base camp, tossed our stuff, and met outside our tent. As I waited for a few stragglers, I rubbed my chin and scrunched up my face as I thought of what to say.
"Yeah, we all really did sign up for this." I huffed a laugh. "We have no fucking idea what's to come other than what we've been told. We're definitely outnumbered here in a very different country than where we come from. As different as the local people are from us, we'll treat them with respect, and kindness, and give them our protection. There's a lot we can't control, but what we can control is ourselves." I

took a moment and looked around at my team, Moore, Brown, Anderson, and Gail. All good men. "None of us are in this alone. We've got each other. I'm going to give you three words, and whenever you feel like you're slipping, I want you to chant them out loud if you can, or in your head if you can't. Use these words they will help bring you back from whatever darkness you find yourself in." I tapped my head and looked at each of them until I knew they were with me. "Whiskey, Alpha, Tango. We are together."

"Hooah," they responded in unison.

"Again," I called.

"Whiskey! Alpha! Tango!" they shouted.

"Hooah," I replied. "Now, hit your bunks. You'll need it.

"Don't be touchin' my lotion." Brown laughed as he ducked into the tent around Moore. I smirked at the men in front of me and couldn't be more pleased that we were here together.

We got this.

"American." Someone touched my shoulder, and I jolted back to the present with my weapon up and ready. I wiped the sweat off my forehead and lowered the gun when I saw the brother's face. "It's time."

I gathered my belongings and hurried toward the front of the house. I glanced at my watch and realized it was only three a.m. He led me outside to where Amina waited. Only her eyes could be seen, as she was dressed in a full head-to-toe Afghan *burqa*. She motioned me to follow her then slipped into Ahmad's truck. I was nervous, suddenly. I knew how risky it was to travel at night, and especially for a woman. I hated to know I risked her safety as well as my own, but I joined her in the back. Two other men sat in the back with us, and I kept my eyes on them.

"It's not far." She encouraged Ahmad to get started. She must have caught my discomfort. "You asked me for my help, and that is what I'm doing."

"I appreciate it." I licked my lips and scanned the darkness for any sign of lights or movement. We were just out of town when we pulled over and Amina jumped out of the truck.

"Beckett, do you have a light?"

"Here." I handed her my flashlight, and she awkwardly held it as she began to climb a hill. I felt unprotected as I followed her with the other two men behind me. A strange feeling crept up my spine; I just didn't know what it meant yet.

Amina stopped suddenly and turned to look up at me. Then she directed the beam of light until it landed on a pile of dirt and rocks. Three larger rocks were placed carefully one on top of the other. "Every man, woman, and child deserves to be laid to rest."

I sucked in a mouthful of air when I realized what she meant. It was Brown's grave. She'd made sure he was buried properly. She'd helped him move on from this world. I dropped to my knees as emotion flooded through me, and once again, I felt the weight of his death on my shoulders.

"No," Amina said from behind me, and I thought she warned the others not to come close. She knelt at my side as I gave in and cried for my friend.

Everything hurt as I let the anger and pain I'd held back for so long pour from me. I hadn't dealt with Brown's death, maybe because I'd been so set on taking down Hill that I used the pain to fuel my fire, but I was damn tired of the burning pit in my stomach, and it felt good to finally let it go.

Once I was tapped out, I took a long, deep breath and sat back on my heels. The heat from the sun could already be felt as it began to rise over the mountains.

"Thank you for this," I whispered. "I've been so scared wondering what happened to his body, I couldn't..." I stopped to gather my emotions again.

"Holding on to what was will never allow you hold on to what is. I'm not saying that to ask you to let what happened go completely, but your friend is not coming back. You are here now, so gather up the twigs and branches and start building your fire and flush out the bad man."

"I can do that." I dried my eyes and ran a hand over my face, letting her metaphor sink in.

"It's what I'm doing." Her eyes lit up, and I knew she was smiling, and I smiled back and felt a little less heavy. She looked down at my arm and tilted her head. "You wear the wolf."

"It was a gift."

"I know." She nodded, and I realized maybe she knew more about me than I thought. After all, Frank had set this up.

"Imdad Jaber spread the word about what you did for his son, Halim. If he gave you the wolf, that means it is what you are. A leader."

"I told the boy a story about how I kept seeing wolves when I was stationed here. We even saw one together."

"Wolves are drawn to their leaders," she said with certainty. "You must let this go and get back to being the leader you are. Everything else will fall into place. It always does." The way she said the last part made me wonder what she meant.

"I'm going to need the body," I whispered.

"Ahmad will help you with that," she stood and stretched her back, "but this is where we part ways."

"Thank you, Amina. I wish I could do more for you and your family."

"No need, my friend. Just get better here." She placed a hand on her heart. "*Inshallah*."

God's will.

ELEVEN

"I promised Ty I wouldn't do anything much while he was away—"

"Say no more." Savannah's face told me everything. She understood. "Zack's it is. Let me check and get a table reserved and all that fun stuff." She topped my mug up with coffee. "I'm the same way when Cole leaves. The more they can keep their heads in the mission, the better."

"Yes." I blew to clear the steam away.

"How are you holding up?"

"I'm fine when I don't let my mind wander." I stopped, as I heard voices. Cole and Moore were talking as they walked through the living room toward us. We both perked our ears to hear.

"No matter what, we have a check-in time. We both

know it's the team leader who does it, but on solo trips it's on you."

"What time'll that be?" Moore questioned.

"Beckett will check in at—" Cole slapped a friendly smile on when he spotted us and switched gears. "Savi, Easton texted he wants to come home. I think a call from Mom will help him get through the last day there." I was pleased to hear the kids would be returning. It felt like they'd been gone forever. I was very pleased that Cole heard my advice and waited to tell the kids about Lexi here rather than at Dusk. They were younger, and it was time to share the news about Lexi and let them start the healing process.

"I will, but," she grinned and pointed her head at me, "she's just as stubborn as I am, babe. Now, finish that sentence you were saying about when Beckett's to check in."

I loved Savannah.

"Very well." He gave her a wary look. "Beckett checks in at eighteen hundred tonight."

"That's ten hours before he must be at his rendezvous spot," I piped in without thought, then pressed my lips tight together.

"Five, actually." He nodded like he remembered he had given Ty permission to share this mission with me. He studied my face a moment then went on. "Alpha-Bravo had to abort their mission. They were ambushed."

"What!" I blurted.

"Not to worry," he held up a hand, "it's fine. There

were no casualties, and it was well away from where they left Beckett. We'll let him know about the change of plans when he checks in." His fingers tapped on the marble countertop. "What else do you know?"

"Doctor-patient confidentiality."

"You're not his doctor."

"When he handed me a twenty, I was." I winked. We knew how to get around the rules.

"She *is* like you." He glared at his wife, who just grinned wide.

"You've bent the rules for me, Cole." She waved him off. "It's what you do when your loved one is scared. Besides, I thought he was in Mexico," she mocked playfully along with me.

"See, now, I heard Lebanon." I tossed my hands in the air.

"You see what I have to live with?" Cole chuckled at Moore. "Anyway, now you know, Moore. Good luck at Camp Green. Training's canceled, so we have the rest of the day off." He turned and walked away.

"Speaking of time off," Savannah chased after him, "we're planning a night out at Zack's."

"So," Moore moved toward the counter, "I was thinking, since Ty's away, his friends should play." He gave me a mischievous smile. "How about that friend's day out?"

"No Ty to cut in on our storytelling? Mm." I raised an eyebrow. "When do you leave for Camp Green?"

"Thirty."

"I'll grab my things."

Moore had to file a bunch of paperwork for the Dark Water team at the head office when we arrived. I was glad he did because it gave me some time to meet the new teammates again in a more relaxed atmosphere.

Lee and Perez were lighthearted and comical. They seemed close and were more than ready to leave the camp and get into training. They didn't stand out to me when I conducted the interviews of candidates as much as…

"Dr. Knight." Gear pulled me aside while he made sure to catch the door for Liza as she hurried by with a quick hello. "I just wanted to say thanks again for what you said during our interview. You made me realize how important this is to me. I gave up my dream last time, let myself get talked out of it because of my family's needs. I had a long talk with my mom and sister, and we all agree that I need this for me. Despite what my sister's got going on, this is my life, and they don't want to hold me back. Since then, I've found them some help, and they both seem happier." He took a deep gulp of air.

"And you?" I couldn't help but feel warmed by his words.

"I feel free. Free from guilt and free to follow my dream, and now look." He held out his arms. "I made it."

"That's amazing, Gear, truly. I'm glad we're going to be housemates. You're going to love it at Shadows."

"I'm sure I will." He nodded politely then joined the others. I watched him for a few minutes and could tell he was much more relaxed and at ease with the other guys.

He joked and laughed. I was happy the weight he carried was gone from his shoulders.

Ty slowly crept into my head, and I suddenly felt the panic of not knowing if he was okay as it took over.

"All finished." Moore joined me, and I focused on him, which stopped the vicious invisible monster known as anxiety. "The new team'll be with us in no time." He glanced over at the guys as they laughed together, and he nodded and smiled. "How about we chat with them a bit then go for some lunch?"

"Sounds good, but any chance we could do town versus here?"

"What? Don't you like their meatball sub, mashed potatoes, and Jell-O?"

I quivered at the thought. Nothing was worse than Jell-O.

"No, but can we take some home for Mark?" I smirked, and he laughed. We'd both been in the kitchen when Mia served some to the kids. Mark took one look and ran off with a girly shriek. Mia laughingly filled us in on his phobia with the quivering mound.

Jellophobia was a real thing—well, at least it was to me and Mark. Not that I was going to share that with anyone. Lord knew the house would use it against me and I'd find my shower stuffed full of it one day. I followed the rest of them outside for some fresh air.

"Moore," I whispered as we gathered at one of the tables, "is that…?"

"Yes," he cut me off when he spotted Dustin, "he was transferred here."

"What?" I felt my bravery kick in, and I went to stand.

"Ivy," his fingers laced around my wrist and gently sat me back down, "now isn't the time." He shifted his gaze to the others, and he was right. We didn't need to drag them into this either.

"Of course." But that didn't mean I didn't keep my eye on him. At one point, he even sat a few tables away, facing me, and ate his lunch. If I didn't know any better, I would have thought he wanted to make sure I saw him.

An hour later, Moore and I sat tucked in a corner of a little coffee shop. I chose my chair purposely, so my back was to the restaurant. If he was anything like the rest of the guys, I knew he'd want a clear view of the place. As much as I wanted to dig in about Dustin and why the hell it looked like he was working there, I had an unusual opportunity to understand Ty a little better. I wasn't about to waste it. We ordered, and he beat me to the punch with a question.

"What made you become a psychologist?"

"Wow, you don't waste any time." I laughed and pretended to have a serious thought. "My father helped me make the decision, but not in the way you'd think. He wasn't exactly a model dad." I grimaced to make my point. "I guess I wanted to help people. Sounds kind of cliché, but I'm one of those who wants to help others, and at the same time it helps me."

"And your father, where's he now?"

"No idea, and I'm good with that now." I gave him a wry smile. "Okay, my turn. How long've you known Ty?"

"High school." He chuckled. "We were both asked out by the same girl. She wanted us to choose, so we did. We both chose not to date her and became great friends because of it."

"That'll teach her." I laughed as I dipped my bread in my soup. "And Brown?" I looked up and hoped I hadn't crossed a line.

"Ah," he cleared his throat, "he was that quiet kid in school, always kept to himself. Then he came out for football tryouts and attempted to tackle Ty, but he wouldn't go down. Ty's like a brick wall, so it was Brown who got laid out. When Ty offered him a hand to help him up, Brown did some weird thing and knocked Ty right on his ass. Everyone kinda held their breath to see what he'd do to him, but he just busted out laughing. From then on, Brown was just one of us."

"My God, men have it so easy. Women are so much more complex." I smiled and thought how true my words were.

"If your ex-fiancé came back into the picture, would you consider him?"

"Oh, that's how were going to play this?" I brushed the crumbs off my fingers.

"I have no walls up, Ivy." He shrugged. "Neither should you."

"Okay, okay." I laughed lightly. I enjoyed his openness. "No, there's no way we could ever work. Besides, I'm a completely different person now than I was back then."

"Is he still in love with you?" I gave him a hard look. He grinned. "Something Ty might have mentioned."

"Maybe, but I'm in love with Ty. He's out of luck on that one."

"Good answer." He nodded.

"What's with Ty and his family?" I held up a hand as I second guessed my boundaries. "Maybe I shouldn't ask that."

"Beckett." He lowered his head and shook it before he smiled at me. "You couldn't be healthier for him, Ivy."

"Why?" Now he had me even more curious.

"Because he's struggled with his relationship with his family for years. He feels guilty about it but doesn't know how to fix it. I'm happy he's now dating the one person that maybe, just maybe, can help him figure it out."

"Maybe I could if he'd let me in and not snap my head off when I ask about it."

"Oh, no, you can't bring it up," he scoffed like I was nuts. "No, you need to dance all around the subject then go through a back door, so he doesn't realize what you're doing."

"I see." I could do that. It wouldn't be the first time. "Good to know."

"Are you staying at Shadows?" He switched topics.

"I am."

"You want kids?" He slipped that in with a quick grin.

"Eventually," my cheeks pinked, "but I'm not in a

hurry." I shifted in my chair then leaned in toward him. "What's Ty scared of? Gimmie something good!"

He was about to speak when his gaze suddenly moved over my shoulder and his expression changed to one of surprise.

"Kit Moore?" A familiar voice had me swivel in my chair. "Oh, my God, and it's Ivy?"

"Shelly?" Moore looked at Ty's sister then at me. "Oh, that's right. Ty mentioned you guys had met."

"Yes, and, um…" She looked like she might jump right out of her skin.

"What's wrong?" Moore asked.

"Well, folks, shit's about to get real. Real interesting, that is." She laughed.

"Why?" Moore said slowly as he stood.

"Because the gang's *all* here." Just by the way she said *all* put my nerves on edge. "If it counts, I'm team Ivy."

"Team what?" I fought to catch up as an older couple approached us dressed in skiwear.

"Mom. Dad," she said with a full-out grin at Moore, "look who it is."

"Kit-lit!" Ty's mother came around the table and threw her arms around Moore. I recovered fast and smirked at her nickname for him.

"Connie, how are you?" Moore got up and glared at me as he hugged her back. "What a nice surprise running into you." He then patted Ty's father on the shoulder. "Richard. I totally forgot Ty mentioned you'd decided to move here."

"And I'm sure my boy was thrilled." Connie's voice dripped with sarcasm. Her gaze swung to me, and Shelly stepped forward.

"Ah, Mom, this is Ivy Knight." Connie's mouth went into an O and her eyebrows took a jump. I guessed Shelly had mentioned me. "Ty's lady-person friend."

"Oh," her eyes went glossy, "so, you're the one that he couldn't stop staring at during dinner?" She stepped back to take me in. "Aren't you a pretty little package."

"Thank you." I shifted at her compliment. "Lovely to meet you both." I quickly looked down at my outfit, suddenly feeling nervous. Though I always dressed my best, I wasn't prepared to meet the parents of the man I'd fallen for. "Would you like to join us?"

"Ah," Shelly's eyes went wide as she gave me a quick look, "do you think that's a good idea?"

"Oh, Shelly-nelly, don't worry so much. What T-Rex doesn't know won't hurt him." Connie waved a hand.

T-Rex? I glanced at Moore and grinned. This was getting good. I'd learned so much in the last three minutes.

"That's not what I meant," she muttered as her father spun some chairs around and they settled in. Connie and Richard began to chat over the menu, and Shelly perched on a chair between her mother and me but didn't look happy. She glanced at her watch and looked out the window at the street.

"What are you doing?" Moore whispered as he got closer.

"Going through a back door." I shrugged as I tossed his own words back at him.

"Ty's not gonna like this."

"What T-Rex doesn't know won't hurt him." I flashed him a killer smile, and he shook his head with a chuckle.

"I had a best friend once," he joked. "We had good times together. I just don't understand why he won't talk to me anymore."

"Oh, please," I waved his sarcasm off, "this is every psychologist's dream." I stopped whispering quickly as Ty's parents put their menus down and turned their attention back on us.

"Please, Ivy, tell us all about yourself." Richard was just as eager to talk to me as Connie was. I spent a few minutes and gave them the gist while they sipped their coffee. I was sure to skip over the part where I lived just up the road.

"She's lovely, smart, and beautiful," Connie confirmed to Richard. "I can see why our boy is so captivated."

Shelly caught my eye as she leaned back and mouthed, "Don't say too much." I understood. I would want Ty to be with me anyway if we were to share anything personal.

"Where is Ty?"

"He's training," Moore cut in. "Ivy and I needed to make a stop at the military camp nearby. We came in town for a quick lunch."

I caught Connie's face slip in disappointment, but she

pushed it back into a smile. "Of course. I know how busy you all are."

"Do you happen to know when he'll be in town next?" Richard wrapped an arm around his wife's chair to provide some comfort.

My stomach twisted into a knot in sympathy. It was obvious these people had moved across the country—to a mountain town, no less—where they probably didn't know a soul just to maybe catch a glimpse of their son on occasion. There would have been a time when I'd have given anything for my father to even want to be in the same room with me.

"I'm really not—"

I cut Moore off. "We might be at Zack's for dinner in a few days." I wanted to soothe their hearts. What was the harm? "Shelly, I'll text you when, and maybe we can all meet up."

"That would be cool." She smiled warmly then glanced nervously at her watch.

"We'd love that. Thank you." Connie placed her hand over mine. "Is he doing okay? Does he need anything? We could do him up a care package."

"Mom," Shelly rolled her eyes but took pity on her and patted her arm, "I'm sure he's got everything."

"I think he's fine right now," I gave her hand a pat, "but I'll let you know if I think of anything."

"Right, of course." She sat back and let out a heavy sigh, then smiled. "Maybe we should send him Binkie." Connie winked at Shelly.

"Mother!" Shelly looked horrified.

"I'm sorry, who?" I pressed my lips together.

"Oh, yeah," Moore snickered, "I'm going to be buried alive."

"Hush, you." I hit his shoulder. "Binkie?" I repeated, and Shelly had to turn in her seat as she started to laugh.

"His childhood blanket. It had a little *la-la-phant*," Shelly used air quotes, "in the middle. More commonly referred to as Binkie."

I covered my mouth, just so happy. "It's like Christmas morning."

Everyone broke into laughter, and we carried on in fun for another few minutes until Shelly stood and said they had to go and catch the bus that was to take them up to the ski hill.

Connie hugged me. "You take care of my boy."

"I will. I promise." I hugged Richard. Shelly hung back a bit while her parents put on their coats. Moore made a motion that he'd be back and walked with them.

"I'll be right out, Mom," she called. "He's going to kill us." She shook her head with a laugh. "I just hope this won't push him farther away. He's not comfortable sharing his life with us."

"I'll do my best to do damage control."

"I know my parents can be a lot, but it's for a good reason."

"Yeah?" I dug. I wasn't overly proud of it, but this family could use some healing.

"I have to be quick, but to give you a window in,

when the recruiters came to the high school and did their pitch, something clicked inside Ty. When he brought the idea back to our parents, they freaked out, they cried, the whole nine yards. In fairness, he did make an effort to look at colleges, but he always came back to the military. What hurt the most was that he joined first then told them. You can imagine how scary that was for them. They'd always supported us in everything we did. I know they just needed time to wrap their heads around the idea, especially when they understood how important it was to him. I mean, their son was about to risk his life and in a whole different country." She sighed.

"I couldn't even imagine."

"When he's on leave, instead of coming home and letting his family know he's okay, he shuts us out. He just carries the guilt around his neck and doesn't see that we all understand and support him now. It's just snowballed. If he could just let Mom and Dad in a tiny bit, they wouldn't be so wounded and stage five clingy. God, even that dinner where we met, fifteen minutes in they relaxed, and we were like our family again." She glanced at the door.

"I'm going to do my best to help," I assured her.

"He'd never admit it, but he needs us, too."

"I agree." I pulled her in for a hug. "I'll be in touch."

"Thanks." She gave me a wave, and I watched her run to the bus. I sat down heavily, so deep in thought I barely heard the little bell in the café ring as someone came in. A reflection in the window had me looking up.

Oh, shit.

"I'll take it by the shocked look on your face you know who I am."

"I do."

"Can I sit?" Her tone was clipped, and I gave a tight nod. "I see you met the family."

"I'm Ivy."

"I know who you are." She looked like a typical New York woman. Strong, confident, and feisty. Not bad things as a rule, but it could be when you were dating their ex, who I would assume she still had feelings for. She studied me for a moment, and her eyes pierced into mine as if trying to dig inside my subconscious. Little did she know I kept myself under lock and key.

"Did you want something?" I tried to push the conversation along.

"Just trying to figure out why he chose you over me."

"I think that's a question for Ty, Demi."

"He was mine for years. We've got history, and that counts for something. I'm the one who waited for him. I was there after every tour."

"You're right, all that counts, and you were there for him before I ever knew who he was. However, as time goes on, people change. Ty changed."

"Don't talk to me like I'm one of your patients." My brows went up, shocked she knew I was a psychologist. "I overheard Shelly," she explained when she saw my expression.

I see.

"Trust me, Demi, if you were a patient of mine, you wouldn't like what I have to say." Her mouth slacked open like she couldn't believe I'd have the gumption to speak to her like that. "Look, I don't know your past, nor do I want to, but I do think you'd want what's best for yourself as well as Ty. So, find someone who loves *you*. Don't hold on to what isn't there anymore."

She licked her bottom lip then leaned forward.

"If you want to play *we're females so let's look out for one another*, fine." She closed her eyes for a moment then locked her gaze on to mine once more. "Let me tell you this. You might think he wants to settle down and have a life with you, but that's just not Ty. He can't settle. He'll leave again." I hated her last comment. It hit so close to home. "Ty Beckett isn't meant for love. He's just meant to fuck." I cringed at her language and glanced around at the other customers. "Why do you think he did so many tours? Most soldiers do one and they're done. Not Ty. He's an addict. He'll just go chase his next fix because it's never enough." Her face softened, and I saw her mask slip for a second. "You'll never be enough, Ivy. He needs a woman like me, always there no matter what."

"Fuck!" I heard Moore's voice as he came back inside, but I never broke eye contact with Demi. "Yikes. Sorry, Ivy. I had a call come through." He slid back into his chair and glanced quickly from Demi to me.

"Hello, Kit." Demi leaned back, her face now morphed in a smile.

"Hey, Demi. It's been a minute. I see you've met Ivy."

"Met, chatted, and warned." She pushed to her feet. "Remember what I said." She smiled, picked up her purse, and left.

"Jesus, Ivy, I'm sorry. Christ, she's like a friggin' vampire. She just appears."

"No problem. I can handle myself." I could, but her comment did leave a little bite mark, though nothing I couldn't shake off. Women could be just as territorial as men. I just couldn't forget that damn packed rucksack and found myself a little insecure.

"Yeah. I know you can. Come on. Let's go." He tossed a bill on the table, and we walked to the truck.

I was quiet on the drive back and felt Moore's eyes on me a couple times. I needed time to dissect Demi's conversation with me. I knew better than to let her get inside my head, but I was caught off guard that she'd been there at all. I wondered what she thought would happen. Did she think Ty would change his mind and go back to her? The events of the day whirled in my head.

"Ivy," he looked concerned, "what'd she say to you?" I played with the strings on my bag and watched the snow fall in the headlights while I chose my words.

"She was just trying to understand me. I can't fault her for that." He pulled in and parked outside of the main house, and as we walked toward the front door, I turned to him. "They've got history."

"If it counts, Ty has zero interest in her anymore."

"I know that." I gave him a reassuring smile. "It's just odd she's still here with his family."

"Not really." He let out tired breath and held the door open for me. "Demi's just used to waiting for Ty. She just needs to get he isn't available anymore."

"That's kind of sad."

"Yeah, it is."

"It's gonna be okay."

Mark suddenly appeared and scooped me up in a hug as I dropped my purse on the table. His look at Moore said it all.

Something had happened to Ty.

TWELVE

TY

An hour before

"I'll go get some water." Ahmad held up the empty bucket. "Be back soon, my friend."

I stood up and nodded at him then wiped the sweat from my eyes. Amina's brother had gone to check on her an hour ago and hadn't come back. He wasn't happy about being asked to help dig up a body. Back on task, I carefully dug about a foot away all around where I thought he was. I didn't want to hit my friend with the blade. It made the job that much harder. I tried to ignore the smell and the knowledge it brought.

"You know," I said to Brown, "for a little woman,

Amina sure dug a good way down to send you off." I tossed more dirt over my shoulder. "Maybe you could get off your ass and help?" I froze as his hand suddenly slid out of the dirt. I'd seen enough dead bodies to shift gears fast in my head, so it didn't affect me, but when it was one of your brothers, it's a shit ton trickier, and I had to steel myself to keep it together. "Well, that's a start." I gave a dry chuckle.

The sun beat heavy on my shoulders, and I hoped Ahmad wouldn't be long. I slumped to my knees and carefully used my hands to dig around Brown's arm to free it up. The earth was hot, and my clothes stuck to my slick skin. There was zero protection from the sun.

I was used to the heat in this country and had grown accustomed to the temperatures, so why was my mind going back to the cool air at Shadows? Back to the lake, the peaks, and the crisp autumn nights. My hands worked aimlessly as my head wandered. Then an image of *her* appeared. Her cool skin and soft lips. I shook my head as I tried to concentrate on the task at hand. "I know, I know, buddy. I've spent a huge chunk of my life here. I thought it was where I wanted to be." If I ever had a doubt, I knew in that moment my heart was back in those mountains.

A short time later, I had all but his neck and head uncovered. I had left it last to prepare myself. As I reached to brush the soil away from his face, a shadow fell over me, and I felt a smidge of relief.

Ahmad was back.

"Can you hand me some wa—"
Whack!
Everything went black.

The smell in the air made me want to breathe through my mouth. We were just a mile outside of one of the little towns that ran along the Kobel River. Green to the country, only two weeks in, and still trying to adjust to the smell and heat of the place. The boys and I had spent two days down in a sewage drain to try to prepare ourselves for what the towns would bring us. It was one thing to train; it was another to live it.

"That's fuckin heartbreaking." Moore dragged his gaze away from the kids who played with sticks in the polluted water.

"Thankfully, they don't know any different," I grunted and sipped some of my water. I wished I was able to share some with the kids, but I only had my canteen, and I knew better than to engage with the locals unless ordered to. God love them, they looked at us with such hope at times, but when they realized you had nothing and no hope to share, it crushed them.

"Fucking savages," Moore growled. "What kind of animals are the Taliban to cut off their clean water supply?"

*"It's hotter than if the Devil was in heat himself,"
Brown sighed, "and here we are with clean water
and they're down there getting God knows what in
that fly infested swamp."
"It's not fair," I agreed, "but our job's to protect them,
let the other teams fix their water issue." I needed
them to try to keep their heads straight. "We've only
so many men."
Brown looked over at me, his mouth gaped as he
mouthed something.
"What?"
"Get up." His eyes were black.
"Why?" I scanned the horizon, but everything was
fuzzy.
"Get up, Ty!" He used my first name, and that
caught my attention, then he bent at the waist and
screamed inches from my face. "Open your eyes!"*

I jerked back to the living and struggled to open my eyes. Sounds came in and out as my head pounded and throbbed with my effort to wake from the dead.

"Get up, Captain!" Brown's voice echoed in my head again. With all my will, I felt something wash over me and I opened my eyes wide toward the sky.

Shit!

I grabbed my weapon on my hip when I heard a noise and focused in on the barrel of a gun that was pointed at me.

Slowly, my head kicked in and I saw the green tape on the handle. I released my grip on the weapon and lowered it. The man nodded as Ahmad moved into view.

"Oh, the American is awake." He smiled at me. "Lucky I come back. You would soon be swarmed once the rats let them know." He offered me a hand, and I stood on shaky legs. "Good thing I brought friends, but the brother never came back." He examined the back of my head. "Good thing it's from a shovel and not a bullet."

"Thanks," I somehow muttered as my stomach rolled. I took in the men around me; they were scattered about like a child's toys in a room. I shook my head as something gnawed at my memory. "How long was I out?"

"Couple hours." He shrugged. "We must move soon. Whoever hit you will bring Taliban." He gave orders to his friends, and they laid out a tarp near Brown's body. "Drink." Ahmad urged water into my hand. "Friends are here to help. Take a minute to rest." I was thankful for his kindness, but all I could imagine was the chopper leaving without me and Brown. I dropped my head and spit at the taste of sand on my tongue. I fished out some painkillers and swallowed them back. That was when I noticed my watch and remembered what Frank told me. I pulled out the tiny pin and activated the tracker. If anything, they'd at least know I was alive.

"See, all pretty. Like a gift." Ahmad's smile grew wide as he pointed to Brown, who was now wrapped neatly in the black tarp and tied with rope. "Sad, yes, but now you and your friend can go home, and we can get paid." I nodded, happy I could take Brown back where he belonged. At least that was something.

"Thanks." I gave a friendly nod to the others as they put Brown's body in the back of the truck then put a fist to my heart to thank them.

"Come, I'll drive you out of town." Ahmad hopped in the truck.

Neither of us spoke as we skirted the town. I stayed silent not because my head felt like it had been cracked in two, but because I knew I was officially finished with this country. I wouldn't return here again, and for once I was all right with that.

"Dress quickly." Ahmad slowed the truck as he handed me some clothes. "We got trouble." He nodded at a roadblock not far ahead. I blinked back my thoughts and was pissed I wasn't more aware of what was happening around me.

"Let me talk. Act sick. Let's hope the rats up the hill didn't let them know you were here in town yet. If they do know, you better be prepared." He nodded at my weapon, and I hid it under the cloth. Leaning my head against the door, I focused on the pain from my head and let that show through.

"Look at this asshole, thinks he's big shit because he has a weapon as long as his leg." Ahmad snickered quietly as we rolled on toward the roadblock. "I bet it's the only thing that's big on him. Good day." He switched gears when the man approached the window.

"Where you going and why?" he barked in Dari, and Ahmad prattled off the information. "Who's that?"

"Very sick friend."

"Show me his face." One of the men moved to my window, and I started to cough and acted like I was about to vomit. It wasn't particularly hard, given that I fought back nausea as it was.

"I wouldn't do that," Ahmad warned. "You see that in the back? That dead man carries a disease that makes parts of your body shrivel up and fall off. He's already lost his." He pointed at me and gagged, and I had to cover my face to hide my grin. "Now it's spreading up his stomach. He'll die soon."

Fuck it.

I let my stomach turn, pulled the cloth down from my mouth and projectile vomited all over the man next to my window. He jumped back, cursing and yelling. He started to rip off his shirt in fear while I quickly covered my face again.

"Get out of here!" The man hit the car, and Ahmad took off.

"Oh, my friend!" He cheered me on once we were well away from them. "That was something." I had to laugh at his enthusiasm even as pain shot through my head as I tugged off the bile smelling clothes and tossed them out the window. "I appreciate that you aimed your mouth at him and not me."

"It was the least I could do." I pinched the bridge of

my nose and tried to clear my head, "Ahmad, do you have a phone?"

"Box." He pointed to the glove box, and I found an old Motorola phone. I noted it was charged partway. I used a secure number, and when the operator answered I gave her my ID and password.

"Frank." Frank's voice sounded stressed.

"It's Beckett."

"Shit." He snapped his fingers, and I heard him call out to Cole. I couldn't help but wonder if Ivy was there too. "Are you good?"

"Just a mild hit to the head."

"He has a concussion," Ahmad called, and I shook my head at him. I didn't need any more attention right now.

"Is that Ahmad?"

"Yes, sir."

"I'll have a medic on stand-by."

"Sir, I'm making my way to the rendezvous. Am I too late?"

"Just get there and keep your tracker on."

"Roger that." I hung up and was relieved to have made contact.

"Thanks, Ahmad." I put the phone back in the glove box and closed my eyes as dizziness came over me again.

I wasn't sure how long we drove when I opened my eyes and saw we were somewhere I didn't recognize. I must have slipped off to sleep.

"Where are we?" My hand flexed on my gun as I looked around.

"You, my friend, would not make your rendezvous on foot." He stopped the truck and looked at me. "I have orders, too." He smiled warmly, and my stomach sank as I wondered what that meant. "See that turn over there?" I nodded. "A few kilometers east, and that is where your friends wait for you."

"How did you know where to come?"

"I have helped Frank in the past, and he has helped me in return. You're a good man, Ty Beckett." He looked back at Brown. "I'm sorry for your friend, but I am glad you will return him to his home." He put a hand on my arm. "You need to let him go once he is laid to rest, and then let this," he patted over his heart, "be free. You must do that to heal, my friend. Trust me."

I pushed my heart down out of my throat and mentally cursed myself for being so vulnerable. I put it down to the concussion.

"Thank you, Ahmad. I'll never forget your help."

"Nor I you." He got out, and I opened my door and stood there a moment as the world tilted. I used the door to help me fight it off.

"Send my thanks to Amina." I accepted Brown's body as Ahmad slid him from the truck.

"I'll tell her and her husband." He smiled.

"But I thought he was taken?"

"She helped you, so Frank helped her." He winked then headed back to his truck. "Take care, my American friend."

I felt a rush of endorphins as I headed toward the

others. The thought that Amina would be reunited with her husband made all this worthwhile. I couldn't change what happened with Brown, but I could change other things moving forward. The sound of the chopper and the dust it spun into the wind made me walk faster.

As I rounded the corner, the men caught sight of us, and they raced toward me to take Brown. Once inside the chopper, a medic began to check me over. I leaned back and let him do his thing. All I cared about was that Brown and I were going home, together this time.

———

The trip back the Washington was a blur of color and sound. It was confirmed I had a concussion. The way my head felt, I had no doubt of that. They took it a little easier on me during my debrief. I appreciated it but made sure they knew I'd done what I needed to do and done it to the best of my ability.

A hot shower, a good sleep, and a hardy meal made everything better. I snagged my phone from the charger and called Ivy's cell. She answered right away.

"Ty?" Her voice sounded small and unsure.

"Hi, it's me." I pressed my hand on the wall as I spoke.

"Are you—" she stumbled as her words rushed out, "are you okay?"

"I am, just a bump to the head, but I'm good." She

exhaled, and my heart swelled, pleased she cared. "I'm back in Washington."

"Good. When will you be home—or, rather, Shadows," she corrected herself.

"Tomorrow. I just have to meet with," I stopped myself as I realized I didn't want to give her more to stress about, "some people. Then I'll be back."

"Good, that's good." Her last word got caught in her throat. "I'm, ah, I have to jump into session."

"Yeah, of course." I suddenly felt a wall between us, and it made me uneasy. "I'll see you tomorrow—" I squeezed my eyes shut. "Ivy?"

"Bye, Ty." The line went dead.

Okay.

As I grabbed my things and headed toward the elevator, I mulled over why she seemed different. I barely noticed I'd arrived at the private hanger where Frank and Daniel were to meet me. We waited for Mr. and Mrs. Brown to arrive.

"For the record," Daniel said quietly by my side, "I'm incredibly impressed with what you pulled off over there."

"It wasn't just—"

"No," he shook his head as he turned to face me, "Ty, this was you bringing closure not only to you but to that boy's parents. Take this as a win, son." He put his hand on my shoulder. "Not only am I impressed, but I'm also honored to have a soldier like you at Shadows. There's no doubt in my mind that Dark Water will be everything we hoped because of your leadership."

"Thank you," I choked out and blinked away the unexpected emotion. My strained relationship with my own father suddenly hit me. I knew with sudden clarity how much I needed to hear that I had done a good job by a father figure. I also knew my father loved me and that I was the one who needed to fix things. I made a mental note as the plane landed.

"Ty?" Mrs. Brown's voice found me as they came into the hanger. "Did you—" She reached for me as Mr. Brown stayed a few feet back. I understood. They'd been through the wringer.

"I brought him home," I told them and stepped back as Frank wheeled in the wooden casket with the American flag draped over the top. "At least he'll be laid to rest here at home."

"Oh." Mrs. Brown put a hand over her mouth and reached back for her husband. He stepped up and placed a hand on the flag. "My dear, sweet boy." Tears leaked down Mrs. Brown's weathered face as she stood next to the coffin and wept.

"You're home, son." Mr. Brown lowered his head.

I cleared my throat a few times, but it was no use. I cried with them. I had to. It was a bittersweet moment for us all. Mr. Brown reached over and tugged me into him. His arms locked around my shoulders as he hugged me. It was unexpected, but I embraced it.

"You did good, kid." He sniffed. "I can't imagine what you went through to bring him back, and for that I'm grateful."

"I'm sorry," I confessed. "I'm so sorry I wasn't able to stop what happened."

"No," he pulled back, "I'm the one who's sorry, Ty. You were his brother. You would have done what you could. If he ever knew what I said to you at the funeral…" He shook his head. "I just had so much pain I couldn't see anything but red."

"I know," I assured him. "Me too." I hesitated, unsure if this was the right moment. I caught Frank's eye, and he gave me a nod. "I wanted to run something by you." I looked at Brown's mother. "By both of you."

"Oh?" She dried her cheeks and came closer.

"I wanted to ask your permission for something. Can we talk?"

They looked at one another and nodded.

My head was killing me by the time I was finished with the Browns. I walked slowly and purposefully the long way down to the cafeteria. As I walked past his door, I listened and heard a chair squeak and a moment later footsteps. My phone rang right on cue.

"Hey, man." I raised my voice a bit as I answered.

"Was the bait taken?"

"Seems so."

"Good." Moore chuckled. "So, how'd it go?"

"I brought Brown home to his parents," I answered as I held the door open for a soldier with his arms full. I used the moment and turned my head just enough to catch a glimpse of him in my peripheral vision as he eavesdropped. "Once the autopsy's finished and the body released, they'll hold a private service for anyone who wants to be there. I'll let you know when."

"Good. I still can't believe you got him back."

"I'm really glad I got him back, too." I continued to hold the phone to my ear as I slowly made my way toward the cafeteria.

"Ready?" Moore questioned.

"Just a sec," I replied quietly as I waited until I could see him in the reflection of the glass door. I needed him close enough to hear. "Yeah, the fact that she's willing to come all this way to testify is—" I ran a hand over my head as if the person I spoke to had interrupted me. "No, the family wouldn't talk, but at least she's willing to. Gotta run, but I'll keep you posted." I was one person away from ordering my meal. "Okay, talk soon."

"Now we wait," Moore said as he ended the call.

I ordered my food to go and made a show of almost bumping into Rivera as I left the cafeteria. We locked eyes, and I gave him a smirk.

"Yes, now we wait," I muttered to myself as I walked away from him.

I slept a lot. I slept the whole flight, and the whole drive back from North Dakota. Daniel and Frank woke me every few hours just to make sure I wasn't dead. It was annoying, but I was thankful they kept an eye on me. Truth was, the concussion didn't bother me anymore. My head felt okay. Maybe I was finally able to settle now that I'd brought Brown home to his parents. I hadn't come back completely emptyhanded.

"You meet with Dr. Roberts in three hours." Frank's voice booked no argument. "Then you need to get another MRI for that head. Any and all symptoms must be reported immediately. Understood?"

"Roger that." I grabbed my stuff from the back of the SUV and smiled as Blackstone and Moore came out to greet me. I heard happy kid screams from up on the hill and noted the sled tracks in the snow. I was pleased to know they were back and everyone was home again. Keith held back but waved at me. He watched his daughter as she played in the snow. I wondered how she and Brandon were doing.

"How are the kids?" I asked Moore as we walked together.

"Happy to be back."

"How's Ivy?" I glanced at Moore as we headed inside. I couldn't believe how good it felt to be back. The air was like silk to my lungs.

"We had a great time." He beamed, and I glared. "Then, when you didn't check in right away, she closed right up. I'm glad you're back, and I know she is, too." He nodded toward her office. "Given what happened, Frank thought it best we didn't tell her exactly when you'd arrive."

"We're circling back to your *great time* with her later," I warned as I dropped my stuff and headed toward her office. Her door was slightly ajar, and I'd seen most everyone already, so I figured she wasn't in a session. I opened the door slowly and looked inside. She was hunched over her iPad scribbling notes. She looked up, and her face twisted into some kind of painful emotion.

I stepped inside, closing the door as she stood, and in three strides, I cupped her face with my hands and slammed my lips to her in a passionate kiss. Her body trembled as she grabbed at my t-shirt and clenched the fabric between her fists.

"Oh, my God," I muttered against her lips, "I missed you." I missed her touch, her taste, her squeaks, everything. "Don't close up on me, Ivy." I was terrified something happened while I was away that changed something between us.

"You didn't check in," she suddenly cried out as she stepped back. She put her hands over her face.

"Hey." I was beyond relieved it was that and not something else that bothered her. I took her hands. "Everything was fine."

"For you maybe, but I—" Tears pooled her in beautiful eyes. "It made me realize—" She stopped herself.

"Realize what?"

"Ty, I'm so in love with you, and I've accepted that you have a crazy dangerous job, but that trip…" She cupped her mouth. "You could've died, and I never could've said I love you."

"Ivy," I pulled her to me, "I know you love me, and you know I love you."

"You don't know what I mean, Ty." She shook her head and gathered herself. "I've felt different levels of love before, but with you, I know. I know without a doubt that we are *it*. Just promise me," she paused again, "promise me you won't do any more trips like that one. I'm new to this whole 'loving a solider' thing. Oh, God, there's a reason I never went for men like you."

"Ivy, Ivy." I lifted her to sit on the side of her desk then stepped between her bare legs. "I promise I won't do any more trips without my team. I'm sorry I scared you. I really am." I nuzzled her neck and started to kiss her, showing her just as sorry I was.

"I was really scared," she said then hiccupped softly in my ear.

"I can think of a way to make it up to you." I slid my hands up over her hips then tugged her panties down to her ankles where she kicked them away. "I promise," I undid my pants and freed myself, "to ground you whenever you feel like you're spiraling." I gently stroked between her folds and watched as her eyes fluttered shut. She grew wet quickly, and I swirled my fingers in her arousal. I lined up and put my hands on her butt and pulled her forward to sink myself deep inside her. "I promise that this," I tilted her chin, so she'd looked at me, "is the only place in the world I want to be." All signs of pent-up nerves fizzled from her face as she leaned back on her hands.

"I missed you," she whispered as I held on to her hips and gently started to move.

"You were with me the entire time I was there," I said with honesty. "Whenever I felt my mind drift off, there you were. In your silk blouse, tight skirt, heels, and that smile that makes me weak in the knees." I picked up the pace a little as I lost my mind in how good she felt.

"Tell me more." She was breathless as her hands moved to get a better grip. She gave herself to me to do whatever I wanted, and I let out a growl from deep down in my throat.

"Last night, I was so hard for you that I needed two showers just to calm myself down."

"Oh, yeah? Did it work?" Her back bowed when I changed angles.

"No." I closed my eyes and tried to control myself. "Nothing works but this."

"Then take me."

I folded over her, grabbed the edge of the desk, and used all my strength to go deeper, harder, rougher, until all she could do was hold on. Her lips puffed hot air over my ear as I repeated how much I loved her. Over and over, I uttered the words until she shook beneath me, and I released everything I had inside her.

All that could be heard was the sound of our heavy breathing, but my words were still there hanging in the air to remind us of what we had.

"God, it's good to be home," I whispered. "This is my home." I kissed her chest above her heart and sealed my words inside it.

THIRTEEN

PAUL

For days, I stayed glued to the cameras that showed my house in Mexico. I watched and listened for anything I could bring to Blackstone. I knew Frank had a few men on this in Washington, but I knew this life better than any of them, and I needed to help.

With the camera footage projected onto a massive screen, I poured myself some coffee. Abby had brought a whole pot down for me earlier along with some sweets. I snagged a sticky pastry from the plate, and as I sank my teeth into its deliciousness, I was struck by how much the people in this house cared for one another. I'd almost forgotten how much these simple acts of kindness made this place a home to all who were lucky enough to live here.

I knew Ty was back. I'd heard Moore mention he'd gone right up to see Ivy. Lucky guy. Talya's face immediately popped up in my head, but even as I shook away the memory of her face, my subconscious defied me. I could hear the sounds she'd made in the back room of that bar as clearly as if it were in the here and now. I closed my eyes and indulged for a moment. The temptation was just too much. The scent of her brought memories of fresh laundry and a hint of sweet perfume. It made my chest ache as I thought of her long, smooth legs. I sighed deeply, then my eyes flew open as I heard Alejandro's voice.

"Are you slipping?" The memory of Talya shattered, and I shot forward to look at the camera feed. Alejandro was in the library. "Get your shit together." He snickered at Filippo. "They're talking about you out there. You're drawing attention to yourself—no, to us."

"Shut up," Filippo barked.

"What's going on?" Alejandro demanded with crossed arms. Filippo rubbed his head, and I tossed my pastry on the table and moved closer to the screen.

"Castillo's called for a party." Filippo pulled at his hair. "*Hijo de puta*, I think he knows that we know."

"Settle down! Do you think we'd be standing here if Martin Castillo knew the truth?" Alejandro stepped closer to Filippo. "Do you think this place would still be here at all if that were true? We'd be dead and this house would be burned to the ground just to make a statement to everyone he knew." He reached back and pulled out his gun and pointed it at Filippo's chest. "We're in this together, *mi amigo*, but if you can't handle it, then I will."

"Fuck off." Filippo pushed his arm away. "The fucking safety's still on."

I smirked as I remembered Ale's fear of blowing off his own junk. He always kept the safety on and always forgot about it. *Real hardcore Cartel member, right there.*

As the evening went on, I felt my eyes grow heavy, so I lay down and watched the screen from the comfort of the couch. The sound of the sliding glass door woke me, and I jerked upright. A blurry Savannah stared down at me as I sat there, and it took a moment to remember where I was. Her kind smile eased my mind as I fumbled to clear my head.

"Paul, I know you want to help the team, but please take a break. Come and join us in the living room upstairs." She nodded toward the door.

"Yeah, sure, okay." I swung my legs and let my feet hit the floor heavily. "I think I need a shower first."

"You said it, not me." She winked. "The new team's here. They just arrived, so you should come up and meet them." She gathered my plate and mug and put them on the tray. "I'll take this for you while you get ready." She smiled and whisked out of the room.

"Right." I dreaded the idea of meeting new people, especially the way I felt in that moment. I left the office and eased into the entertainment room then flipped down the panel in the wall and slipped through into the hidden stairways. I was pleased the Logans hadn't changed the passcodes. Only Blackstone would know about them, anyway, I reasoned, and of course Savannah. I was pleased I remembered the way to my room without having to engage with anyone on the way. The Logans hand-built an entire back way to move about the house unseen so we could move prisoners, move to different rooms, or flee to the escape room if, God forbid, anything was to happen. I climbed the stairs and smiled at Sue's private room that Savannah used as a quiet place to hide from the boys in the house. I stopped to admire Sue's, Savi's, and now Oliva's names carved into the wood showing generations of women who used this little oasis, and the water ring of Aloof's fishbowl. The memories the house held were truly amazing.

I kept moving then punched in the code to open the wall door to my bedroom. Once inside and the door was flush with the wall again, I dropped my clothes and headed for a much-needed shower. It was nice that they kept everything the same. They had no idea what that meant and how I wasn't just a picture on the wall.

The living room was full of energy as I entered, and I walked toward the others, glad I felt more like myself. I chuckled when I spotted Aloof's bowl on the mantel of the fireplace, another secret Olivia let me in on as she had seen Mike return one night with a new goldfish. I wondered what number they were on to keep him alive for the kids. Ty had begun to introduce the new team members who arrived early this morning to everyone, and when he spotted me, he hesitated. I realized he was unsure as to how to introduce me.

"Hi, I'm Paul. I work for Frank," I called and moved closer with a smile and a nod.

"Lee. Nice to meet you." One of the guys stepped up and shook my hand. Mark suddenly cracked a joke, and the attention went immediately to him. I silently thanked him. Everyone stood around and chatted, and the sound of ice cubes and laughter soon made me feel at home again. I enjoyed these times with the family, and I appreciated Savannah's effort to bring me back to the fold.

"Hey, Perez," Lee called, "you gotta work on your dismount." The new guys laughed at that, and I knew there was an inside joke there as Ty joined in. "Gain will kick your ass next time."

The conversation turned to training and how Ty had wasted no time in getting the guys ready. They'd been up on the mountain with Daniel several times already today, and Lee joked again about who was better at what. I knew Ray had been training with them at Camp Green as well. Sounded like Dark Water were more than prepared to head to Mexico. I was impressed that Ty had found some good men. They obviously fit well together. He made it a point to say how they were already a solid team and he was happy how they'd come together in such a short time.

We were only days away from our big strike against the Cartel. We all hoped it would be one of the biggest dents made in Cartel history so that Dark Water was ready put my mind in a better place. My attention was pulled by raised voices.

"I can beat you up there with one hand behind my back, Gain!" The guy named Perez hooted, and soon the whole Dark Water team clamored out of the room with bets called along with shouts of encouragement and rude remarks.

"And just like that, they're off." Mark grinned at me, clearly as impressed with Ty's leadership skills as I was.

"Nice to see he's taking his job seriously." I nodded and grinned back.

"Bringing in Beckett was one of the best things Daniel and Frank have done in years," John said. "I know he's being standoffish with you right now, Paul. Give him time. He'll warm up." We all stepped up to the window to watch them rush in the direction of the hill.

"I get it. I lived as the enemy."

"He's just got his own shit going on," Mark added. "His head's a little preoccupied."

"But if you want to really win him over, get to know Ivy." John nodded. "She's great, and Ty really values her opinion."

"Good to know." I eyed Ivy as she chatted with Savannah near the kitchen door. "How long have they been dating?"

"Started dating?" Mark shrugged. "No clue, but the moment they met, sparks flew." He waved his hand. "You know the friggin' power of this house. It's like Disneyland when they pump the smell of food in the air just to get you hungry. I swear Shadows does that with hormones." I chuckled at his interesting analogy; it was kind of true.

We stood in silence as they came into view again and watched them zigzag up the steep trail on the side of the mountain. "That was us not that many years ago." I laughed. "We so wanted to please Cole and be the best we could be. Crazy how time flies, and don't even get me started on the wild curve balls it throws at you." I shook my head at their agreement.

Mark turned as one of the twins raced by. "Hey, Liam?"

"Yeah, Dad?"

"Do me a favor and grab me my blue jacket from the hall closet."

"Do I get a cookie if I do it?" The kid's eyebrows went up.

"So, there's no doubt he's your kid," I muttered playfully.

"A boy after my own heart." Mark shrugged. "Yeah, bud, there's two in it for ya."

"Deal!" He ran full tilt down the hall, and a moment later we heard him shriek. Savannah's snort of laughter could be heard from the kitchen, and Mark shook his head.

"You got your nephew with that *thing*!" he called.

"Sorry, bud!" Savannah couldn't stop laughing. "No one's exempt from the house games!"

"That thing scared the crap out of me." Liam tossed his father's jacket at him.

"Blame your father." Savannah raced by holding the friggin' contraption.

"I know she was tryin' to get me." He snickered under his breath. I chuckled and once again enjoyed how light this house was even in the darkest of times. It sure had its charm.

"Speaking of which…" I knew I could screw with Mark a little. It was well overdue on my end, and I knew Savannah would approve. "Did I see Abby and Doc lip locked outside last night?"

"Nope," he shot back.

"It was the funniest thing, and his hand was so far up her—"

"How are you settling in?" He switched topics on me so fast I squinted and pretended I wasn't pleased by his change in topic.

"Fine."

"Good." He nodded at someone behind me just as Catalina hit my shoulder.

"Suck it, sucker. You're it." She gave me a devilish twinkle and raced off as everyone in the room broke out in laughter. Even Liam raced out of the house so fast he was a blur.

I glanced at John, Mark, and Cole, who all had laughed as she scurried off.

"I see…" I felt the warmth that ran through the room with the knowledge that Shadows was in full swing of a new prank mode. I flipped them the finger and went to find Olivia again. I knew she would at the very least fill me in on what the hell I was now a part of.

———

*P*unch, *punch, punch.*

I ducked, hit, and bounced my way through a boxing lesson. Olivia had given me the scoop on the giant game of tag the house was in on. I was already in strategy mode on how to make the next move. She'd shown me the board, and I'd seen who the last person was that needed to be tagged. I might just win this game.

I felt the need to clear my head before I settled in to watch my house in Mexico.

Out of the corner of my eye, I saw Ivy quietly speaking to Mike about something.

"Keep your head with me," the instructor ordered. He probably thought I was checking her out. Ivy was beautiful, but she was much too young for someone like me. Besides, I knew who she belonged to.

"Give me a moment." I dropped my arms and shook out my shoulders as I moved to the ropes. "Hey, Ivy, can I bother you for a second?"

"Sure." She waved at Mike then headed toward me. "What can I do you for?"

"I was hoping you and I'd have a chance to talk later."

"About anything in particular?" She tilted her head,

and I could almost feel her energy as she studied me. "Or are you hoping to win Ty over through me?" She raised an eyebrow with a ghost of a smile.

"Am I that easy to read?"

"No, John just mentioned it upstairs." She chuckled.

"Hilarious," I rolled my eyes and leaned some of my weight on the ropes, "but I need his trust, and right now I don't think I have it."

"And you think gaining mine would help convince him?"

"It's a worth a try."

The subject of our conversation stepped in the side door at that moment and came up behind Ivy to plant a kiss on her temple. He took a quick glance at me, and I moved my weight back off the ropes.

"Hey," he greeted her warmly, "I was lookin' for you."

I was uneasy about how our conversation might have looked to him and took a step back.

"How was training?" She sagged into him lovingly, and I remembered how Talya used to do that with me. "You were out there early."

"It was great, and the guys are in good form. Ray did a great job. They're ready."

"Like you had nothing to do with it." She laughed. "Any steam left in that body?" She lifted both her brows, and I suddenly felt awkward standing there. Ty pulled her into him.

"Always."

"Good." She pulled back and nodded toward me. "Why don't you hop in the ring and show Paul here what you got?"

"What?" His face fell.

"That's not what I meant, Ivy." I shook my head.

"Look," she held up a hand, "since I arrived, all I've heard about is how Shadows is the best because you're all the best. This is supposed to be a brotherhood. If there's mistrust or hard feelings, there's no brotherhood. You can't fight out there if you're not okay in here. So," she took Ty's bag from his hand, "get in the ring, and you two duke out your shit and move on. I'll not be part of the generation that screws up this house."

"Can we clap for that?" Mark stood from the bench. "Because I'm clapping for that." He started to clap, and Mike joined him. I saw John put down a weight and move closer.

"This is why we love Ivy!" Sloane called from the corner of the room where she'd been stretching. Ivy crossed her arms, and I gave her a slow nod, then she directed a look at Ty, who was not pleased at being put on the spot.

"She has a point," I told him. "You have a problem with me. We do it here or out there."

"Fine." Ty disappeared and returned a moment later wearing shorts and sneakers. "Let's get this over with."

The instructor gave us the rules, we bumped gloves, and we started to circle each other. He immediately went in for a jab to the ribs. I blocked it, but he set another blow and got me. The kid was quick and packed a mean hit. I was impressed.

"Nice hit."

Again, he came in, faked a punch, and hit my thigh. I used his technique, but he was ready for it. Clearly, this wasn't his first time in a ring.

"Ty," Ivy said softly, and to my surprise it got him talking.

"I know you were a good man, Paul—"

"Am," I corrected.

"But you have to see it from my point of view." He bounced, around and I could see his frustration with me come to the surface. "Where's the line?" He jabbed my jaw, and I shook it off.

"What are you talkin' about?" I huffed as he sent in another, hard.

"The line, Paul. The line between the man you were and the enemy you became. Is there gray there?"

"No gray. Just black and white." I ducked to avoid another jaw shattering jab.

"Sam Duggan," he started again, "one of my buddies from training. Was a smart guy," he huffed. "Climbed the ranks fast." He gasped as I faked him out and hit low. He recovered quickly. "Three years in and ended up a POW. Took five weeks to find him." He danced and shot me a good one in the head.

"That all ya got?" I said as my head spun. "What are

you goin' on about, this Sam guy?" I danced around him as I tried to find an opening.

"He flipped, that's what." He dodged. "They got to him while he was in there. We never saw it comin', and he led them right to us."

"Ooff," I huffed as he slammed me when I let my guard down at his words.

"Lost two good men that night. They brainwashed him into thinking he was one of them." His hands fell as the heaviness of what he just shared weighed on him, and we both stopped. "Sam was a friend, a good soldier, but now he sits in a prison cell because in those five weeks he let them get inside his head." He tapped his head with his gloves then ripped them off and tossed them over the ropes. "You were there for over a decade." His eyes burned into me. "You see where I'm goin' with this?"

"Look, I get it. But I'm not Sam," I assured him. "It's unfair for you to compare us."

"No, you're right, it isn't," he shrugged, "but I can't help the way I feel."

"Then we have a problem here."

"Yeah," he huffed, "we really do."

"Now what, Doc?" Mark chimed in.

"We can do this two ways." Ivy put her hand on her hip. "You two keep talking, or I'll have to call in Doc."

"She plays dirty," I muttered under my breath as she held up her phone.

"She's not bluffin' either." Ty swiped a hand over his face.

The door swung open, and Savannah stepped in. She froze as they all looked at her.

"Out!" the guys all yelled out in unison.

"Wow, you guys are a comedy act." Savannah rolled her eyes but never wavered in her step as she approached the ring. "One, Cole isn't here, so…" She flipped us the bird. and I knew she'd caught the humor. None of us could let the moment pass without reference to the last time she got in trouble in the ring years ago with Cole. "And two, I know better than to interfere with whatever you got goin' on here." She twirled her finger at us. "Ty, I was hoping to talk to you. I need a little insight on the guys and what they might like to eat."

"They're in the middle of a session," Ivy said, and Savannah's face lit up. "So, he'll be a bit."

"Oh?" She stood next to Ivy. "Just what kind of session?"

"These two need to clear the air." Ivy stared at Ty and me as she tossed Ty's gloves back over the rail. "And they're far from done."

"I got a better idea." Cole had entered quietly behind Savannah and shot her a look that she ate up with that award-winning smile reserved only for him. He dropped two duffle bags on the floor. I figured they both planned a workout. "You two either clear the air here or spend a night on the peak."

"Shall we?" I held up my hands, ready to fight, and he didn't miss a beat. He tugged his gloves back on and took a quick shot at my chin. I just managed to block it. We sparred for the next hour or more. I lost track of time, my body ached, and we both dripped sweat and began to slow down. Our swings lost their power, but neither of us stopped.

My phone rang, and I glanced at it as I recognized the ring. Ty took advantage and landed a solid punch.

"Will he answer it?" John shouted, and Mark hooted.

"Game's yours." I ripped the Velcro away from my wrists and dropped the gloves. I stumbled out of the ring and grabbed my bag. Ty swiped a water off the stool and eyed me as I took a breath to steady myself then answered it.

"What have you got?"

"I…" He paused. "I found out who killed Lexi."

"Hang on." I picked up my bag, aware that everyone stared. I pushed open the door to the showers and glanced in to be sure it was empty before I responded. "Go on."

I listened as my blood turned cold. Tears fought their way to the surface, and I lowered my head as I tried to keep control of myself. I was supposed to have protected her, but I'd let her down. I let them all down. The memory of that whole night flashed in front of me from the ambush at the convoy, to racing through the streets with her, to the moment she was shot, to…

How did I not know?

"I'm sorry, Eric." He used my fake name, which meant he didn't trust where he was. He was taking a risk even to call me. "I'm sure this is a lot to take in."

"I'll be in touch." I tossed my phone into the sink and covered my face with my hands and let out a silent sob.

"You okay?" I looked up to find Ty in the doorway.

"No, not really," I confessed and lowered my head again. I hated that my emotions were at the surface and caught in my throat. "That was my informant in Mexico." I cleared my voice, but it didn't help. "Jesus." I drilled my fist into the mirror, and he moved closer and leaned his back against the wall to face me. I turned to him and ignored the blood that now ran from my hand, glad of the pain.

"What's goin' on?" Ty asked quietly.

"Every woman who was moved through that tunnel went through me. She was sold to my buyer, then we made sure she went back to the States. It was a smooth, clean-cut operation. Then the one time it goes wrong, and it's *his* wife. I thought I'd done everything right. I played my cards perfectly." I snatched my phone and held it up. "And now to find out who it was, who killed her." I felt tears rim my eyes. "I could have stopped it."

"I understand that feeling." He held my stare. "I kept my team alive until the very end, and then just like that, Anderson and Gail are killed and my friend Brown was shot in the head by one of our own. Those last moments play over and over again in your head. You replay it and replay it to try to think what you could have done differently."

"Shit. You hear about shit like this happening, but I've

never known anyone who personally went through it. Does it ever stop?"

"Not so far." He pushed off the wall. "Guess it'll keep going until we find a way to make it right and stop it. Guess it's up to us to do that."

"I can tell you date a doctor," I mumbled.

"She's the best part of me." He started for the door.

"Hey, Ty?" He stopped and turned around. "I guess if we're gonna take these fuckers down, I need to know we're good."

"Yeah," he leaned forward and held his hand out for a shake, "yeah, we're good." I waited for him to leave, took a few deep breaths, and focused on getting my head on straight.

I quickly showered then changed and made my way to the office. I found my box of belongings and dropped it on the desk. Cole had given me this room to use as an office. I knew it was a safe place to watch the cameras and keep my things.

I dug around and found the USB stick where I'd downloaded the recordings from the house. I was thankful I'd taken it with me before I left for Castillo's on the night of the auction. It was old school, but uploading anything would have been too risky. I dug farther and found my old wallet. I pulled it apart and fingered out the sim card I'd hidden between the pieces of leather.

I pushed it into one side of my laptop along with the USB stick. I clicked on the icon and started to download the voice messages from my phone to the stick. Once everything was moved over, I did my best to organize it. Since I'd decided to share it, I decided to hold nothing back.

It was time.

I tucked it and a few other pieces in my pocket and went upstairs. I walked through the house to check where everyone was. Some of the guys were in the living room, the kids were outside making snow forts, and the girls were chatting it up in the kitchen. They showed me the cookies they'd made for the kids to decorate later with Abby and June. Cole swiped a finger taste of the frosting, and Savi took a swat at him with a dishtowel.

"Hey, Logan?" I called as he ducked her towel with a laugh. "A minute?"

"Yeah." He kissed Savi, and she scowled at him as we headed for the door. "Are you and Beckett good?"

"Yeah. We're good."

"Great. So, what's up?"

"I think it's time I talked to Keith." He glanced down at the USB stick, player, and earbuds that I'd pulled from my pocket. "I, ah," I glanced around, "got a call from Chili."

"Oh?" Cole looked concerned.

"I'd like your permission to let Keith know first. I think I owe it to him."

"Understood, and I agree, but I want to be second."

"Roger that."

"He's out with the kids," Savi said as she popped her head in from the other side of the door. Of course, she heard. Cole shrugged at my look, and I had to smile. I waved at them both as she put her arm around Cole's waist, then I grabbed my jacket and slipped out of the front door.

The cold air helped clear my head, and the sound of the fresh snow as it crunched under my boots took my head to happier times. I looked at the footprints that led down to the lake. The kids' shouts could be heard from the top of their sledding hill. I grinned at the rainbow of food coloring that decorated the girls' snow castle.

I knew the men at my house had watched me press the tile on the wall many times. I also knew they thought it was a second lock to keep the basement door secure. It actually triggered a mic that recorded every moment of what happened down there. I knew that if I ever returned home on my own or if my cover was blown and I had to leave quickly, either way I'd need to prove whose side I really was on. I'd had hidden mics installed the first week I moved in. Not once did I regret having them. Especially now.

As I rounded the boathouse, I found Keith. He sat on an Adirondack style chair and nursed a steamy mug of coffee. It took him a moment to realize I was there.

"Room for one more?" I pointed with my hand still inside my pocket.

"Mm." He nodded, still in thought. I picked up a doll dressed in bright snow gear and gently set her upright on the table and took the chair next to him. I knew how the girls were with their babies.

"How's Reagan holding up?"

"Not sure." He blinked away a memory and focused on me. "She's not really talking."

"I can't imagine what she's going through."

"No one can." He sipped his coffee, and we both watched a deer as it walked across the lawn. It stilled for a moment then lifted its head. Three smaller deer soon appeared and followed her once she knew it was safe.

"Keith. I wanted to talk to you about something, but I'm not sure if it's the right time."

"It is." He didn't miss a beat.

"Okay." I tried to think of where to start. "When we sold Castillo on the idea of getting everyone together for a big event, I had to show proof that Lexi was alive, or he'd never believe me."

"Okay." His throat contracted but his eyes stayed locked on the deer. "And how did you do that?"

I took a deep breath and hoped he'd see what I was going to offer him was a gesture to help him heal and not something to cause him more pain.

"With this," I pulled out the USB stick and set it on his armrest. "I recorded everything. I even bugged the room she was kept in." I paused to gauge his reaction, but he sat like stone. "She left you a message," I could hardly push the words off my tongue, "after she was shot." I sniffed and stomped down on my emotion. "I promised her I'd give it to you." I hesitated. I needed him to know all of it. "There's a lot more on there. I want you to have it all. I want to give you everything from the moment she arrived until the very end. I don't want you to ever doubt my loyalty. I was and always have been your brother." I set the earbuds down next to the recorder then stood as he eyed it. "Then, when you're done, I'll answer your next question."

"Which is?"

"Who shot your wife."

FOURTEEN

T had my phone up to my face as I slowly made my way into the kitchen. I concentrated on the email I was interested in. It was about a conference I hoped to take in California in the new year. I heard the voices but didn't take them in right away until I heard my name mentioned.

"…the bar you and Ivy went to? We could set the trap…" Moore stopped talking when I rounded the corner, lowering my phone.

"What's going on?" My gaze moved to Ty. His tight t-shirt made his arms look even bigger. *How is that even possible?*

"We planted a seed to trap Hill before I left for Washington," Ty answered, "and now, we're ready to act on it."

"Great. When and where?" I was more than interested in bringing that guy down. It was personal now.

"Nope," Ty shook his head, "not this time."

"Come again?"

"I won't put you in the middle of this."

"It's too late for that, Ty."

"Agreed, Ivy, Hill isn't stable," Moore chimed in as he tapped his head to make his point.

"Oh, is that so, Moore?" I gave him an *as if* look. I was a psychologist, after all.

"Yes, and it makes him dangerous. Who knows what he'll do next."

I looked between the two of them and studied their expressions. "I will not be written off just because I'm not a soldier."

"You're being written out of this because you're my girlfriend and I don't want anything to happen to you."

"Where was this when we were in Washington together at that bar?"

"That was different. I was there to protect you. It just happened to work out that time that we could go there together, but now Moore's here—"

"Now that Moore is back, I'm no longer needed." I put my hands on my hips. "I'm just expected to stay out of it?"

"That's not what I meant."

I tried not to get upset, but the truth was it bothered me. We'd worked well together up until now, and it made me feel more connected to Ty. I was more than just a girlfriend. I knew I was capable, and I wanted him to see that. I also didn't want to argue with him in front of Moore.

"Well, I'm glad I know where I stand in all this." I skipped the coffee and headed down the hallway.

"Hey, wait." Ty chased after me, and I turned and drew in a controlled breath. "I'm sorry I upset you."

"I don't want to be a Demi," I blurted and blinked when I realized what I'd just said.

"Demi?" He shook his head, baffled that I went there. "Where's that coming from?" Shit. I closed my eyes; this was not the time. "Ivy?" He folded his arms, and I internally kicked myself.

"What the heck has Demi got to do with anything?"

"When you were gone, Moore and I were in town for lunch and ran into your family." His mouth went slack as his eyes widened. "Shelly and your parents. They were headed to the ski hill and stopped for lunch. They seemed lovely," I added, worried that his face was like stone. "Anyway, after they left, and Moore went to walk them outside, Demi found me."

"Oh, really?" His tone was clipped. "And what did she have to say to you?"

"She said she just wanted to meet me and…"

"And?" His eyes drilled through me.

"And she warned me that you don't love people, only your job." I waved it off. "I know that's not true. I know you two were purely physical," I assured him. "But, Ty, besides all that, what I really mean is that when you and I were working together trying to find out stuff on Hill, I really loved it. We have a lot more than just a physical relationship."

His arms dropped to his sides, and he sighed. "How many times do I have to tell you that what we have is different than whatever she and I had?"

"You don't have to tell me. I know we are, but I need you to know I want what we had when we worked together before. It made us different. We were a team."

"First, you and I," he flicked his finger between us, "will always be a team. As for Hill, I won't stop you from helping, but I won't put you in harm's way, ever. Especially when it comes to actually taking him down." I relaxed my shoulders at that, as I saw it from his standpoint. "There's that physical," he stepped close and tipped my chin back with his finger, "like I'm going to beat his ass to the ground, then there's our kind of physical." He leaned down and brushed his lips over mine.

"Hummm, I like our kind of physical." I smiled under his lips and slid my arms around his midsection as he took over my mouth. *Let it go, Ivy. He's only trying to protect you.*

"See, we make a great team," he murmured and dove deeper.

The alarm on my smartwatch rudely went off. I had to get to my next appointment.

"I have to go," I huffed.

"Are we good?" He searched my face.

"We're good." I smiled honestly. "Thanks for taking

the time to explain it to me, and for wanting to protect me."

"I will always protect what's mine." He kissed my fingers then let me leave. I loved the fact we communicated and tried to clear the air in the moment rather than let it fester inside. *Look at us being all grown up.* I chuckled at the thought.

I found Keith sitting on my couch as I went into the office.

"Gosh, I'm sorry, Keith. How long have you been here?" I moved quickly around to my desk to get my iPad. Scoot was sitting in his spot on the arm of the chair, and the *where the hell were you* look he gave me made me raise a brow at him. Keith didn't move; he just stared toward the window. "Keith?" I walked over to him and realized he had earbuds in, and his eyes were glossy. As he realized I was there, he pulled them out and clicked a button.

"Hey, Doc." He gave me a sad smile and sniffed. "Sorry. Your office was quiet, and I knew we weren't meeting until later, so I used the time."

"No problem at all. Please feel free anytime it's not in use." I went back and unplugged my iPad from the charger, turned my phone to vibrate, and settled in the chair across from him. Scoot seemed more than ready to start the meeting.

"Sorry I'm late." My uncle rushed in. "I hope you got my message, Ivy. I'm here to observe you today." We both glanced at Keith, and he nodded his permission with a shrug.

"Thanks." I smiled warmly at Keith. "Sure, take a seat, Doc." After he settled, I pointed to his cheek. "Ah, you got a little something." He took a tissue and dabbed at his skin then turned bright red as he realized it was lipstick.

"Well," I focused back on Keith, "where would you like to begin?"

"Let's start with my wife's last few days." He set a small recorder on the table between us as I looked up at him, confused.

He took a few moments to fill me in, and I blinked at him as I wondered how he stayed so calm.

"I won't lie, that's the last thing I expected." I tried to smile, but really, I was more than a little concerned about his mental state after he apparently listened to some pretty dark stuff. I knew the Blackstone guys were a different breed, but literally hearing your wife's last words, not to mention her death, was on a whole different level.

"You can come in anytime, Doc." Keith waved him over. "I want you to hear this, too." Doc did get up and moved closer but didn't comment. Keith remained hunched over the table.

"Keith," I looked at him and waited until he looked up at me, "would you say you're better or worse after hearing all that?"

"Shockingly, better." He gave a small shrug.

"Good." I nodded and let my gut guide my next question. "Why?"

He rubbed his forefinger and thumb together, and I

could see he was choosing his words carefully. I caught his drift.

"Keith, it's okay." I stopped his thoughts. "You've got my word if you share something dark with me, I won't pull you off the Mexico mission."

"Ahh," my uncle started to speak, but I shifted my gaze to him quickly.

"My patient, my rules." I wouldn't let him interfere. The mission was too important to Keith, and to even suggest he shouldn't go would cause him to completely clam up. We'd never know the truth about how all this really affected him.

"Understood." Doc fixed his glasses and pressed his lips together with a nod.

"This whole thing is certainly heavy." I pointed to the little listening device. "It would be unfair not to expect you to have a strong reaction to it. But I know you got this," I reassured him. "So, this place right here," I indicated the room, "is your safe space. Let me in your head, and let me help."

"Yeah, okay." He flexed his neck and wiped his hands on his thighs then leaned back into the couch. "I've been trying to sum it all up in my head." He looked up. "She went from a fighter, to breaking down, to seeing clarity in what she did. How she wronged us, I mean. Our family. Then she acknowledged the consequences of what she'd done."

I noticed my uncle seemed impressed by his explanation, but this was Keith with me. He opened up, trusted the process, and found solace in my kind of therapy. Sometimes you just needed to spew the ugly on the wall, hurt something, then move on.

"You know people will sometimes say *they'll have a lot of explaining to do at the pearly gates*?" I nodded. "I think being in that basement was like that for her. She told Paul things about us that makes me see she was truly sorry about everything. And then there's her final words to me." He leaned forward, tapped two buttons, and hit play.

"Tell Keith," Lexi's soft voice filled the room, "I loved him the best way I knew how. It was far from perfect, but it was the only way I could." She coughed as she took a breath. "Find someone, someone," *cough-cough*, "who will love you and our babies." There was a pause. "I forgive you, Keith. With all my heart, I forgive you."

I blinked to clear my eyes and looked at the tears that streamed down his face. I glanced quickly over at Doc and saw him mop at his eyes with a hanky.

"In her final moments, she was selfless, and she forgave me for not coming home. It's always been there between us," he looked up at me, "I know it was. All those years ago when I let her down when her parents were murdered." He used the back of his hand to dry his cheeks. "That's the Lexi I fell in love with." He smiled, and a chuckle broke from somewhere inside him, then he broke into a sob immediately afterward. "For her to say those things," his breath caught in his throat, "what it did for me inside," he hit his chest, "it's like I know I'll be okay, and our kids will be too. I know she loved us. She couldn't help who she was." His voice cracked, and he leaned forward over the recorder and let go of all the emotion he'd tried to hold back.

I joined him on the couch, wrapped my arm around his shoulders and cried with him.

"Let it out, Keith. Let all the guck out," I whispered. "She gave you the gift of closure, and not many ever get that."

My uncle stood and placed a hand on Keith's shoulder and bowed his head. We stood there in solidarity and gave him the time he needed to grieve for his wife.

———

"That was certainly…heavy." My uncle came back into the office. He'd walked Keith out of the room and watched him as he went down the hall. "Paul was waiting for him by the stairs. I'm glad he has the support of his brothers."

"He's going to be okay." I nodded.

"I'm impressed, Ivy. You handled yourself extremely well."

"I was taught by the best." I sniffed as I fluffed up the pillows on the couch, only to have Scoot jump up and push them back down again as he made himself at home. "I have to admit the last hour wrung me out." I pursed my lips and blew out a whistle of air as I sat down.

"Ivy, I'm retiring, and I can't think of a better person to take over for me here."

Wait. What? Where did that come from?

"Take over? You're retiring?"

"In a way, yes."

"You can't retire." I looked at him in shock.

Was he mad?

"I can, and I think it's time. Well, maybe not full-time." He adjusted his glasses as he often did when there was more he wanted to say. "I'm getting older and have a few things I'd like to do."

"Such as?" I looked at him with wide eyes.

"Such as pull back on my duties here. I will, of course, still work with Dark Water until they bring in someone. But the timing of your situation and how well you've fit in here couldn't have come at a better time. You've earned the confidence of everyone here, and—"

"Why did you dodge my question?" I folded my arms as he cleared his throat.

"You may have noticed I've been a little distant lately."

"Yes, but I just figured you were off in a dark corner with someone. You know, getting it on with the nanny." I wiggled my brows at him as I pointed to his cheek, and he glared, hating that I'd caught the lipstick earlier. "Don't be such a prude, uncle. I'm happy for you." I laughed. "If you want to move on to something different, do it. But I'm not the one you'll need to convince. You have like a hundred sons out there who won't let you leave easily."

"There's really only one I worry about." He looked at the door, and I figured he meant Keith. "But right now, I need you to focus on getting Blackstone ready for this trip to Mexico. I'm not pulling any stops with Dark Water. This will be their first mission, and it's not just them going, it's also Quinn's team Dusk and Mills' team Eagle Eye." I knew that General Frank Brandon had started team Eagle Eye years ago, but his skills were needed in Washington. He since stepped down, and Mills had taken over the team. Frank kept in close touch with the men, and I knew he still itched to get back in the action.

"Jesus," I huffed, "I know they're going after Castillo, but do we really need all our men to take him down?"

"Our guys have special skills," he nodded, "but best you don't know all the details." He leaned over and kissed my temple. "Now, I have some calls to make." He left as my own phone vibrated on the desk.

It was Shelly.

I read her text a few times and wondered what I should do, then I remembered Savannah's offer and headed for the kitchen.

"You know, baby girl, if you eat this banana for me, I'll give you a cookie." June glanced up at me as I came in and took the stool next to Reagan. June mouthed, "Won't eat, won't talk."

I reached over and plucked a marker from where she'd been drawing.

"Did you ever hear about the dolphin that turned into a flower?" I picked up the banana and showed it to her then made motions with it as if it were a dolphin.

"No, and dolphins are blue, Miss Ivy," she whispered and continued to color in a puppy in her book.

"Yes, most are blue, but there's some very special ones that are yellow." She gave me a quick look, and I knew she was curious. "Yup, and these yellow dolphins can turn into a flower. May I show you?" She nodded and watched me draw two eyes and a happy face on the top of the banana. I used the tip of the stem as the beak. She smiled a little. "Yellow dolphin." I slowly peeled back the skin and used a paring knife to slice the banana into slivers while keeping the base of the banana whole. "Ready?" She watched as I lifted it and set it straight up. The thin sliced pieces bowed under their own weight and formed into a flower.

"That's pretty. Can you show me something else?" She had brightened up and was talking, and I could see the relief on June's face.

"Of course, but you have to eat this, before I can do another." She reached for it and slowly peeled the petals down and ate them like string cheese.

"Thank you," June whispered as she fixed a bit of hair that had escaped her elastic. We both looked toward the living room as laughter erupted. I checked it out. The Dark Water team played a card game, and they seemed to enjoy poking fun at each other as they played. I gave a satisfied nod.

"Do you like to color, Reagan?" I turned my attention back to her.

"I like to draw more."

"Do you think you could draw me a picture of something? Anything you want. I have a whole wall above the table in my office that needs some decorating, and it sure could use a picture."

"Okay." She pushed her coloring book aside and started to draw something. I knew drawing was a perfect insight into a kid's head. I didn't give direction on what to draw so I could see where her head was in the moment. Savannah came in the front door, and I waved to get her attention.

"I'll be right back, okay?" Reagan kept drawing. "Once you're finished with your banana, I'll show you how apples can become frogs."

I made my way over to Savannah, who looked over my shoulder at Reagan.

"Did you get her to eat?"

"She just needed food to be fun. Takes her attention away from her thoughts." I shrugged. "Listen, I was wondering if we could do Zack's tonight."

"You had me at Za," she laughed. "Yeah, for sure. Everything okay?"

"I kinda met Ty's parents without him. He seems to be apprehensive about spending time with them. Now his sister's trying to plan something, and I want to get him to go. Maybe if he knew everyone was coming to Zack's afterward?"

She grinned. "Smart."

"It's hard navigating between I want to help but not stepping over a line," I confessed.

"Say no more. I'll set it up." She waved her arms. "This is my jam."

"Thanks." I turned to leave then swung back. "You still owe me that secret." I made a motion toward June.

"That'll just be the cherry on top of tonight's events." She winked.

After I got Reagan to eat half an apple and a peanut butter spoon, I headed outside where I found Ty, Mark, Moore, and Gear cleaning weapons in the shed that Ty and I had christened a while ago.

"Am I interrupting?"

"Nope," Gear grinned, "just making sure all is right before we head out."

"Right." I smiled back, as he was such a friendly guy, but I felt my stomach twist at the idea of them going. "Just wanted to let you guys know you're going to Zacks's tonight, but we're heading there first."

"A night out," Mark hooted. "Sounds just about right."

"Zack's?" Gear looked confused, and Moore filled him in. "Will there be women?"

"It's a ski town. There's all kinds of fine ladies there." Mark smirked playfully but immediately frowned when he caught my glare. "It's not like I took home anyone's number." He gave me a sly look.

"Mark," I scowled and shot my gaze over to Ty, who stared at me, "you're a shit disturber."

"Just a minute here." Ty pointed his rag at him. "That's the second time you've brought that up, Lopez."

"It was nothing, Ty. You already know." I rolled my eyes, happy that Ty already knew and didn't find out this way. "Remember Olivia's friend introduced me to her father?" He nodded darkly. "Mark and I were there," I pointed to Mark then back at me, "when they were leaving on their Girl Scout trip, and that's when he gave me his number."

"And she took it," Mark added.

"What's the big deal? She's hot." Lee came up behind me and snagged some rubber bullets from the counter. They all looked at him while my cheeks heated. "What? She's not my doctor."

"No, but she is your team leader's girlfriend," Mark pointed out.

"Oh, dude," Gear laughed, "it sucks to be you right now."

"You got a hot girlfriend, Beckett." Lee shrugged.

"Thanks, man." Ty chuckled and returned his attention to me. "Hey, guys, could you give us a minute?"

"And that's our cue." Mark didn't waste any time. He hustled them toward the door.

"Hey, Mark," I called as they left, "payback will be a bitch."

"Bring it, Doc." He winked as he closed the door. I moved closer to the heater in the corner for warmth.

"So, this guy gave you his number?"

"Yes, which you knew about."

"Did you keep it or call him?"

"Yeah, actually we have a date tonight." I smiled a seductive smile. "No, of course not," I laughed, "but in fairness, we weren't officially dating at the time."

"And then you met my family?"

Okay, so we were clearing the air right now.

"Yes, I did, and they were lovely."

"Anything else I need to know?"

"Need to know?" I pretended to think, and he put his weapon down on the table next to him. "Your sister wants to meet up with us at Zack's for dinner." I saw his reaction and held up my hand. "Before you say anything, all the guys are going tonight. Maybe not for dinner, but they'll be there for drinks right after."

"Is that so?"

"I'd really like us to go, Ty."

"Why?"

"Because you met my mother. It's only fair I get to meet your family, too."

"But you've already met them," he tossed back at me. It wasn't really a jab, but there was a clip in his tone. "Why do I feel it's a setup?"

"Ty," I took a deep breath, "I'm not blind to why they're going through me to get to you, but it would mean a lot to me if we could see them tonight, together." I put the emphasis on the last word. "If that's me crossing a line, I'm sorry."

The bottom of his shoe tapped on the floor as he studied me, his lips pressed into a straight line.

Shit, I pushed too far.

"Make it for eighteen hundred." He gave me a tight nod.

"Six?"

"Yeah." He picked up his weapon and started to clean it again.

"I'll let Shelly know." I was so excited I decided to risk one more comment. "Ty, I really like them. I'd do anything to have family like yours. They're so desperate to spend time with you."

He never made another comment, just continued to rub something off his already gleaming weapon. I gave a little sigh and decided to leave it alone. I had accomplished what I wanted to do. As I walked past Mark, I glared at him, and he gave me a sheepish grin as he hustled the guys back inside.

That night, I wore a plum sweater dress that Savi loaned me. She called it her lucky dress. I didn't allow my brain to focus too much on just how she got lucky, but I needed all the luck I could get tonight. I'd paired it with tall boots, and a pea jacket that just hit my knees. When Ty appeared, he was dressed in jeans, a tailored wool coat, and a ball hat. It was cold as he took my arm once we got outside, but thankfully the Shadows trucks had the best of the best when it came to heaters, and it warmed up fast. Ty didn't talk much on the way there, but he kept a hand on my thigh. As usual, he watched the mirrors like clockwork.

Zack's parking lot was busy, but I knew he'd saved us the best table in the back, thanks to Savannah, who'd called ahead to make the dinner reservation for us.

"Hey," I turned to him by the side of the truck,

"thanks for letting me in a little more." He leaned down and kissed me hard. He swiped his tongue against mine.

"Damn, Rowe, look who we have here," someone shouted at us. I turned to see two Redstone police officers coming toward us.

"And they gave you badges?" Ty laughed as he wrapped an arm around my waist.

"Who might this pretty lady be?" one of them asked.

"This is Dr. Ivy Knight." Ty looked down at me. "Ivy, this is Rowe and Beam. We go way back."

"That we do." Rowe leaned forward and shook my hand. "Lovely to meet you, ma'am."

"You as well." I smiled at the two of them. It was always nice to meet any friends of Ty's.

"Congrats on the job, guys." Ty pointed to their uniforms.

"Nice to be here and not over there." He glanced at Ty, and they both made a face of understanding.

"Where's Jay?"

"He got in, too. He's just gone to visit family. His mama is real sick. He'll be back, though."

"Send him my regards." Ty urged me forward. "See you around."

"You too, Beckett."

"They seem nice." I tried to keep Ty's thoughts level as we approached the restaurant.

"They're good guys," was all he gave me.

We were met with a burst of warm air and a delicious aroma. I glanced at the "deal of the day" and hoped what

I smelled was the smoky sausage and mushroom pasta it promised. My mouth watered at the thought.

I spotted Ty's mother, Connie, across the restaurant. She nearly leapt out of her chair, but thankfully Shelly put a hand on her arm to stop her. Shelly whispered to her, and she seemed to rein herself in.

"You look good, Ty," Connie said as he leaned in for a hug and her eyes closed as she drank in the moment. My heart hurt for her, but I knew it would take baby steps. It was why we were here. Careful baby steps.

"Thanks, Mom," Ty murmured.

"Ivy, you look lovely."

"Thanks, Connie. I'm glad we could meet up."

"Me too."

We said our hellos to his sister and father.

Ty took my coat and hung it under his on the coatrack then pulled out my chair and waited for me to get settled. I noticed his father watched with pride that his son was so well mannered.

"Is this new?" Ty eyed my dress.

"Borrowed from Savi."

"Well, I hope she doesn't want it back." He gave me a quick, private, hungry look, and I was pleased. I knew he was okay if he could still be playful.

"So, Ivy," Shelly had waited for everyone to order before she jumped in and took the lead on the conversation, "how long have you two been dating?"

"Well, let's see, now," I tried to think when things went official.

"A few months," Ty offered curtly, and Shelly threw him a look, unimpressed by his tone.

"Well, at least we know at this dinner you won't be checked out. You know, with her here at the table and not over there by the window." She gave him a shit-eating smile, and I held my breath.

"That's true." He nodded. I was shocked he took it so well. "So, Dad, got any fishing in?"

"Oh, ah, no, not yet." Richard stumbled over Ty's unexpected question. "Still getting the lay of the land."

"There's a great spot just a mile up the road," Ty went on. "You should check it out sometime."

"I'd love to hear more about it." His dad's eyes lit up as if in that one simple moment, things had changed, and it had made his whole year worthwhile.

"Ivy, has your mother been to town to see you?" Shelly asked, and her face let me know she was happy how things were going.

"No, regretfully, not yet. Soon, I hope." My stomach twisted for a moment at the mention of my mom. I was such a mama's girl, and I hated to be away from her. At least I knew Reid checked in on her often and had friends checking as well. "I haven't seen her since we were in Washington last month."

"We?" Shelly asked.

"Yes, I had to go to Washington, and Ty was there for work. Since we happened to be there at the same time, Ty offered to drive me."

"I bet *he* did." She chuckled, and he rolled his eyes at his sister. I caught his smirk, and so did Shelly.

"So, you met her mother, Ty?" Connie's face said a lot.

"I have."

"So, this is pretty serious?" She pried a little further.

"Very," he confirmed. "I love her." His hand landed on mine, and my eyes went wide with shock. I wanted to burst with warmth. I certainly hadn't seen that coming.

"No. shit," Shelly snorted. "I mean, the kitchen could have exploded at that last dinner we had, and he'd barely have noticed he was so busy watchin' her."

And now I'm blushing.

"That's wonderful, son." Ty's dad smiled and smacked the table, and he and Connie exchanged looks of complete surprise.

"And you, dear?" Connie finally got some words out. "Do you love my son?"

"More than anything," I assured her. I beamed at Ty, who sat and studied us all, his face smug that he'd caught everyone off guard.

"Please, have some kids so my daughter has someone to play with." Shelly laughed, and the smug look disappeared. Ty took a quick mouthful of water and choked.

"I love the idea of a little one running around with his own little *binkie*." I couldn't help myself. I pressed my lips together to try to stop the laughter that bubbled up from inside.

Ty's face went murderous as he looked from his sister to me.

"I love those ones with the little la-la-phants in the middle." I let the laughter go and could feel my face turn red as I gasped for breath.

"You're all dead to me," Ty hissed, and the whole table erupted in laughter so hard people started to look over at us. "You think that's funny?" He smirked at me. "Just wait!"

"Remember, Ty, I'm not the only one who was here that day. Moore was here, too."

"That's right." Ty looked thoughtful. "He kept that conversation from me too. Well, that's two people who may not show up for work tomorrow morning."

"You're soo funny." I tossed my napkin on the table. "Please excuse me. I'd like to wash my hands before we eat." Really, I just wanted Ty to have a moment alone with them. Ty instantly turned into Shadows mode, so I rested a hand on his shoulder. "We're at Zack's. I've already waved at Jake so he knows I'm here. I'll only be a moment."

"It's the bathroom, dude," Shelly teased him. As I started to walk, I heard her add, "Unless she's in some kind of trouble. Oh, my God, are you her bodyguard? Are you like Kevin Costner and she's Whitney?" I had to stop and look back.

I laughed. "You never know."

"Why are you so weird?" Ty sighed, but he stayed at the table.

I took a few extra moments in the restroom. I was so happy about how things were going. I couldn't stop the grin on my face as I glanced in the mirror and thought of what Ty had openly shared with his family. I put on a little more lipstick then headed back.

When Ty spotted me, his shoulders relaxed, and he stood as I approached to pull back my chair. I hoped they had a good talk while I was gone.

"Ty was just about to tell us what he's doing now." His father directed the comment at me as I settled in. I looked expectantly at Ty, and he jumped right in. He kept things on the surface and explained that his time in Afghanistan was over. He spoke a little about his last tour. He even mentioned how he was able to return Brown to his parents. Once Connie shot me a worried glance, but I gave a little shake of my head to assure her that all was okay. He bantered with Shelly and even let out a belly laugh when she poked at his friendship with Moore.

It seemed the brittle eggshell Ty had built around his relationship with his family had cracked open, and it all just seemed to flow smoothly out. He looked happy, and the lines around his father's eyes as he smiled at his son showed just how much they'd needed this.

"So, Ivy," Shelly leaned over when Ty was in full swing conversation about their mom's hope to add a library to the new house they bought, "sorry for the joke earlier about the restroom. Ty explained everything."

"He did?"

"Yeah, it makes more sense now, the way Moore kept watch on the exits when we were at lunch." When I looked at her, she shrugged. "It runs in the family. We notice stuff like that."

"What'd he say?"

"That given what they're doing on their special ops missions, it leaves you and a few others exposed to some of the dangers here." That was more than I ever expected Ty to share with them. "I haven't said it yet, but thanks for making this happen. It'd be really cool to have you in the family."

"I've always wanted a sister." I leaned in and gave her a hug.

Ty's face was full of life, and it almost brought tears to my eyes at how carefree everyone looked in that moment. To others, it looked like we were a big, happy family enjoying a dinner. But I knew they were a family in need of repair, and tonight, the first step had been a big one.

When the others arrived, the volume in the place had risen to one of a family dinner in Italy, and it was the most spectacular thing I'd ever witnessed. Moore was pulled in for hugs and kisses by the whole Beckett family, and I noticed Mark somehow weaseled his way in for some himself. He reminded me of a golden retriever. He wanted to soak up as much love as possible. It was rather endearing, especially as I knew some of what he'd gone through as a young boy.

"Pull up some more chairs," Cole called. "We've got

more family here tonight!" No one wasted any time, and the scrape of chairs as they made room for Ty's family made me smile.

"Ivy." Savannah rushed over to me and grabbed my hand. "Okay, you ready? Because now's the perfect time to tell you about June." *Oh, the secret!*

"Yes!"

"So don't turn around yet, but she's over near the table by the door." She pointed carefully, and I nodded that I could see her. I also noticed that Mark watched us. He seemed to know something was up by his slitty-eyed look at Savannah. "Do you see *it*?" she asked as I studied June's mannerisms as she chatted. I took in the way she dipped her head and smiled coyly. There was no denying the sexual sparks.

"Oh, my god," I mouthed with excitement under my hand.

"Been going on for months now."

"Does Mark know?"

"Nope, I'm sure he doesn't," she whispered, and we both glanced at Mark as he studied us from his seat at the table.

"Oh, Savannah," I placed one hand on my chest as I squeezed her hand, "if I could have this one, I'll forever be in your debt. That little frigger tossed me under the bus today, and I'd love nothing more than to take him down."

"He's all yours." She smirked darkly, and we both turned to stare at Mark. His face suddenly went from quizzical to terrified.

"Holy all that's female. Something's happening, Cole!" Mark called out to his brother, who shook him off like a tick.

"Let the fun begin." I shrugged happily and began to silently make up scenarios I could use on Mark.

"Hey." Ty pulled me into his chest as we made our way toward the restrooms a bit later. He cupped my face and stared into my eyes with such intensity I felt the heat grow deep down in my belly. "I'm not afraid to admit when I'm scared, and the thought of tonight scared me to no end." He paused, and I wondered where he'd go with this. "Jesus, Ivy, the weight you lifted off my chest." He took a breath. "I know it was my own guilt that caused it. I never thought I could get past it, didn't know how."

"Ty, I just…"

"Just listen, please, Ivy. I need to say this. You are the light to all the dark parts of me, and I—" He struggled to speak while I fell even harder for this man. "Thank you for the push. You're right. I just needed to face it, and tonight I genuinely laughed with them, and, fuck, I want to show dad that fishing spot." His face lit up and he looked ten years younger. "That's all because of you."

"I'm glad I could help." I sagged into him and let the joy warm me up.

"I've thought about it a million times since I met you, and I'll wait a little longer so's not to scare you, but Ivy Knight, I'm gonna make you my wife."

"I won't say no." I met his lips halfway, and we sealed our words with a sexy kiss.

"Hey, lovebirds!" Mike broke our moment. "We got the call. Time to ship out."

Well, the night was almost perfect.

FIFTEEN

PAUL

"Does everyone know exactly what they're responsible for?" Cole's voice was sharp and cut through the silence of the room like a knife. We were thirty minutes from the Mexican border, in a safehouse, with only a short time before one of the biggest moments in Shadows' history. "If not, speak up now because we can't have one single mistake. We're not just taking down Martin Castillo, we're taking down a major tier of the Mexican Cartel." He looked around the room at us. "That means each and every one of you needs to be on the same page. We're not leaving a man down in that God-forsaken country." He stared at all of us. "Everyone knows who their mark is. You get in, make it happen. Get out."

"Hooah," we all called in unison. *Well, some of us.*

"Since when did Shadows start working with the Italian mafia and California bikers?" Mills, team leader from Eagle Eye, muttered behind me. I turned around as I got his concern and couldn't blame him.

"It's not just about Castillo and his men." I wanted to set his mind at ease. "There's a lot more to it. It's about who else they've been working with." *And who else they've affected in the past*, I thought as I eyed Trigger. I knew from Mike that Castillo had helped Trigger's father run a drug operation a while back. So, Trigger and his club had a personal stake in this. I also knew Castillo was his mark. I was more than fine with that.

Before we left, Cole had explained the details to most of us. Some of it was on a "need to know" basis but none of it was particularly a secret. It was just complicated, especially with Frank and Team Eagle Eye. He needed to keep Frank in the dark as much as he could about just how Devil's Reach and the Capris were involved, as Frank needed to turn his head to a lot of it. He'd opened up to me about it all, because we both knew this was the last operation I had left in my career. I wouldn't go under-cover again and couldn't show my face working with Blackstone. It would be too risky given who we were at war with.

Mills was a good guy, and I sure as hell didn't want Eagle Eye to think anyone at Shadows was purposely keeping details from them. When he nodded toward the window, I followed his look and waited. I wanted to know what was on his mind.

"Yeah, well, I know that guy's Elio Capri, and he's a bigshot in the mafia, and those guys are his cousins. How're they involved?"

"I'm not sure of the connection there, exactly." I scrunched up my face as I thought. "I know Castillo somehow got hold of Rosa Coppola. She'd pulled some dirty deal on him or something." Mills looked at me, confused. "She's the last remaining member of the Rome Syndicate, and Elio Capri's been on the hunt for her for a while now. When he heard of our mission, he offered to help since he wants Rosa bad. I guess he threw out a reward for her, and Castillo's such a puffed-up asshole he took the bait and Capri got an invite to the party."

"So, is all this the new normal?" Mills scratched his head.

"No," I chuckled, "it's not normal, but the truth is we need all the help we can get on this one. So, here we are." Mills shook his head slowly, and I clapped him on the back. It was a whole different kind of war we fought these days, and we all had to go with it. Maybe Mills had a point, though. Maybe it *was* the new normal.

"And what about Devil's Reach? What's their in?"

"Grim Gates."

"Sweet Jesus," he shook his head, "the life you lived."

"Yeah, well, look where it brought us." I grinned, and he smiled and popped a fist bump then got up and walked over to join his team. I knew he'd be okay with it all. These guys were the best of the best.

I failed to mention to Mills that Chili had already put

out the word on Castillo, and anyone with a vendetta against the son of a bitch had been invited to join the op. Castillo was done.

My friend Sal approached his brother Dylan, who agreed to be our eyes at the house. Turned out Castillo had messed with Dylan's daughter a while back, and both brothers were happy to help. Dylan oversaw the ongoing maintenance of Castillo's escape tunnel, and he kept an ear to the ground. Because of him, we knew the rotation of the guards and when they switched shifts. He really proved his worth when he told us where the weak spots of the house were.

"Good?" Cole asked as he leaned on the wall next to me.

"Yeah," I assured him. All was well with me. I just itched to move.

I glanced at Cole then checked the time. We had a few more minutes before we all left in different directions. I took a moment to think about all the people who were here with us.

"Just odd. I mean, my two worlds are about to collide." I shook my head at that.

"Odd doesn't even begin to describe this." Cole looked around with me.

Team Dusk and Team Eagle Eye were going over the property map. Trigger, Brick, and Rail, old motorcycle friends of Mike's from California, were in heavy conversation with Italy's mafia king, Elio Capri and his two cousins Niccola and Vinni.

"It's sure hard to wrap my head around." I whistled quietly in amazement. "How you pulled all this off, Cole, you never cease to amaze me."

"Be glad Frank chose not to hear some of the details," Cole huffed. "He may have to claim selective memory later."

"Dark Water and Blackstone mesh surprisingly well when you consider they haven't had a lot of time to prepare." I'd been impressed with that, and Cole nodded his agreement.

"You took your kid's gum?" Ty's voice drew our attention.

"No. Well, it was mine to start with." Mark held out a piece toward him, but Ty shook his head with disgust. I smirked at the ridiculous wig Mark had on, and Cole chuckled.

"Some things never change."

"Nope." Cole sighed.

"So, I guess you got to work with Elio after all," Ty said to Keith as they walked toward us.

"At least I'm not crossin' any lines this time." Keith glanced up at Cole and I could see there was more to that story.

"Keith." Trigger suddenly appeared. For someone so large, he was quick on his feet. "I got ya somethin'."

"A gift?" Keith eyed the black box tied with a red ribbon. Trigger held it out in his tattooed hand and waited for Keith to take it.

"Yeah, figured a shot to the head or nuts would be too

simple." He shrugged as Keith took it from him. "You do you, man, but consider it a gift from my playground." I chose not to ask any questions. "However, you decide." He flipped his floppy Mohawk out of his face. "DR has your back."

"Thanks, Trig."

"No sweat, man." Trigger turned and walked back toward his guys.

Keith watched him go then opened the box and let out sharp laugh and held it out to us. "It's a ball buster." He held up what looked like a small bear trap with razor sharp teeth. It looked like when released it could easily tear away your manhood in its jaws. "Thoughtful of him," he glanced over to where Trigger stood with his men, "but it's not who I am." He tucked it away in his jacket, and I felt Cole relax a little.

"Hey, Mike," I moved to his side and kept my voice low, "how much did Trigger tell Grim about me?" That moment at the bar when he gave me his car still played with my head.

"Trig?" Mike nodded him over.

"Yeah?" He eyed me.

"How do you know Grim?"

"Well," was all he offered.

"You have history?" Mike folded his arms.

"A long one, yes." He studied me then and decided to add a bit more. "His family has a few hotels on the Vegas Strip. I have my business just off the Strip. Our paths cross frequently when he's in town."

"How much did you tell him about Eric?"

"What you said to." He spat to show his dislike of being questioned. "That Blackstone needed Lexi out by whatever means necessary." He looked at me. "Though he has his suspicions."

"Meaning?" I questioned, and he squinted at me and looked pissed. "Look, I'm just concerned that I need to worry about Grim. I don't want anything to mess up the operation."

"He suspects you maybe flipped sides because of the girl." He stroked his beard as he looked at me. "It happens." He looked around the room. "He saw you carryin' her. He's just tryin' to figure you out."

"Fair enough." It made sense. Trigger lit a joint and inhaled as he pocketed his lighter. Then he scrunched up his face and looked at me again.

"Grim's not someone to fuck with, but he wouldn't cause you shit unless he figured you deserved it."

"Thanks, man." Mike was satisfied and eyed me to make sure I was good. I nodded.

"You boys ready?" Rail, one of Trigger's crew, came up to us. He reminded me of a happy feral cat. His eyes danced with excitement as he held up a notebook. "Got my flipbook of kills." He held up the book where he'd glued in the mugshot pics of who our targets were and flipped through them with his thumb. He must have swiped the pictures from Cole's board at the meeting earlier.

Mike chuckled. "Inventive. I hope you took the right ones."

"I was real careful." He grinned and flipped the pages again as if he couldn't wait for the party to start. I had to laugh.

"Rail, get over here." Trigger pulled Rail away from us.

"They're an odd bunch," Mike laughed, "but they've always had my back. Blackstone's too." I held up my hand as if to say I wasn't one to judge.

My watch vibrated, my two-minute warning to start hauling ass out of there. I put my hand on Keith's shoulder and looked straight at him. "For Lexi."

"For Lexi," he repeated.

I left the house and tested my coms again once I got outside.

"Raven One to Fox One, do you read?"

"Read you loud and clear, Fox One." I smiled as I opened the door to the pickup truck. Man, I'd missed that. The tiny receiver sat low in my ear, and its flesh color hid it from sight. You'd be hard pressed to see it even if you looked for it. Frank had some pretty cool hookups with the Secret Service.

I turned the engine over and watched as the others dispersed in fancy cars, Land Rovers, and two badass looking motorcycles. *Shit, if Frank could see us now.*

As I made my way across the border, I left Paul in America and shifted my brain back into Eric mode when I was waved through. I took a deep breath and picked up speed as I made my way south toward Rosarito. Not long later, Cole checked in that he'd made it across with Blackstone and that Dark Water wasn't far behind.

I glanced down at myself. I wore a wrinkled dress shirt and sunglasses, and with my inch-long wild hair, I hoped it made me look like I'd been off the grid for the last while and hadn't had time to worry about what I looked like. I downed some water and tossed the bottle on the passenger floor. It rolled on top of some food wrappers I'd scattered there. I needed it to look like Lexi had traveled here with me. Even some female clothes were tossed in the back. Deception was everything, especially today.

The pickup truck sounded like thunder when I shifted it into third gear to make it up the hill. I hunched over the wheel as I made my way through the narrow streets then up toward Castillo's over-the-top white mansion.

"Approaching the gate." I kept my voice low. I had to remember not to use formalities as I kept them all in the loop.

I gave my name to the guy at the gate, as I didn't recognize him. He gave the truck a once-over and muttered something incoherent into the radio, then the gates swung open.

I parked, got scanned for weapons, and was escorted inside. It wasn't lost on me that Castillo didn't greet me outside or even once I entered the house. He wasn't a fan of me to begin with and clearly trusted me less now. Given the number of guards in the place, he wasn't taking any chances. For once, Castillo played it smart. I wondered just how long that would last.

"Where's the girl?" One of Castillo's men, one I particularly detested, got up in my face.

"None of your fuckin' business. Where's Castillo?"

He just glared at me and didn't move.

"I've been on the run, *estupido*," I acted annoyed. "I need to know what I'm walkin' into. I still don't know who ambushed me before. Maybe you'd like to tell me?"

His jaw ticked, and he rolled his eyes like the punk he was. "Go upstairs." He waved at me.

I made my way toward the stairs, then took two at time and scanned the area as I went.

"Eight guards in the front and two at the base of the stairs." I spoke quickly into my com. "I'm on the second floor and—" I stopped hard as I came face to face with Alejandro.

Shit.

This was one of those moments you could never prepare for. A moment that could take down everything, ruin the entire operation.

"It would take one word and you'd be finished," he growled. "Blackstone."

"That works both ways, Ale," I warned. "You'd go down with me."

His face was a study of confused emotion. He licked his bottom lip as he considered his options. We stared each other down.

Suddenly, Grim Gates stepped out of a doorway and

eased himself between the two of us. He shifted his gaze from me to Alejandro. The ice in his drink rattled as he moved close to Ale and placed a hand on his shoulder. Alejandro looked uneasy but didn't react. Grim was a big player, and Ale knew to respect him.

"We all have choices to make tonight," Grim purred darkly. "Choose wisely, boys."

Ale waited a beat then shrugged him off, and, with a look at me, he disappeared down the stairs.

Grim studied me hard for a few beats then moved past me without another word.

"Jesus." I let go of the breath I held. I had managed to dodge that bullet.

Cole's voice came into my ear. "We're moving into position." It made me breathe easier. My brothers were close.

I shook off the last few minutes and made my way to the 'party' room. I snagged a glass of gin and tonic off a tray as I entered and nearly choked on the smooth drink when I caught sight of Trigger and his biker pals.

They looked like they just stepped out of a James Bond movie. It was a far cry from the ripped jeans, t-shirts, and leather cuts they normally wore. Trigger glared as he caught my expression, and I quickly shifted my attention elsewhere.

I looked around, taking note of who was where. Elio Capri and his cousins in their flashy tailored suits and shoes that probably cost the price of a car were on one side. I noticed Vinni kept a close eye on Trigger and wondered if they had history.

I scanned the faces and wondered if she was here among the dirty rich. Talya was my weak spot, and I couldn't pretend not to hope she'd be here, yet at the same time hoped she wasn't.

Chili kept his distance. He talked to Roman, doing his part by keeping him near the window. Alejandro and Filippo were nowhere to be seen. I hoped they'd make like wall flowers and stay out of the way.

"Good evening." Castillo stood at his beloved podium like the God he thought he was. "Tonight is about making a statement that you can't touch the best of the best." I swallowed back my scoff. "I am the best, and I'm here tonight to prove that." He held out his arms to the room.

I felt eyes on me and caught Grim's intense gaze. He was hard to read, and I'd known even before my talk with Trigger that he was a dangerous man and not someone to trifle with. I nodded at him to try to deflect him. I wished I knew what went through his head in that moment. He was popular with the ladies, and once again I was glad Talya wasn't on his arm. Tonight, he seemed to be alone and was focused on me.

"Please, everyone, enjoy a drink," Castillo called, and I pulled my eyes from Grim. "I only need a moment, as my friend has arrived." He motioned to me as he stepped down, and I hesitated then followed him. Chili caught my eye just as I stepped out of the room.

"Moving to the office. Castillo's ahead of me," I whispered.

"Copy that," Beckett said over the radio, as he was second in command.

As I followed Castillo, a door opened and one of his men entered with Rosa Coppola. She looked frail, but her eyes told a different story as she took me in. She was ushered toward the stairs.

"Those stairs are steep, Mrs. Coppola. Step carefully." I addressed her clearly so our guys would hear and know where they were taking her.

"Shut the damn door!" Castillo ordered as he swung around and stuck a finger in my face. "Where the hell is the girl?" Two of his men pointed their weapons at me. I knew our snipers were close by with their scopes focused on this room. I put a hand up to my ear to make sure they knew not to shoot. I needed to control the scenario.

"Castillo, take it easy. I came to this party because you asked me to. I'm here unarmed, and I want the same outcome you do. You'll get the girl. All I want to know is who the hell ambushed me that night in town."

"How dare you try to play me!" he shouted like a child. "Prove to me she's here." His face turned red. I nodded and moved to the window then motioned for him to come and look.

"Red truck, by the curb." It took everything inside me not to smirk at Mark in his wig and coat as he sat in the front seat. He sat low in the seat to downplay his size. He played his part well as he wiggled around and held his "bound" wrists up to his mouth as if to try to untie them.

"Tell the bitch to look up at the window."

"How? Should I yell? Or should I have given her a phone?" I snapped back. "Like I said, I came alone. You don't believe me, send someone down there and find out for yourself."

"Tomas, get her." He waved a hand, and one of the men left the room.

"I kept my end of the bargain." I folded my arms. "Now it's your turn."

"Fine." He whirled on his heel and marched out the door, and his men followed us out. "If we're going to do this, we're doing it right."

Castillo burst into the main room so quickly some of the guests jumped.

"We have a go, boys. I repeat, we have a go," I said quietly while all the attention was on Castillo.

Castillo turned to look at me and raised his arms in the air. "You wanted answers on who ambushed you in the city that night?" he shouted so all could hear, and Trigger moved to stand close behind him. Elio nodded at his cousins across the room, and they slowly moved in. A vision of panthers in the night popped into my head. "Let me share with all of you just who that was." He swept his arm with a flourish, and Grim stepped forward to take the spotlight.

What the hell?

"You think I didn't figure you and Chili were playing

me?" Castillo's eyes flashed and his lips pulled back in a hideous grin. "A bonus death will be your appetizer for this evening, folks. The Blackstone wife, and now…" He let out a dramatic laugh as Grim stood with his gun pointed at me. Then in a smooth transition, Grim swung it in an arc so it now pointed directly at Castillo.

It all happened so fast. Trigger pulled a knife and went to slash it across Castillo's neck, but Grim shot first and blew a hole in Castillo, just missing Trigger. Elio pushed a gun into my hand as I took cover. Shots flew as pandemonium broke out.

"Rosa was moved upstairs." I shouted at him, and Elio bolted out of the room. Vinni and Niccola plucked men off as fast as they could aim their weapons.

Suddenly, the tall windows that lined three sides of the room burst inward all at once as Blackstone and Dark Water crashed through them. I lost sight of Chili.

Trigger and Brick went after Roman and his wife, while Rail pulled two huge handguns out from somewhere and started shooting. His joint hung from his lips as he hooted with a big-ass grin. "You need to go!" *Bang! Bang!* Two of Castillo's men flopped to the floor. "Yeah, son, you gotta go!" He whirled around as though high off the kills. His laughter rang out. "Yup, you're in my book, too!" *Bang! Bang! Bang!*

Fuck! He looked like he lived for this shit.

I snapped off a shot and took out the despicable guy who worked for Castillo. I couldn't lie; it felt good ridding him from this life.

I ducked and moved for new cover, and when I popped up, I saw Trigger and Grim back-to- back as they fired. Not once did they miss, but for every two they took down, another two entered the room. Eagle Eye and Dusk had stayed outside to take care of the perimeter. We only needed to take out targets who were inside the mansion, but they'd come well supported, and well-armed.

"You want to tell me who the hell this Eric guy really is?" I heard Grim shout to Trigger over his shoulder.

"I could, but where'd the fun be in that?" Trigger tossed his empty gun and pulled his knife. "I'm out. Time to slaughter." He lunged at a guy and stabbed him in the stomach then kneed him in the jaw, and as he slumped, he slashed his knife into the side of one of the two who had Keith trapped between them. Keith grinned his thanks as he grabbed his gun off the floor and shot the other one.

I ran toward John as he struggled with a huge guy on top of him, and as soon as I got a bead on the guy's face, I popped two in his head. I grabbed John's arm and pulled him to his feet then helped him to a nearby wall to catch his breath.

I whirled around and saw Ty in a fist fight with a man twice his size. Trigger got there first and stabbed him in the back, but the man was a beast, and he whirled on Trigger, only to get popped twice in the back by Rail.

Ty's back was turned as Filippo aimed a gun at him. I steadied my hand and drilled a bullet into Filippo's ear. Ty spun as Filippo fell, and he gave me a tight nod then moved on to drive a fist into another guy's stomach. He grabbed a weapon and shot another man as he went for the door.

"Ahh!" I heard from behind me and spun as one of Castillo's guards held a lamp over his head about ready to smash it down on me. Before I could line up a shot, Grim tackled him to the ground and snapped his neck like a twig then shot another guard without so much as a glance at me. I took cover behind a toppled table and took in my surroundings.

Piece by piece, Castillo's empire was being brought down. I watched the fight with interest as I noted the different fighting styles. We'd been trained to fight quick and clean. A shot to the brain or heart. If need be, we'd use our knives to end a life the best way we could. Devil's Reach liked it up close and personal, their kills more violent and bloody. I cringed when Trigger and Brick came at one guy and sliced his neck open on both sides, and blood spewed. Rail had given up on his guns, and his knife flashed as he threw it expertly at a guard who tried to run. He pulled it from his back then wiped it on his pantleg. He'd lost his suit jacket somewhere, and his white shirt was stained red.

Grim liked to use his hands. He snapped necks in practiced moves and chopped with his hands at the throat or nose to bring his opponent down. As I watched, I swore he looked over at me and smirked as he popped the guy's shoulder out of joint then yanked the man's arm around his neck like a scarf.

Clearly, these guys liked to inflect pain.

I popped a bullet into the man who ran toward me, and he took two more from Cole before he crumpled to the ground.

Then, as fast as it began, everything went still. The sound of heavy breathing filled the air as we all slowly stood.

Mills checked in. "Clear for the moment."

"Roger that," Quinn said after him. "Clear for the moment."

I tuned in to a strange sound. Keith dragged someone along the floor until he reached the center of the room. Then he pulled him to his knees. An eye for an eye, I thought when I saw who it was.

"Did you kill my wife?" Keith stood above him, his arms heavy at his sides, his hands in fists. The rest of us watched justice about to be served. Truth be told, all of us would have loved a piece of this guy, but this was Keith's moment.

"*Sí*." Alejandro smirked up at him. Blood ran from his swollen mouth. "I followed them." He cast his gaze at me and switched to English. "That traitor." He spat on the ground. I flexed my fingers on my weapon. "You were different with that *chica*, Eric. I watched you. You loved her." I huffed. Little did he know just how important she really was to me. She was Keith's wife, therefore she was family. "Business comes first. You always said that. But you were fucking things up with Castillo all because of a woman," he hissed. "So, I shot her in the stomach so you could watch the life drain from her body." His face was ugly with hate.

Whack!

Keith drilled him in the jaw and sent him flying backward toward Mark. Mark pulled him to his knees again as Keith moved forward. Alejandro groaned but managed to raise his head and look up at him.

"Get it done, Keith," Cole ordered. "We need to move."

Trigger stepped up behind Alejandro and grabbed his crotch to suggest the device he'd given Keith. Keith squinted at the big biker then shook his head and pulled out his gun. He aimed it slowly and deliberately at the center of Alejandro's stomach.

"Sorry I can't stay to watch."

Bang!

Alejandro slumped back on the floor and held his hands to his midsection while his own blood flowed from his body. His breaths came in gasps as Keith turned to walk away. The guys followed. I waited for Grim to be out of earshot then bent down so he could see me.

"Ale," his painfilled eyes looked up at me, "I didn't love Lexi the way you think. She was my sister-in-law." His eyes widened as I grinned at him. Fuck, it felt good to say that out loud. "I hope the rats get to you before your soul leaves your body."

I raced to catch up with the others. "Cole," I snagged his arm, "Chili?"

"He had orders from Frank to get out the second

everything went down." We started to move through the house. "He can't be compromised. He's still useful here."

I understood and was relieved as I jumped into one of the pickup trucks that Eagle Eye and Dusk had started and readied for us. It was a tight squeeze, but we were running out of time.

"Go, go, go," Cole called over the radio, and we tore out of the driveway and down the hill to the main part of town. I eyed the church that once had brought me little pieces of home and was glad Chili had passed along my gratitude to the priest. He'd also made a large, anonymous donation on my behalf. A small sum, really, for what that place had brought me over the years.

"Crazy to think you lived here for ten years," John shouted over the engine noise. "You sad to leave anyone behind?" I cleared my throat and shook my head as I allowed myself to remember Talya once more.

"Not really."

"Too fuckin' hot here," Mark chimed in. "I couldn't do it."

"Agreed," I said then pointed as the truck in front of us came to an abrupt stop. Ty's head appeared out the driver's window.

"Ah, Logan, we have problem." I strained my neck to see what the holdup was.

Several police cars and at least ten uniformed officers had made a barricade across the road.

"Shit," Cole muttered. Mark suddenly slapped a pair of handcuffs over my wrists, and before I could react,

John pulled a sack over my head. I hoped they had a plan. I could see just fine through the fabric.

"We need to look legit," Mark whispered.

"Raven One to Shadows. We've run into a police barricade on the perimeter of town." Cole's voice was heard by all of us through our coms as he radioed Daniel.

"Copy that, Raven One. Stand by." There was a brief silence, then, "Help is on the way."

We watched Ty as he pulled his truck off to the side while two officers pointed high-powered rifles at him. The officers signaled at us to do the same.

When all four trucks were pulled over, we were told to exit and get on our knees. I was worried. This wasn't how things normally went down here. The Mexican police usually just wanted money. You paid a fee and moved on. I wondered if Castillo's snitches around the city had already put the word out we were here. A uniformed leg appeared, and the sack was roughly ripped off my head. I squinted and pulled away as if in fear. I knew it looked like I'd been roughed up and hoped he'd think it was from the guys. I'd taken a few blows back at Castillo's.

"Who is in charge here?" he asked in English.

"I am." Cole stood, then, to my surprise, so did Ty.

"Me too." I could tell Cole wasn't expecting that.

"So, you two are to blame for that?" He pointed behind us toward Castillo's house up on the hill. We had set it on fire in hopes it would draw attention to the house and not to us as we made our escape.

"We had orders to extract this one." Cole nodded at me. "Things just went a little south."

"What he do?" the officer asked.

"I married his sister," I chimed in, knowing they loved a good story. The officer laughed as I got a hit to the shoulder from John. Which I was sure he enjoyed.

"There's a bounty on his head, for killing a politician and his wife," Cole explained. "We made a deal with your people to come in, extract, and get out with just him."

"I never got word of that." The officer shrugged. "Tell me more about this bounty."

It always came down to money.

"Twenty thousand, still breathing." Cole nodded.

"That's a lot of money." The officer turned back to buddies with a chuckle. "Why don't we do this. You give me fifteen thousand, and I'll let you leave, still breathing, of course." He smirked at his comment. I could see Cole weighing his options. We sure as hell didn't have that kind of money on us.

"We have to turn him over before we get the money." Cole raised his shoulders in a shrug.

"This is a problem, then." The guy pointed his weapon at Cole.

"Maybe I can do you one better." Ty stepped forward and peeled back a corner of his vest.

The man's eyes lit up, and he moved away from Cole and over to Ty, who held up two pieces of gold jewelry.

"These are worth more than the bounty." He handed a chain to him and tucked the other one back in his vest.

"I've spent time in the Middle East and central Asia. I know gold will get you a lot farther than cash."

The officer tossed the heavy chain back to his buddy, who studied it carefully. All the rational questions that should have been asked went out the door. All they saw was yellow.

"It's real." The guy tossed it back, and I noticed Moore shake his head slowly.

"Give me both and we have a deal."

"Both?" Ty took a moment.

"Hey, that's all we have, man." Moore looked pissed about the situation.

"Deal." Ty held up a hand toward Moore and passed over the other chain.

"Very good decision." The officer nodded then turned and waved the barricade to be moved. Then they all jumped in their cars and whisked away.

"And I'm the pimp?" Moore laughed as they walked toward their truck.

"I don't wear 'em." Ty smacked his shoulder, and Moore snorted as they climbed in.

I shook my head at all the ways that could have gone sideways as I left them and veered toward Cole who waited by our vehicle.

———

"Well, shit," Mark laughed with relief as we boarded the plane that would take us to Washington, "that was one hell of a trip, boys."

"It was," Keith huffed as he took a seat. "What's with the gold, Beckett?"

"It's fake. We'd buy it in bulk from India," Ty dropped his bag at his feet, "and barter with it. The younger Taliban always fell for it. It was useful in certain situations."

"They didn't know any better." Moore grinned.

"It saved our asses a few times." Ty nodded and took his seat.

"And again today," I added. "Thanks for that." I reached out and hit his shoulder. "It was a risk, but it paid off."

"Gadar for the win again." Moore whooped, and they both laughed.

"How's it feel?" John sat next to me. "I mean, I understand this was your last mission."

"Truth, pretty damn good." I smiled at him. "It's been a ride, but I'm ready."

My body and mind needed a reset, and the idea of doing that at Shadows with my family was exactly what I wanted.

SIXTEEN

"Who knew staring at a green wall could feel so good," Moore muttered with his face in a trance-like state.

We'd just been through three hours of intense debrief here at our Washington headquarters then were pulled into another hour because of the police incident. Our brains were like Jell-O, and I would have given my left kidney to be anywhere in a room with Ivy rather than here in this airless place. She grounded me in ways no other could.

"Hey, Beckett," Lee moved so he could see me around Moore, "when do you think we can get out of here and back to Shadows?"

"My guess would be tomorrow morning." I yawned as

a door opened.

"Your team is dismissed, Beckett. Go get some lunch, do whatever, just keep your phones on." Frank waved us off. Somehow, I willed my feet to move. Lunch was just what we needed to fuel up again. We decided to take a walk and find some hole in the wall pub and take a few hours for ourselves since we weren't on duty.

The lobby was busy with people coming and going, and we waded through hassle toward the door when I heard a man getting frustrated at the front desk.

"I demand you tell me where she is!" His face was red.

"Sir," the young officer looked to be on his last nerve, "like I told you a few weeks ago, like I told you every week since, and like I told you yesterday, I cannot and will not give out that information to just anyone."

"I'm not anyone. I'm in your logbook. You can see for yourself I used to be here all the time to visit Dr. Knight." He placed both hands on the counter to calm himself. "I understand that you're new, but I've been through this door countless times to see my fiancée, Dr. Ivy Knight. I demand to see General Frank or someone who can answer my damn question."

That stopped me short. I told the guys to hang on as I walked over.

"Everything okay here?"

The officer looked at me in shock. "Major." He saluted. "Sorry, sir. I didn't realize you were here."

"Not a problem. At ease." He relaxed. "I'm only here for twenty-four," I explained then looked at the man who was eyeing me up. "Major Beckett." I offered a hand. "What can I do for you?" He didn't reach to shake my hand. His face twisted in an unpleasant expression.

"Ty Beckett?"

"Correct."

"I see her taste has changed," he muttered as he stood straight. He seemed to check himself. Perhaps he realized he was being rude. "Bronson Fitzpatrick, *Dr.* Bronson Fitzpatrick," he corrected himself.

I didn't think my day could get any stranger, but here we were.

"You're the ex-boyfriend," I confirmed.

"Ex-*fiancé*," he corrected me, "and you must be the *new* boyfriend."

"I am, and how do you know me?"

"Ivy's mother said she'd moved on. She mentioned your name." He looked around like he waited for someone to appear. "I recognize you from the video." He held up his phone to show the TikTok video from when Ivy and I were in Washington. I nodded. "I know she was or is in some kind of trouble, and now she won't return my calls. All I got was a text message saying she was all right and that I needed to move on."

"Okay, well, she's not here, but I can assure you—"

"I'd prefer to speak with her in person."

"If she's not picking up your calls," I shrugged, "that's her choice not to speak with you."

"I need you to get her to call me. I need to know she's all right."

"*Mr.* Fitzpatrick," I held up a hand as he tried to correct the Mr. to Dr., "I can promise you she's fine. Whatever was going on before now has been handled."

"Well, where is she? I have a right to know," he demanded.

Now he was starting to piss me off, so I lowered my voice and spoke clearly and concisely.

"No, you don't have a right to know. You aren't together anymore." He went to speak, but I cut him off. "You have my word that she's safe and sound. She has a new position where she's surrounded by good people."

"But—"

"She's happy, so let her be happy by moving on. It's not your place to worry about her anymore." I added with a pointed look. "That's my job."

"I see."

"Now, please stop bothering these men and let them do their job." I nodded over his shoulder at two people who waited behind him. "It was nice meeting you, Bronson, but your time here is over." With that, I went to join my team, and Moore gave me a look.

"Who the hell was that?" he asked while the other guys moved close, all ears.

"That is Ivy's ex."

"What the hell's he doin' here?"

"Looking for her, apparently." I rubbed my temples. "Let's go get some beer." We made our way outside and found our way to a local Irish pub where we ordered some pitchers for the table.

Green and red Christmas décor was draped over some kegs that lined the walls, and a tree stood next to a small stage where a man strummed a guitar. It wasn't overly busy but was just loud enough to know we could speak freely without being overheard.

"So, Beckett," Lee called across the table, "now we're alone, what are your thoughts on living at Shadows?"

"I love it." I poured myself a glass of beer. "Not a place I ever thought I'd end up, but I'm thankful I did."

"Any part of that have to do with a certain blonde doctor?" Moore teased, and I couldn't control the smile that broke out over my face.

"I gotta say, that was the most unexpected part of life at Shadows," I admitted.

"Yeah, nice find." Perez winked at me. "She seems really cool."

"Yeah, she is." Moore handed me a bowl of peanuts. "Funny, and isn't afraid to give him shit when he deserves it."

"That's true." My mind conjured up her beautiful face. It had kept me going the entire time we were in Mexico.

"How do you think Keith's holding up?" Gear asked. He was the sensitive one in the group, and I admired that.

"I think now he can make his peace." I twisted the glass in my hand to clear it of condensation. "Now comes the hard part of moving forward." Everyone sat in silence as we allowed ourselves another moment to think. The new guys didn't know Lexi and barely knew

Keith, but the fact they had him on their minds at all spoke volumes. I held out my drink to the center of the table. "To Lexi being in a better place, to Keith finding justice, and to our first mission together as Dark Water."

"Hooah." We clicked glasses.

We switched topics, and soon Moore and I sat back and let the guys shoot the shit. This was where we'd learn the most. Gear wore his heart on his sleeve, Lee loved any woman with a pair of long legs but was respectful about it, and Perez apparently was getting over a recent breakup of his own.

We enjoyed our drinks but knew we'd regret the pub food. We all looked forward to the house dinners that awaited us back on our mountain. We grabbed our stuff and walked back toward headquarters.

"I think we did good." Moore smiled at the three men ahead of us who laughed and carried on like old friends already.

"Holy shit," a voice called. It was Jay, who'd gotten one of the police jobs in Redstone. "Moore, hold on." He raced across the street. I forgot his parents live here. "Man, I've been trying to get hold of you forever!" He looked at me then at the rest of the guys. "We need to talk, now." He looked at Lee, Perez, and Gear, unsure of who they were.

"You can speak in front of them." We were a team now, and they needed to know everything for us to be solid unit.

"I didn't trust leavin' a message." Jay looked at Moore. "This," he shook his head, "is wild."

"Okay, out with it." What the hell else was this day about to throw at me?

"Lopez came to the station and spoke to us directly, about what happened with Hill and your girl." I didn't know he'd done that. "I'm just going to jump right into this. Everyone's aware that something's up with Hill and Rivera, and the fact that Dustin disappeared to Camp Green has everyone talkin'."

"Yeah, that was a shock to us, too." Moore waved for him to go on.

"Okay, so, I was running an errand for Frank a few days ago at Camp Green, and Dustin was there asking for you."

"What did he want?"

"He wanted me to pass a name on to you, Josh Johnson from Fresno, California. He's actually living here now. Works as a clerk at HQ, and he's had a few run-ins with Hill. I guess Hill's been running his mouth again, and Dustin thinks he might be next." He lowered his voice at the end.

"What the hell!" Hill was losing it.

"Ty, remember how you and your girl went to that bar, The Rusty Nail?" He stepped closer.

"Yeah."

"You spoke to the bartender, right?"

"How'd you know that?" An uneasy feeling prickled down my spine.

"There were lots of people there that night. Hill and Rivera included. I know your girl spoke to them, but they also saw you speaking to the bartender—well, owner."

"Pam," I added.

"Yes, Pam. Well, she must have found out something because she was found murdered in her apartment."

"What?" I couldn't believe what I was hearing. "Pam's dead?"

"Yeah, and I can tell you that Hill showed up late for his shift that night. I only know that because one of my buddies was pissed, as he got called to cover him. Poor guy was late for his own brother's wedding because of it."

"Holy shit." Moore's face mirrored mine. "Ty, we need to do something."

"Truth is, this shit is gettin' dark." Jay's eyes were big. "I really don't want any part of it, but Ty, you've always had my back, and I miss Brown, too. So, I'm passin' along what I heard, and I still will if anything else comes up. But I'd really like to keep my job and stay hidden in those mountains, so if it's just the same to you, I want to step back from this as much as I can."

"I really appreciate you stickin' your neck out for all of us, Jay. Your name'll never be mentioned."

"Appreciated." He shook my hand. "Good luck, fellas."

I closed my eyes; I knew it was now or never to deal with Hill.

I turned to the others as a plan formed in my head. "I

think I have an idea how to end this shit once and for all."

I spent the next thirty filling in the others.

The guys were quiet as we loaded into the elevator and rode to the eleventh floor where Frank's office was. The expression on our faces was enough to keep people out of our way as we headed down the hall and marched through Frank's open door. Team Blackstone was there in conversation with Frank.

"What's wrong?" Cole stood the moment we entered. The mood in the room shifted instantly.

"Remember when you said whatever means necessary to deal with Hill?"

"I do."

"Oh, shit," Frank muttered but didn't interject. I swung my gaze across the room.

"Paul, are you up for one more last mission?"

We spent the rest of the day and into the evening planning and gathering everything we needed to bring this thing to an end. It wasn't easy, but once we got hold of Josh Johnson and he shared what he'd found out, everything started to fall into place.

"It's pretty fucked up." Lee stretched then leaned back on the couch. Frank had lent us his conference room, and we made full use of it. "All this because of his over-inflated ego."

"Call me crazy, but I'm disappointed there wasn't a better reason." Gear shrugged.

"It's why no one saw it." I shook my head. "There really wasn't any reason. It's why he was able to hide what he'd done for so long. I mean, when someone's killed, you look for why. Crimes of passion, crimes of greed, and all that."

"Guy kills for nothin? That's nuts." Keith paced the room.

"His brother consistently bailed him out of trouble. He helped create the monster. Then each time he got away with it, it probably fed his ego more, made him feel powerful, maybe. That's something Ivy and the Doc might be able to figure out." I shrugged. "All their lives destroyed for what?" I waved my hand at the photos of Hill's victims taped to the board. I felt a punch to the gut when my eyes went to Brown then Pam.

"Beckett," Frank stood in the doorway, "Hill and Rivera have been spotted in town."

"Really?" I couldn't believe it.

"Well, I kind of made some calls for it to happen." He cleared his throat and glanced around the room. I knew the tension between Frank and Blackstone was still rocky over the whole situation with Paul, but there was work to be done there. "They were told they had interviews for a job they'd both applied for. Told them they'd been overlooked." He made a face. "I pulled a favor, and they'll be here tomorrow at fourteen hundred. They asked Lindsey, at the front desk, to make dinner reservations for them afterward at a seafood place down by the water. Once I know the time, I'll let you know."

"Thanks, Frank." I shook his hand. "I appreciate everything you're doing here."

"It's time to end this."

"Agreed," Keith piped up and gave a tight nod to Frank, who closed the door behind him as he left.

"All right, boys," Cole flipped the whiteboard around, "how do we want to do this?"

My brain was fried by the time I made it back to my room. I showered and ordered something to eat. Snowflakes fell against the window, and I wished I was back at Shadows in front of the massive fireplace, with Ivy.

I placed my glass of scotch on a square coaster and slowly eased my big body down onto the tiny couch, a loveseat thing that I hoped wouldn't break under me. I wiggled to find a comfortable position and tried to sort out my thoughts. I tapped my heel as I ran through everything we'd talked about. Tomorrow was the day I'd waited for, hoped for.

Nothing could go wrong because we had only one take on this. I tried to shift my head into work mode. I couldn't let my stress about the importance of this mission play on me. Usually, I had no problem with my focus, but this time it was different. Maybe it was because we weren't a few inches underwater or lying somewhere in a hot hellhole while we waited, but whatever it was, I just couldn't concentrate.

I closed my eyes and was shot back into a memory.

"Drinks are on me!" Flex yelled happily. He slopped some beer as he held it high, and almost fell from his

perch on the barstool. Everyone cheered at the top of their lungs. Moore gave me an eyeroll, but the idea of a cold, crisp beer made my mouth water. We were fresh on block leave, I'd had no sleep, and still picked the odd grain of sand from my teeth no matter how many times I brushed. It was nice to be back, but I knew in a day or two the itch to go back to Central Asia would be as necessary as my next breath.

I glanced at Anderson, who had that all too familiar thousand-yard stare, and I let him be. Anyone who served understood that look all too well. I chuckled darkly to myself; it didn't take much to know which guys had just arrived on block leave. We all had our backs to the wall and our heads on a constant swivel.

"Cheers to one year ago today," Moore raised his beer to the center of the table, "when we left the land of the free and stepped into what could only be described as World War Three." We clicked glasses and took a moment to digest that we'd all made it back in one piece.

"To our fearless captain." Brown tipped his bottle at me, and the others followed. "You led us there and brought us back, and I couldn't be more thankful." Though I appreciated the compliment, it wasn't correct. "No one guy can do that. We're a team, and it takes a team to survive over there."

"Let's make a pact." Anderson leaned forward. "Every time we come home, we have a drink here,

same table, same shit beer," we all chuckled, "and make a toast to getting out alive."

"Deal," we all agreed. As I looked around the table, I couldn't help but wonder who might not be here next time. I shook off the thought as I tuned in to my reality. I was their captain. It was my duty to make sure they got back. If any of us couldn't be here, it had to be me. The captain could never be the last man standing.

"If one of us isn't, though," Anderson pointed a finger at all of us, "you better nail the son of a bitch who got him to a post, so we all can have a turn at him."

"Agreed!" we all shouted.

"You goin' home tonight, Brown?" Gail rolled the label he had peeled from the beer under his palm.

"Yeah, home to my own bed where none of you fuckers can breathe in my face with your stink-ass breath." He laughed, and my chest tightened.

Home. I dreaded that thought.

"Hey, man," Brown leaned over so the others couldn't hear, "don't go back to your cousin's basement. You know you always got a room at my place. My parents'll lose their minds if you don't at least spend the first night."

"Thanks." I felt my mood shift, and I knew I needed to sort my thoughts out alone.

Loud laughter drew our attention over to Hill and Rivera at the bar. Two pompous assholes if there ever were any. Their captain, Flex, stood nearby and watched as they made a show of doing tequila shots off some chick's tits.

I stood and patted my pocket.

"Shit, boys, give me ten. I need to grab something from my truck. The next round's on me."

They hit the table and cheered. As I walked by Brown, he reached out and put something in my hand.

"Back door." I slipped the key in my pocket and gave his shoulder a pat as I slipped out into the cool night air. Brown and Moore were my brothers and were the only ones who knew how much guilt I carried. I didn't know what I'd do without them.

I yanked open the truck door and let out a long-controlled breath while the silence seeped into my head. I flipped on the radio and sat back.

The ache in my chest returned when a small red Ford pulled in. My head immediately went to my mom, and I reached for my phone. My mind slipped back to the expression on her face just before I went out the door. I remembered how she'd cried that she loved me and how hard she'd hugged. I saw my father's face again, and the fear of what I was about to do was written all over it.

I shook my head hard and let the anger back. Other families were proud to know their son wanted to fight for their country, but not mine. They were just scared. They hated that I'd joined JROTC and hated it even more when I left for ROTC. Shortly after

*that, I was packing for my first twelve-month tour,
and I never looked back.
They didn't get it; I was made to be a soldier. To do
more and be more. I looked down at the phone in my
hand and shook my head. I tossed it on the dash then
slammed the truck door as I headed inside to buy
that round of beer. I couldn't let my parents know I
was back. Not yet.*

I blinked back the memories and found my phone once again in my hand. Without hesitation, I made the call I should have all those years ago.

Two rings, and the call connected.

"Hello." Mom's voice filled my chest with instant warmth. I tried to speak and instantly regretted the call as my voice caught in my throat.

"Mom."

"Ty, honey, is that you?" The happiness in her voice made me feel guilty.

"Yeah," I croaked and brushed a pesky tear away.

"I'm so glad to hear from you. Is everything okay?" She picked up on my mood. "I heard you were back in Washington."

"I am." I took a deep breath, and everything inside me started to loosen and untangle. "We just got back and are here to debrief." I gave her the truth; she deserved it.

"Hopefully a successful mission." She kept her tone easy, which I appreciated. "When do you head back home?" The word *home* and what that meant to me now seemed to open a door I didn't even know I was behind.

"Mom, I," again my words stuck, "I'm sorry that I closed myself off from all of you when I joined the military." She went silent, and I heard her sniff.

"Ty, you don't have—"

"I do, Mom. It's long overdue." I used the back of my hand to catch the tears and was pleased I was alone at that moment. "I know how much you didn't want me to join, and when I did, I know it crushed you all. Coming home became harder and harder because I know I was a disappointment. I channeled my guilt into work, and I let nearly a decade go by without you." I paused to gather my words.

"I'm happy where I am now, Mom. Way happier than when I was in Afghanistan. I never thought I'd say that, but I am. I want you in my life, and I want you to know the woman I love. I want you to be there and be a grandmother to our kids. I'm so sorry for what it did to you, Dad, and Shelly. I'm gonna make up for lost time."

"Ty," she stopped my rambling, "sweetheart, how could you ever be a disappointment to us?" Her voice trembled. "Look at the man you've become. You fight for what's right, you work hard, and now you've let someone into your heart who I know loves you back just as much. Yes, we were scared as hell when you left, but you're our baby boy. What parents wouldn't be terrified of their son leaving to fight in war?"

I felt the last of the tightness in my chest go as she

spoke. It all slipped away as she shared her feelings with me.

"Sure, we were a lot when you came home, and made a fuss over you, but that was because we were so happy you were home safe. That's my right as a mother. The only disappointment we felt, Ty, was when you didn't come see us and pulled away. If we didn't want to see you, do you think we'd have left everything and moved lock, stock, and barrel to Redstone, Montana?" She laughed lightly. "Though I can tell you no part of me misses the city."

"True," I huffed with a hint of lightness to my voice.

"We clawed our way back into your life, and now it's up to you to let us in."

"I want that."

"I want it, too." I could hear her smile through her words. "Can I ask you something?"

"Yeah."

"Will you say hi to your father?" I grinned and knew he probably hovered around her like a bee.

"Yeah, I'd love that."

This was just what I needed.

PAUL

The teams were staggered throughout The Salt Line-Navy Yard, one of the more popular seafood restaurants in town. Sloane apparently loved the place and recommended the chowder when I spoke to her about where we were going. She also made sure I knew exactly what I needed to do and say to keep things legal. We couldn't afford any mistakes.

Moore and Mike took tables in the outdoor seating area under the heat lamps while Mark and Ty went inside and took seats at the back. Close enough to watch but not be recognized. Gear and I were the ones who were to play out phase one of the plan. Mainly because no one knew I'd returned from the dead and Gear was new to the city. The others went to get ready for phase two.

"What can I get you?" The young waitress smiled at

Ty, then looked down at the device in her hand, ready to take their order. Our radios were tucked in our ears so we could talk freely between tables and not look suspicious.

"I'll have a bowl of clam chowder, please." He handed her the menu.

"Oh," Mark purred, and his pleasure came across loud and clear on the radio as he studied the menu. I smirked from across the room. I knew we shouldn't have let him come, but Ty had to learn that when there's food involved, so was a Lopez. "I'll have that, too, plus," he held up a finger while he squinted to think, "a side of fried clam bellies and some Parker house rolls." He flashed her one of his famous smiles, and I shook my head. We all could pack away a lot of food, but Mark was an endless pit. It was comical that he hadn't changed one bit.

"They're here. Approaching front door." Mike's voice filled us in on what we couldn't see. Mike wasn't an easy man to miss, and I was concerned about him when we arrived. I needn't have worried. He was dressed in a black hoodie with the hood up because it was cold, which helped to conceal his tattooed body. He had positioned himself perfectly so Hill and Rivera wouldn't spot him as they walked by the enclosed glass structure.

Hill was Ty's age but would have some knowledge of who Blackstone was. After all, Blackstone were a legend. There were some who knew what we looked like. Frank and Daniel had done a good job of keeping our identities quiet. But if you met Mike Irons once, you'd never forget him.

I swore the energy in the place shifted when Hill walked in. If you didn't know to watch, you'd have missed Ty square his shoulders and his left leg start to bounce. When he caught me tap my thigh, he stopped moving, lowered his head, and used the beak of his hat to shield his face. Mark was deep in his fried clams, but I knew the guy was keenly aware of what happened around him. His demeanor never changed as he continued to eat.

I started to talk as Hill got close to our table. "I don't know, some guy named Hill." I caught Hill waver in his step and shoot a look back at Rivera, who looked at him, confused. I continued with my role. "Ever heard of him?" I never once looked away from Gear.

"Nope," Gear used his napkin to wipe the butter from his thumb, "but I know Josh, and he's known to run his mouth after a few beers." He shook his head and played his part perfectly. "Remember when we were at that bar in New York and that girl was all over you and he got pissed?"

"Yeah, and he knocked his damn beer into my lap." He closed his eyes. "Asshat."

"Maybe, but he got to go home with her, so by my book, he won."

Hill took the booth behind me and Gear and indicated to Rivera to sit and keep quiet. "He's listening. Keep talkin'," Ty said quietly over the radio.

"Anyway," I sipped my water, "Josh says he's got some video proof that this Hill guy went after that bartender." I lowered my voice like I was mindful of those around me.

"The Rusty Nail chick?" Gear leaned forward.

Ty spoke again. "Hill just mouthed the words *what the fuck* to Rivera."

That's right, take the bait.

I gave a little more. "Yeah, he wants to show me what he's got. He doesn't know who else to trust. He plans to take it to General Frank and wants me to go with him."

"Unbelievable," Ty hissed, "Hill can't help himself. He just turned so he can hear your conversation better. His mouth's open like he's catchin' flies. Can't believe what he's hearing."

"Ah," Gear fumbled for a second, "why you? Why not go straight to Frank?"

"I don't know, but he's scared shitless. I think he's afraid Hill will make him disappear. If you know what I mean."

"Shit, yeah. I'm just tossing this out there," Gear sounded worried, "but do you even want to see it? I mean, from what Josh said, Hill's batshit crazy. How do you know after seeing whatever's on that tape you won't land in a shit-pile of trouble yourself?"

"Not saying I won't." I rubbed my face and put more feeling into it. "Josh needs a friend right now. He's flippin' out. If we could do that for him, shouldn't we?"

"Hey, when did this become we?" Gear's voice went up. "I don't know."

"How about this. We'll just meet up, calm him down, then take him over to HQ and leave it at that."

"I don't like being involved at all, and I sure don't plan

to watch any tape." Gear pushed his plate away with a clatter. "But whatever, I'll go with you. What time?"

"Just a sec. I'll text him." I sent a text to Mike outside for show, and Mike replied. At the *ping,* I pretended to read it. "He says seven. That's about an hour from now. I told him to meet at my brother's place first. I'm house sitting, so he's not around. That way we can talk to Josh and get him to calm down. If all seems legit, we go see General Frank."

"Where's his place?"

"Forty-two fifty-two Clay Street Northeast."

"All right, let's get out of here." Gear and I shuffled out of the booth and made our way outside.

"Paul and Gear are on the move," Ty narrated for us. "Mike and Moore, stay put outside. Hill and Rivera haven't said a word to each—" He paused, and I could hear Hill yell something. "Well, as predicted, Hill's temper just kicked in and he punched the table. Rivera is looking around as a few people are staring."

"Fuck, take it easy." Rivera's loud voice boomed over the radio mics.

"Rivera just warned Hill to shut up." Ty went on. "Now they're talking, something about following you." Ty could read lips just as well as the rest of us. "Oh, nice," he hissed, "the waitress came over, and that asshole tossed a bill at her and waved her off. What a pig. Her face is red as a beet."

"Can I get you anything else?" The waitress's voice grew loud, so I knew she was at Ty's table.

"Just the check, please." I heard Ty's chair squeak as he moved. "Listen, I know those guys, and they're jerks. Don't waste your time on them."

"Jerks isn't the world I'd use." The waitress sounded angry now.

"Oh?"

"Psycho, maybe?" She paused. "They're talking about stalking someone at their home. Why do I get all the freaks?" I looked at Gear, who smirked. We could hear her footsteps as she left.

"I guess we got our answer." Mark chuckled as his fork clattered against his plate. "I think that went well."

"Yeah." Ty chucked. "Were you even here for it? You were so busy sucking back all that food." He couldn't let an opportunity go to give Mark a hard time.

"I was playing my part," Mark scoffed, "and I played it well, I might add. Someone had to look like they were here for the food. Guys," he spoke clearly but quietly through his radio, "let the record state that Ty is leaving a half-eaten bowl of chowder behind."

"Wow." Ty laughed.

"That's a sin in my world, by the way."

"Hill and Rivera just made a beeline for the door." Ty went back to business. "Bait taken, boys. Good to go?"

"Roger that," Mike replied. "They're pullin' out now."

I placed a quick call, and the driver Frank had arranged for us soon pulled up in the van, and we piled in. On the drive across town, Mike and Mark peppered Ty and Moore with questions about Hill and what happened that night with Brown. You could tell Ty appreciated their need for detail. It was important for us to know just what kind of man we were up against.

"If this doesn't play out," Mike turned around to look at Ty, "you know I got you covered. Trigger would gladly step in and wipe them both off the map."

"Don't think I didn't consider it." Ty nodded and looked out the window. I bet he really had thought about Trigger at some point. "Maybe even throw a bit of Grim Gates in there too," he added.

"I'm sure he'd be up for it." Mike gave a dark chuckle.

"Speaking of which, what happened to him?" Moore chimed in. "One minute I was watching him shake hands with Elio Capri in the hall, and the next he vanished. What's their connection, anyway?"

"The Gates and Capris go way back. They both work for, well…a different side of the law than we do." Mike tapped his fingers on his knee as he thought. "Elio would have left immediately after and flown back with Rosa Coppola."

I had no idea that Grim knew Elio Capri, but I really didn't know that much about Grim.

"And Grim?" Moore asked.

"I guess you're in this now," Mike muttered and turned to look at me.

"It's fine." I waved at him to go on.

"Grim's family business is in Vegas, but he works for them out of Mexico. You know what I'm sayin? I'm sure you've cultivated friends to do your job." Moore nodded at that. We'd all had to make that choice in our line of work. We'd befriended more than a few young Taliban members to help the cause. They were usually forced into working for the Taliban in the first place, so it wasn't difficult, and we tried to make it worth their while. It might look bad on our part, but that was the way of the world. "Grim's not someone you wanna be close with, but he's someone to keep in your back pocket. He'd help us out if we needed him."

"And Trigger?" Moore kept going.

"Trigger's a friend. He's proven that many times." Mike paused to think. "He's helped me and Cole, and the others time and time again. And I'd drop anything and help him, anytime. Off the books, of course. Cole even introduced Savi to Tess, Trig's wife. Says a lot." He nodded and folded his arms.

"Sure does," Mark chimed in.

"As for Trigger and Grim, they have their own history," Mike continued. "I've never asked. I just know that both of them and the head of the Italian mafia had our backs when we needed them the most."

"And if they want something in return?" Moore asked.

"Then we cover the flag and return the favor." Mike turned and held his gaze for a beat then sat back and stared out the front.

"So, same rules apply here, too." Moore nodded his understanding.

We pulled up a few blocks away from the house. I called Keith as Ty and Moore hopped out and opened the trunk to grab a few things. They took off down a side street.

"Are you still on them?"

"Yeah," Keith huffed. "They circled the street a couple times and parked around the corner."

"Roger that." I kept my voice even.

I met Gear on the sidewalk, and we went inside to pretend to wait for Josh. The house was dark except for the living room and kitchen. The TV flickered with a video game, and we put a couple beer cans on the table.

We had a photo of Josh Johnson and used Keith to play the part. He fit the description best. He arrived in an old Chevy and got out awkwardly. He was dressed in a bulletproof vest, a sidearm was tucked in his waistband, and he carried a laptop in one hand. He looked around as if scared then walked up and knocked on the front door. Keith was keen to be part of this, and I knew he channeled all that happened over the last days into it. He needed action and, I sure understood that.

I opened the door and gave a quick scan of the neighborhood as if I was nervous.

"Hey, Josh." I stepped back and let him in.

"Okay. You sure it's all right?" Keith rushed his words and looked around. He then moved to the kitchen and stood where his mark was. The lighting was enough to keep his face in shadow. From outside, you'd only see his torso and the computer. Gear sat on a chair near the table but stood as Keith came in. They made a show of shaking hands, and Gear offered him a beer. Keith declined it. I put a hand on Keith's arm as if to assure him that he wasn't alone in this.

I heard a noise, and Cole, who stood in a dark corner, indicated that Hill was coming around the back. I nodded from where I stood at the counter. I turned on some music to make it as easy as possible for Hill to see he'd have the advantage and could sneak in without being heard.

The townhouses were close together, but this house was on the end of the row with easy access to the back yard. We guessed that was where he'd try to come through.

Keith continued to play his Josh role and moved back and forth on his heels like a man scared to death. Keith put the laptop on the counter and began to open it, but I put an arm out and shook my head while I waved for him and Gear to move into the living room. Cole stayed low as he and Mark moved into the hallway.

I flipped on a lamp in the corner and picked up a photo album and opened it. I held it out and pointed as if to show them someone's picture. I made sure my back was to the corner of the living room and I faced Keith. This allowed me to see part of the kitchen and allowed a small line of sight into the dining room.

My radio suddenly crackled, and it took everything in me not to react to the noise. If they were watching me, they'd have enough experience to know what a misfunctioning radio flinch looked like. I glanced around for a moment as the guys studied the book. I couldn't spot

John or Cole, but I caught movement and saw the sliding glass door behind Keith's shoulder slowly open a crack, and the tip of a gun caught the light from the kitchen. I signaled with my eyes to Keith that he was there. We both kept our heads down as though to focus on the photos.

"Wait, yeah I remember him." Gear looked up, and his gaze flicked over to the reflection in the window just to the left of me. "He served with a buddy of mine from high school."

"Yeah, that's him," Keith, aka Josh, murmured as Hill inched through the door without a sound. Hill reminded me of a snake, silent but ready to pack a deadly blow.

"In position." John's soft voice found its way through the radios as Hill, dressed in a hoodie and jeans, moved through the dining room and headed for the laptop on the counter.

"Hold tight," Cole whispered. "Let him pick it up and turn to leave."

Gear kept the conversation moving while I faked my attention on him. It was hard not to move when I knew Hill was a mere fifteen feet from me just on the other side of the wall.

That wonderful adrenaline rush washed over me, and it felt like it had years back when we were about to move in to rescue a young woman who'd been presumed dead for nearly a year.

"I know in my heart she's still alive," Cole had told us just as we arrived at that house in Mexico. "Always trust your heart and gut. The two will never steer you wrong," he'd said.

"Confirmed he has the laptop." Mike interrupted my thoughts, as a giant spotlight lit up the entire house. The team's shadows became large as they moved in. I grabbed my weapon and pointed it at Hill's head.

"Hands up! Turn around, Hill!" I shouted as I quickly moved in on him. "There's nowhere for you to run." Slowly, he lifted his head, and Mike reached forward and ripped back his hood.

Shit. I turned to Cole.

It was Rivera.

EIGHTEEN

TY

"Beckett! Behind you!" Brown's voice echoed off the mountains from thirty feet away. I turned just in time to see a Taliban member with a machete above me. He lunged to take a swipe at my stomach, but I rolled to the side and kicked his knee and he fell and dropped the knife. He sprang right back up and was on top of me in a flash. His hands circled my neck and pressed hard, blocking my airway. I beat his side with one fist as I used the other to desperately try to break his hold with a quick drop of my elbow. He was huge and outweighed me by a lot. His grip only tightened, and I started to see spots. Suddenly, he jerked upward, and his hands fell from my neck. His

eyes went wide while a horrible sound escaped his lips. Cool air rushed down into my lungs as I gasped and gulped it in.

"Ahh!" Brown pushed the machete deeper between the guy's shoulder blades then hauled him off me. He dropped to his knees to see if I was all right. "Jesus, Captain, if you really want to die, try to pick a better way."

"I'll remember that." I coughed as I tested my voice. "Thanks, man." I took his hand, and he helped me stand.

"I've always got your six, you know that." He smiled, and we ran together to catch up with the rest of the team.

Brown's smile stayed with me as I heard the door open. The light flicked on as the door closed behind him. The lock was turned, and his keys clacked as they hit the decorative bowl on the hallway table. I watched as his shadow grew large as he entered the living room then shrank and disappeared as he flipped on the table lamp at the bottom of the stairs.

"Shit." Hill jumped when he spotted me in the leather chair in the middle of the room. "At least my gut was right." He smirked and calmly removed his jacket and tossed it on the banister. "I take it my brother isn't home?" He eyed the stairs, and I watched as he tried to piece together the afternoon and night's events.

"Nope, he's currently being questioned about his involvement in the bartender's death." I held his stare.

"They'll find nothing." He shrugged as he tried to play it cool.

"There was an eyewitness who spotted him leaving her apartment very shortly after she was killed."

"Right." He nodded as if to humor me.

"Thanks to Josh's footage from his father's tattoo shop, we've got a nice clear shot of him as he left. Oh, and I understand there's some audio of him talking to you." I pointed my finger at him. There wasn't any audio, but there could have been.

"Mmhm."

"But the best part of all of this," I leaned my arms on my legs, "is the testimony we got."

He rolled up his sleeves but stayed where he was. "You think I bought that? You think I believe for one second that someone from that Afghan village came forward, traveled all the way over here, just to testify about what happened to some random soldier?" He snorted and leaned against the side table, full of self-confidence while I dug my nails into my palms. "The truth is," he went on, "Brown was losing his shit and was going to shoot me. I was protecting myself and those around me."

"So, you claim self-defense?"

"Of course. You were there. You saw it."

"What I saw was an egotistical asshole who couldn't let the fact that Brown embarrassed him in front of a woman go unpunished. I saw a coward hiding behind a weapon who saw an opportunity to kill and took it, even though a brother was at his lowest point." I slowly stood.

"The fuck you say to me?" He pushed up to his full height, his face like a belligerent schoolyard punk.

"You can only bully for so long, Hill, before someone who can't take the guilt anymore spills the beans and tells the truth." A lazy smile spread across my lips. "Bullies don't develop real friendships, Hill. Lying's only worth it as long as they get something out of it. You're a narcissistic asshole who let his ego get too big. He sold you out."

"Who?"

"Dustin." His eyes flared, but he didn't accept defeat. Not yet.

"He's such a loser." He waved me off. "No one would believe a word he said, anyway."

"Maybe not, but they'd believe this guy." I held up my phone and played a video that Cole sent me.

"Come on, man. I'll tell you whatever you want."

"On that last day in Afghanistan, who shot and killed Brown?" Hill's face turned to stone as he watched in horror as Rivera sang like a canary.

"Hill killed Brown, shot him in the head." Rivera started to sob. "Beckett had him under control, but Hill had a hate-on for Brown." His eyes pleaded. "He took the opportunity to take him out."

"And will you testify to that?" Frank's voice.

"Yes, to that and everything else."

Hill suddenly reached behind the table then cursed as he raced across the room to the bookshelf and cursed again.

"You think I wouldn't have done a sweep of the place first?" I snarled. "Come on, Hill, give me a little credit." I looked at the phone. "Or maybe a lot of credit." I shrugged and gave a humble smile.

"Fuck you, Beckett," he hissed. His eyes darted everywhere as he tried to think of a way out of the situation. "That's just one fucking person. Rivera's lying!" he spat.

"And Dustin too?" His murderous face swung over to me. "Yeah, Dustin also came forward. Your dear brother had some pretty juicy stuff upstairs in his safe. Quite incriminating. And now Rivera." I clucked my tongue. "I think that means you're gonna be street meat for the guys behind bars. I mean, when they find out you killed one of your own while on duty." I whistled. "I wouldn't drop the soap if I were you."

He bolted for the door, and I shook my head as he backstepped into the room again with his hands up. Moore had a rifle pointed at his head. Frank stepped slowly through the door with Cole and Paul right behind him. The lights from the MP squad cars lit up the place like Christmas morning.

"It's over, Hill," Frank commanded then looked at me and whispered something to Cole. They turned their backs to us and left. The others who had come with them followed. Someone closed the door behind them.

I stepped up and got in Hill's face. "We made a pact

years back that if something bad happened to one of us at the hand of someone else, the rest of us would make that person pay."

"Eye for an eye, right?" Hill opened his arms. "Do it!"

"See, that's the difference between you and me," I poked his forehead with my index finger, "I have a conscience."

"You better back off," he growled and took a step closer, and I prepared to swing, "or I won't make the call to my guy who's watchin' your girlfriend right now at Zack's." Everything around me went silent at the mention of her name.

"He's lying." Moore snickered behind me.

"You want to risk that?" Hill stared at me. "It wouldn't be the first time I got to your girl." One side of his mouth rose, and his eyes sparkled with malice. "She's wearing that blue silk blouse, the one where the top button always slips open, and a sexy as sin skirt."

"Regardless," Moore whispered, "she's not alone, Beckett."

"While you rot in prison," I towered over Hill, "spooning with a sweaty horny toad, I'll have that woman for the rest of my life."

"We'll s—"

I made as if to turn away but swung with a full round-house and drilled my fist into his nose. Blood spurted as I felt a satisfying crunch. He yelled in pain as he flew into the wall and lay slumped with his hands over his nose. He gave a wail as Moore stepped up and drilled the butt of his rifle into his ribs. I threw another punch, and it landed square on his jaw.

"That's for Brown," I spat then grabbed his leg and twisted his knee hard, and he screamed in pain.

I had to stop myself. I could have done worse, and truth be told, I wanted to. I wanted to break a bone for every life he'd taken. He didn't deserve to die; he deserved to waste away to nothing behind bars. His brother too, but his time would come. Moore grabbed my shoulders and pulled me toward the door.

"We kept our promise, Ty," he said as Hill curled up in the fetal position. "We aren't like him."

I knew he was right. We'd gotten justice for Brown and a little for Ivy too. At that thought, I grabbed for my phone, suddenly filled with fear for her, but she didn't answer. I knew Moore was right. She'd never be left alone, so I tried to relax.

Within the hour, I paced the small VIP lounge at the airport. Frank got us out on an earlier flight. I didn't give two shits what happened to Hill anymore so long as he got locked up. My only concern was Ivy. My team and Blackstone took up most of the lounge. I paced and dialed and paced again, but I couldn't reach her. Moore watched me, and his face grew more and more anxious.

Cole was on the phone with Abby, John was talking to Sloane, and Keith had his son on the line.

"All right, here's the scoop." Cole walked up to me. "At the last minute, Doc needed Ivy's help, so Daniel went to Camp Green without her. It took a while for Abby to figure that out. She'd thought Ivy was with Daniel and had gone to Camp Green. We're sure the reason her phone isn't tracking is because it's dead."

"And Doc's?" I stepped closer to Cole, and his gaze made a twitch toward Mark. It was very slight, and he controlled it well, but I caught it.

"Abby's gone to check why he isn't answering. She'll get right back to us."

Keith jumped in as he pocketed his phone. "June's with the kids outside."

"The wives are out shopping," John reported, "but are heading home right now just in case. She's not at Zack's, so Hill's full of shit there."

"Okay," Cole nodded as he took in all the information, "our flight leaves in ten. Let's get to our gate and get the hell home."

"You saw that?" I muttered to Moore about Cole's hesitation.

"I did, but remember he's been through this shit before. If he's not telling you something, it's for a good reason." I started to speak, but he shook his head. "You know I'll go dig."

"Thanks."

I was going crazy not knowing. I was sure it was a lie, Hill's last effort to screw with my life, but...

"Hey, come on." Moore hit my shoulder as he stood, and we slowly boarded the plane. "She's gonna be okay," he assured me as we took our seats. I wanted to believe, but as every moment went by, I felt my gut twist tighter.

Was her phone really dead? Keeping your phone charged was one of those things that Shadows was strict about. Ivy wasn't one to be slack about things like that. At least I didn't think she was. So why wasn't she answering her phone? And where was Doc, and why didn't he answer either? What was it that Cole hadn't shared with me? My head was about to burst.

I didn't even notice we were in the air until the captain spoke. The flight was only half full, and I got up to pace as I waited for the WIFI to connect. My phone lit up, and I leaned down to show the screen to Cole then tapped the button and moved to the back of the plane.

"Ivy?"

"Hey," she sounded concerned, and my heart pounded painfully in my chest, "I'm sorry I missed your calls. I was doing some research on my phone and drained the battery dry. I had it charging in the truck on that big battery in the back while I helped Doc. I wasn't thinking. I'm so sorry." I closed my eyes and leaned my forehead against my arm. The flight attendant next to me eyed me as she set up the drink cart but didn't say anything. I took a much-needed deep breath.

"So, you're home?"

"No, we're at the market now. We had dinner at Zack's earlier." My head snapped up. "What's going on?"

"What are you wearing?"

"What?" She chuckled, but there was still a level of concern in her voice.

"Ivy," I tried to focus as the blood rushed through my ears, "what are you wearing?"

"That blue blouse you like, a skirt and a jacket." I stood so quickly I banged my head and Moore was suddenly at my side.

"Sir, you can't be back here," the flight attendant started to say, but Moore whispered something, and she slipped away with the cart.

"Where's Doc?"

"He's just paying for something." There was a pause. "Ty, you're starting to scare me."

"I don't mean to, but Ivy, do you have your earbuds?"

"Yes."

"Slip one of them in your ear and put your phone in your purse."

"Okay." I heard some rustling, and a moment later I could hear everything around her. Classic Apple ear pods picked up all the background noise and then some. "Now what?"

"I need you to quietly tell Doc 'code yellow.'"

"What—" she started to say but must have thought better of it. "Okay, one second." Despite the roar of the engine, I could still hear her heels click as she walked. I could hear her whisper something.

"Very well," Doc responded, his voice clear and cool as could be. "Time to leave, Ivy."

"Don't hang up," I warned her as I waved at Cole to come over. I held the phone away from my mouth as he leaned in. "She and Doc were just at Zack's, and she's wearing the exact outfit Hill mentioned."

His face paled as he slipped into work mode. "Keep her on the phone. Doc knows not to go home but to head to Zack's."

"Ivy—"

"Reid, why are you heading back this way?" She used Doc's first name, and I could tell she was nervous.

"Can't use the back roads without backup," he explained. "There's too many blind spots and high rises."

"Ty," her voice was off, but she kept it calm, "I would feel a whole lot better if you could explain to me what's going on."

"Hill's in custody," I knew better than to lie, "but before he went, he told me he had someone watching you. I'm not sure if it's true, but I want to be sure."

"So, he *could* be lying?"

"Maybe, but he knew what you were wearing and where you just ate."

"Okay," her voice became muffled then went clear again, "tell me what to do."

"For right now, stay on the line and do what Doc tells you." When I turned back around, Cole and Mark had the few scattered passengers from the back moved toward the front of the plane. A few of our guys were on their phones.

"The pilot's a buddy of mine." Cole gave a quick nod toward the flight deck. "He's okay with the shuffle. Told him we just needed some space and didn't want to disturb the passengers."

"Ty?"

"I'm still here."

"Where are you?"

"I'm about thirty-two thousand feet up and headed your way."

"Hello, ladies and gentlemen." The male flight attendant's voice came on. I'd seen him in the first-class section earlier. "I'm sure by now you've noticed the big grizzlies in the back." He made light of our size, and a few passengers turned around and laughed. "Please don't be alarmed. They are US military heroes." The crowd clapped with appreciation.

"We'd like to thank the passengers who kindly gave up their seats to give them a little room while they sort some things out. So, while they work, they'd like us to treat you to a drink or *two* and a meal on them." Again, the crowd cheered and hooted. "Ladies, think of it as a blind date with a handsome soldier, and gentlemen, you just kick your feet up and enjoy the beer these big guys can't." Mark joined in on the laughter with that one.

"There's never a dull moment here on American Airlines," the attendant warmed to his role, "whether it be the roller coaster ride of turbulence or the GI Joe hunk of the month calendar in the back."

"We're at Zack's now," Ivy whispered, and I tuned out the flight attendant.

"Walk, don't run."

"We're inside, and Zack is here."

"Good."

"Beckett, it's Zack. I'm taking Ivy to the back office."

"Thanks, Zack. I'll be in touch."

"Ty?" Ivy was back on the phone. "What now?"

"Now you stay there and wait for me."

The flight felt like it took forever. Cole had the local police do a run-through of every nook and cranny of the town, but the truth was if someone was there already, they'd probably not be noticed. Redstone was a tourist town, and there were plenty of strangers.

We grabbed our luggage and ran for the chopper Cole had arranged for us. Once we touched down, we raced across the park. It was nearly two-thirty in the morning, and the town was quiet. I knew the locals wouldn't be fazed to hear a chopper in the middle of the park. Blackstone had run drills here before. I led the race across the grass, down the street, and into Zack's parking lot.

Zack opened the door as we got there.

"She's okay. She's in the back office with Doc."

"Thanks, Zack." I hurried down the hall and took a deep breath before I opened the door. There she was, sitting on the couch. She looked beat. When she saw me, she pushed to her feet and flew into my arms. I hugged her tight and breathed her in. I'd so missed the scent of her.

"It's okay," I assured her. I knew I was telling myself that more than her. "Are you okay?" I looked at Doc, and he gave me a nod.

"Just a little rattled, but nothing a good night sleep can't fix." Ivy smiled up at me, and I kissed her hard on the lips. "Can we go home now?"

"Doc," Cole called, "a minute?" I looked up and watched Doc leave with Cole. Then I took her in my arms one more time. A few minutes later, I tugged Ivy along behind me as we went to join the others.

"Look at you causin' shit." Mark wrapped an arm around Ivy, taking over so I knew she'd be okay.

"Pot calling the kettle black much?" She rolled her eyes.

"Okay, fine, you got me there," he gave in, "but let's talk about how you let your phone die."

She groaned, and I raised an eyebrow at her. *Yeah, you broke a house rule.*

Later that night, when we were finally alone and the fireplace was lit, I climbed into bed feeling mildly better after my shower. She curled into my side and rested her head on my shoulder. Her arm draped over my stomach as she mindlessly circled a finger around my side.

I leaned down and kissed her head as I relished the fact we were both okay. The logs in the fire popped and sizzled and gave off a nice warmth. I began to relax as I sat mesmerized by the flames.

"Can you tell me now?" she whispered.

"Pat Rose, a PI from Yellowstone."

"Really?"

"Yeah, Hill hired him to watch you. Rose was under the impression he was hired to catch you in the act of cheating on your husband. Hill." I nearly spat the name and felt acid prickle my tongue. "He'd been around for a couple days. We don't think he ever attempted to follow you here, or it would have been noticed. The guys know to take different routes to the house, and with all our checkpoints, they'd have known if someone was following. He must have been watching for you in town."

"I can't believe someone followed me at all. At least he wasn't dangerous."

"He might not have been, but Hill was."

"True." She hugged me closer as she let that sink in. "Kind of gross he made up that we were married. Yuck. He's really pathetic."

I glared at the ceiling. "At least we have enough to put him away for the rest of his miserable life."

"That must feel good."

"It does, but I'd rather have Brown back."

"Just make sure you live for both of you. That's the best way to honor him."

She was right, but I still felt unsettled and amped up for thinking Hill would leave Ivy out of it. He'd already taken great lengths to shut me up. I'd underestimated him. Shit, he'd killed Brown for merely embarrassing him in front of a woman.

"I'm sorry, Ivy. Tonight must've scared you. I'm pissed I didn't see that coming."

"It did," she said quietly, "but I knew you were out there, you and the guys. I focused on that, and it really helped."

"I can't imagine how different life would be right now if I hadn't come to Shadows. It was a lifesaver for me. The fact that it also brought me you, I still find amazing. You're all I want now. I won't let anything happen to you, Ivy. I promise."

"I know." She tilted her head to look at me, and her gorgeous eyes held me captive. Then they creased as she smirked.

"What?"

"I was just thinking." She rolled to face me and then slid up to straddle my hips. Her weight felt amazing on my erection. "How proud that PI would have been if he'd brought Hill pictures of his *wife* cheating on him, with *you*."

"About as proud as I was when I corrected the PI that you were mine." I slid my hands up her bare legs and around her tight little ass. Her pink teddy dipped wonderfully low, showing off her plump breasts and erect nipples.

"That I am." She leaned down and caught my lips while her hips started to move. "All yours, T-Rex," she whispered across my lips, but I grabbed both wrists and gently pushed her back.

What the hell.

Then it hit me.

"I'm going to kill Shelly!"

She laughed as she tried to scramble off the bed, but I caught her hips and was on top of her in a heartbeat.

"What else did my sister tell you?" I tickled her side, and she laughed harder. "You two are never allowed to be alone without some kind of supervision."

"First, it wasn't Shelly!" She tried to breathe.

"Who was it?"

"Second, Kit-lit was there too!"

"Oh, shit, someone is going to die." She tried to wiggle free, but I snagged her again, pushed her teddy up, and slid inside of her without warning. She gasped and moaned at the same time.

"If this is what I get for not telling you secrets, yes, please." She raked her nails down my back, sending a delicious shiver through my nerves.

"I have not forgiven you," I whispered as I kissed her neck, and she chuckled, "but given that I haven't been inside you for what seems like forever, I need to ground myself."

"I couldn't agree more," she sighed.

"I have something to tell you," I confessed as I flicked my hips, getting deeper. "I realized something about you."

"Yeah?" Her hands ran over my shoulders, and I closed my eyes at how nice it felt to be touched.

"Mm," I kissed her jaw, "you're making me better."

"You couldn't get any better," she breathed and wiggled against me.

"No, I mean it may sound funny, but what I mean is I think I'm a better person now."

"You're a great person, Ty."

"But I'm better because of you. Wanna know why?"

"Okay." She arched her back to let me in further.

"I was struggling back at the hotel, you know, about Brown, and you know what I did?" I stopped moving and stared down into her glazed eyes. "I called my mom and apologized for how I'd treated her and the family since I left years ago and how I want them to be in my life from now on."

"Really?" Her eyes lit up and she made an effort to focus.

"Really. That only happened because of you. You showed me what I was missing and how to let go of the guilt."

"Ty," tears rimmed her eyes, "I'm so happy you did that."

"I'm happy, Ivy." I blinked at what I said. The words sounded strange, almost. "I'm happy." I tested them out again. "Happy that I have my family back, that I'm here and have a new team, that we got justice for Brown, but most of all, happy I found you."

Before she could respond, I sealed my lips over hers and started to move again. Slowly. I wanted her to feel my words, not just hear them. Ivy was a game changer for me, and so was this house, these people, everything. I'd known how much I needed to deal with Brown's death and my family. I just didn't realize how much. Letting people go and letting them in was the ticket for me to feel free.

Ivy's breaths began to pick up, and she pushed on my chest and rolled us over. She took over and rode me from above. She was so sexy, and I loved to watch her. She grabbed my hands and put them on her hips. I helped rock her hips, moving her in the direction I wanted. I grinned at her when, despite being on top, she gave me control.

She lifted slightly and squeezed her thighs, moaning through a climax. I let go and floated away with her. It wasn't worth bringing up that I met her ex or that he made a scene where she used to work. Ivy needed to move forward, and she'd made it clear to me that I was her future. Everything else was just white noise.

I didn't remember when I fell asleep, but when I heard the pitter patter of little feet outside the door, I was instantly awake. I wondered idly why kids always woke so early and took a moment to sympathize with their parents. I glanced at Ivy and realized she was still out cold. I knew she didn't have to work today, so I quietly got out of bed and gently tucked the blanket up to her chin.

I tiptoed to my closet to get something I'd ordered online. My old rucksack caught my eye, and I gave it a moment of thought. It deserved that. It had served me well. It even took a bullet for me once, but those days were over. I reached for the package I was after, then with a last glance at Ivy, I left the room.

I headed downstairs. As I entered the living room I

ran into Mark's boy, Ethan. I held up my purchase and watched as his face lit up.

"Oh, my God." Ethan drew in a deep excited breath. "What's that?"

"This?" I grinned. "Only one of the best Nerf guns on the market. And this, my young friend, is what will help take down your father." I bent down on one knee and helped him put his arm through the strap. "Wait until you feel the power of what this bad boy can do."

"You're the coolest uncle ever." He fist-bumped me.

"One more thing." I held up my phone to show him the camera. "Your dad's in the entertainment room."

"Copy that, Major." He gave me a serious salute then raced off. Truth, I had a soft spot for Ethan. His twin brother, Liam, was Mark reincarnate, and most of the attention of the house ended up on him. But there was something in Ethan that I could connect to, and I was glad...

Zip zip zip!

"The hell!"

"Sorry, finger slipped!" Ethan waved from the bottom of the stairs as he raced off.

Ugh. Kids.

———

I grabbed a thermos in the kitchen and topped it off with hot coffee. I put on my boots and a jacket and headed for the lake. I'd seen Keith sitting on the dock from the window. This was his first morning home since Mexico, and although I knew he liked his alone time, I wanted to check on him.

Tripper turned to look at me as I got closer, and his jaw moved. Keith was feeding him pieces of donut. Those two seemed to have quite the bond.

"Morning." I stood next to Tripper and gave him an ear scratch.

"Morning." He kept his gaze on the lake. "Want to sit?"

"Yeah." I brushed the snow off the chair and settled in. "Want a top-off?"

"I would." He leaned over, and I filled his mug to the rim. "Ivy get much sleep last night?"

"More than I thought she would."

"She's tough."

"She is."

"I think it's time we had a chat." He eyed me. "Daniel had the same one with me when I was chasin' after Lexi, and I feel it's only right I do the same with you."

"I'm listening."

"This place," he waved around, "is pretty amazing, isn't it?"

"Yeah." I looked out at the lake and nodded. "Sure is."

"It's a blessing." He patted the pup's head and rubbed his hands to show the doughnut was gone, and Tripper immediately settled at his feet. "But not everyone who comes to live at Shadows can make it work, no matter how much we want it for them." I let his words sink in because they were true. "I hate that she is, but Lexi needs to be our reminder that this life is hard, unpredictable, and unfair sometimes for our wives and children. We get to come and go without a thought, but they give up a lot to be here. They're under constant surveillance even when they aren't here."

"That's true."

"All I'm saying is, be careful falling in love," he whispered. "This place isn't for everyone. No matter how much they love you and promise they're fine, they might not be. This place can eat away at them and corrode their love."

We sat in silence for a bit as I chewed my lip and he ruffled Tripper's ears.

"Any suggestions?" I knew Ivy was open with me, and she seemed to share with the other women. My thoughts were that she would be happy here, but Keith had just been through it in the worst way. Any advice he could offer, I'd gladly take and use.

"Check in often, make time for her, not just at the house, but take her out, to town or wherever. Make sure you keep in touch with the other wives and be open with them. Ask them if they can connect with her. Don't get lax about that as time goes by. Lexi sealed herself off from them all, even Cat. That was a huge red flag, as they were the closest. But most of all," he looked at me again, "see it before it's too late. I hid from it. I didn't want to see it." He turned to look out at the lake. "Because I knew it was over." I felt instantly cold at that. It washed through me as I saw the pain on his face.

We sat in silence again as I mulled it all over. I wanted Ivy to be happy. She deserved the world, and I intended to give it to her. No matter what it took. I couldn't imagine how it felt for Keith to get that call about Lexi, and I never wanted to.

"I'm sorry, Keith."

He let out a deep breath and licked his lips. "So am I." He sipped his coffee, and we both settled in and watched the frozen lake in silence.

NINETEEN

"Oh, Ivy," June cooed from the doorway of the hotel, "you look gorgeous." I ran my hands down my dress and smiled at the fabric. I really did like this dress. A lot had happened over the past few days, and my head still spun with it all. "Just wait until your mother sees you."

"Thanks, June. Would you mind?"

"Of course." She helped me fasten the chain that held a small locket that had once belonged to my grandmother.

"Have you seen Ty yet?"

"Handsome as ever." She winked. "You two will make the perfect pair."

"Ty in a tux? Yes, please." I laughed. "Zack's here

too?" I lifted a brow at her in the mirror and saw her blush.

"Of course. He's running around making sure everyone's well looked after." She pressed her lips together in a tight smile like she couldn't hold it in anymore. "Things are getting a little more serious than I ever expected."

"I've been told that happens." I grinned at her as she tried to regain her composure. I took one last look in the mirror.

"Ivy, actually, I wanted to have a quick word with you about something?" I stood immediately and studied her face. "It's Doc. I think he might just need a little Ivy."

"Of course." I followed her out of my room and across the hall to my uncle's room. She knocked lightly and opened the door with a keycard. Doc stood in front of the window, looking outside.

"I'll leave you to it," she whispered, and I slipped inside my uncle's room. "Penny for your thoughts?"

He turned, and his gaze fell over my dress. "Well, look at you," he whispered lovingly. "My goodness, my little lady. I'm reminded of the time you and Alison dressed up for one of those fancy parties you dreamed of attending."

"Hardly," I laughed, "but I'm pleased you remember."

"I remember every part of your childhood, because as far as I was concerned, you were my little girl. My little lady with your blonde pigtails and big, happy eyes."

"I was happy because I had you, too." I moved closer and hugged him tightly. He let out a little sigh when I pulled away. "You okay?"

"I guess I just got to thinking."

"Yikes," I teased, and he swatted my arm.

"Times like these just make you reflect on the time that's passed. Makes you wonder why you wait so damn long to do the right thing."

"Time is only wasted when you realize that, so do something about it." I fixed his tie, and he nodded as he grabbed his jacket.

"As always, you're correct." He reached for my hand and tucked it under his arm. "All right, enough of all this. Let's go enjoy this memorable day."

"Let's. I just need my coat." We walked together back to my room where he helped me with my long, cream-colored cloak. Then we left the hotel and made our way across to Zack's restaurant. It had been closed for the day due to this special occasion.

"These are for you." Savi immediately took control as we entered. She swept off my cloak and hung it on a hanger and handed me a bouquet of traditional white roses, dusty miller, and hypericum berries for a pop of color. It was seasonal and elegant. "Okay, Reagan and Easton, hold hands and don't walk too fast," Savannah directed as she propelled them out the door when the music started. Everyone stood and made a fuss over how adorable they looked as they walked together. Having the kids involved was just what they needed after everything that had happened. "Now, Tabby and Gabriella, here are your petals. Make it rain." She grinned and sent them out next. We'd decided we weren't going to go all out. Simple was the key, simple and light for this day.

"You missed your calling, Savannah." I chuckled. It amazed me how at ease she was in organizing such an event so quickly.

"Missed?" She scoffed. "Please, this is what I live for. Wait until you get home and see what I've done with the house."

"Should I be nervous?"

"Not unless you hate Christmas." She laughed as she smiled at Olivia and Brandon, who were prepared to enter next. They looked stunning side by side. "Loving all of this." She fussed with the white handkerchief in Brandon's pocket. "And when do we use this?"

"When any of you saps decides to shed a tear." He dripped with sarcasm.

"Pretty much, yeah." She laughed and urged them forward. She looked back at me. "You ready?"

"I am."

"Good, because it's my turn." She called out to the wives, and they all lined up and disappeared into the room. The music and murmurs from inside filled me with excitement. I turned to my uncle.

"How lucky am I?" He beamed.

"The luckiest." I kissed his cheek, took his arm, and on cue, we walked down the aisle together. I looked toward the man who held my heart from the moment he saved me from that panic attack in the middle of the night. His gaze found mine, and he mouthed *I love you* as I took my spot next to the others.

The music turned, and we all looked down the aisle at the woman who'd won the heart of my dear uncle.

Abigail.

She wore a beautiful red dress, just a shade deeper than the rest of us wore, and a radiant clip held up one side of her hair. Her heels were to die for, patent leather and shiny. *Thank you, Savannah, for bringing those babies into my world.* But best of all, Abigail simply glowed with excitement as she held tight to Mark's arm. I was so happy for her. Even Mark seemed to be at ease as he handed her off and took his spot next to Cole.

A moment before the ceremony started, Ty caught my gaze and gave me a wide smile. His eyes practically danced. It amazed me how much he'd changed. A lightness had found its way to his center. He'd finally shed the sadness and guilt he'd carried for his lost brother and was at peace. I knew part of his newfound happiness had to do with him letting his family back into his heart.

Best of all, I found myself falling in love with him all over again.

I blinked back my happy tears and focused on the words that would forever bind my uncle to the woman he had loved for years.

It was perfect.

After dinner, the tables and chairs were pushed aside, and the music started. The kids danced, and their laughter brought smiles to the adults around them. Even Brandon seemed to be happy, and I grinned as he grabbed his sister's arms and danced her around the room. I caught Keith's eye, and he pointed to his phone just as mine buzzed.

> Keith: Thanks for getting us through this, Ivy.

I put a hand on my chest and patted it as I smiled back at him. He nodded then hopped up and grabbed Sue's hand and tugged her to the dance floor.

"I always knew he'd make a great uncle." Shelly pointed with her head over my shoulder toward Ty. He had her daughter in his arms and a silly grin on his face. Luna shrieked and clapped as she touched the balloons he pulled down close for her to reach. She bounced around in his hold, and he laughed as he held on to her for dear life. "It really means a lot that we were invited. I know he wants us to be a part of this new family he's inherited. It's hard to get my head around it, but Mom and Dad are thrilled to be included as well. We're happy for him."

"I had no clue who was all coming. My uncle would have reached out to Ty to invite family, and I'm thrilled he did." She nodded and looked around the room.

"You'll be happy to know Demi is gone. Mom had a talk with her."

"Really?"

"Yeah, basically, she told her she deserves to find happiness, but not with Ty. They always thought Demi was who he wanted. Now they see the real Ty again when he's with you. He's happy and back to who he used to be. Once Mom saw that, let's just say she wasted no time in letting Demi know it was time she moved on." *I really like Ty's mom.* "Mom's claws will be out now if she ever tries to come back. She'll protect her young." She chuckled.

"I appreciate that she did that, and I do hope Demi finds happiness."

"Just not with Ty."

"No, I can get scrappy, too."

"That was such a good answer." We both had a good laugh.

"Who's getting scrappy?" Ty tried to hang on to Luna as she did a nosedive toward her mom.

"Me." I chuckled as Luna grabbed a fistful of her mother's hair.

"Why?"

"If anyone gets between us." I held up my hands and pretended they were claws.

"No one's getting between us." He dropped a long kiss.

"Get a room." Shelly laughed. "Come on, Luna, let's go find something stronger than punch." She gave her brother's shoulder a smack then left us alone. We sat at a table and sipped our drinks.

"You want house pranks, you've came to the right place." Olivia had me looking over my shoulder as she stood near the dance floor.

"Who are you talking to?" Savannah peered down at her curiously. Clearly, she caught what I did.

"Fynn." Olivia showed her the phone screen, and her mother rolled her eyes with a laugh.

"Be sure to tell him about—" She stopped and looked at Ty before she leaned over and whispered something.

"Yes!" Olivia grinned.

"The women here give me the chills sometimes," Ty joked, and I shrugged in agreement. "So," he watched the party with me, "what do you think of all this?"

"I think it's perfect. Exactly what they wanted. Less is more, and I love that Savannah honored their wishes."

"She did a great job, and what a great place to have it."

"Couldn't be better." I chuckled. "Zack's just makes everything better. It's where we all feel safe and happy. I couldn't think of a better place for this to happen."

"I was kinda surprised they didn't have it at Shadows." He thought out loud.

"I understand why they didn't. Shadows would limit the guest list. My mother wouldn't have been able to attend, nor your sister or parents."

"Very true." He rested his chin on my shoulder. "Zack's really is the best place in Redstone."

"It is." I beamed at the happy couple then at Ty as he tugged me onto the dance floor. *Die a Happy Man* by Thomas Rhett burst through the speakers as Ty pulled me tight.

"Look at that." I pointed with my chin toward the mocktail bar. "Aren't they just having the best time?" Ty grinned as he looked over at Olivia and Brandon. They were perched on stools with fancy drinks in their hands. They both seemed to be enjoying making fun of their family on the dance floor.

Ty nodded. "Nice to see him with a smile on his face."

"He's going to be just fine," I agreed.

The kids barely stopped until Cole noted Ethan's big yawn and scooped him up and draped him over his shoulder. Normally, June and Abby would leave and take the kids home to bed. Tonight, it had been arranged for some of the house staff to do that. Soon, all of them had been kissed and hugged and bundled up into cars. We watched them drive off with their escort, and we all walked back inside to enjoy the rest of the evening.

The guys had all hit the dance floor with their respective partners. Gear seemed to be asking one of the waitresses to dance, and Zack moved in and took her tray and encouraged her to go. He was such an awesome man, good to everyone, including…I watched Mark smile at Mia, but it dropped when he saw Zack take June's hand to dance.

"The fuck," Mark mouthed to Cole, who shook his head for him to chill.

I chuckled and leaned my head on Ty's shoulder and breathed him in. I closed my eyes and hugged him tight.

"Greatest escape ever," he whispered in my ear. I drank in his love and rubbed his back gently.

Connie, Ty's mom, smiled at me as she danced with Richard. The look in her eyes told me that everything was right inside. She blew me a kiss then looked up at her husband and said something that made him smile.

Three songs morphed into one and we never broke rhythm. Neither of us wanted to let go. We stayed locked in each other's arms. This was a night we never wanted to end.

Snow fell softly but steadily as we left Zack's. I was pleased I'd packed my tall boots, as the snow was already up my ankles.

"It's so peaceful out here." I held out a hand to feel the snowflakes as they prickled my warm skin.

"Come with me." Ty pulled me in the opposite direction of the hotel, then through a little walkway out toward the main street. "Apparently, every year, the stores and restaurants decorate for Chris—" He stopped as I cut him off while I took in the scene.

"Oh, my God," I whispered at the Thomas Kincade painting in front of me, "it's gorgeous."

"It really is." We moved into the center of the quiet street and admired all the colored lights. All different sized trees lined the storefronts. Some were decorated with red and gold bows, some had oversized ornaments, some had ribbons. Dean Martin's *The Christmas Song* came on over Zack's speakers that could still be heard throughout the street.

"Shall we check it out?" He offered his arm.

"Let's."

A toy store two doors down had a pretty gold train

that chugged around a beautifully decorated tree in their window.

"You know, Doc said something to me recently, and I can't get it out of my head." He covered his heart with his hand. "Love comes to people in many ways. Sometimes it's a slow burn, sometimes you see it coming, and sometimes it's a force that knocks you completely off course. It's how you choose to accept it that determines your happiness."

"His was a slow burn, let me tell you." I laughed as I leaned toward the window and admired a brown teddy staring at me from between the branches.

"And you were a force," he said behind me. "You came into my life like a storm, and I couldn't see anyone but you." He took my elbow and turned me to look at him. "I don't want anyone but you."

"I don't want anyone but you either, Ty. I—"

"Hear me out, okay?" I nodded, "I did something a few days ago." My stomach gave a little lurch. "I asked your uncle and mother for their blessing." *What?*

"Woow," my head pulled back at that, "Ty, isn't it a little soon to be talking about marriage? We haven't even been dating a year."

"And they said yes," he ignored my minor freakout, "because love doesn't wait for you to be ready for it. If your soul was meant to connect with mine, then who are we to deny it? I love you, Ivy. I want you to be mine because I want to be yours."

"I, ah," I stumbled as his words sank in. He stepped

back, pulled a small white box from his pocket, and went down on one knee in the snow.

"Will you marry me, Ivy Knight?" He opened the box, and a stunning princess cut, white gold ring sprinkled under the Christmas lights.

I stopped and took a moment. I listened to my heart. Yes, it was soon. I thought of my uncle, who had waited so long to find and accept love. *Don't wait too long to be happy*, he'd recently whispered in my ear. Ty made me happy—incredibly happy.

"Yes," the words got caught in my throat as my eyes prickled with unshed tears, "I'll marry you."

"Really?" His eyes lit up as he stood and plucked the ring from the box. He slipped it on my finger. "Geez, I had a whole backup plan," he admitted with a grin. He took my face between his warm hands and kissed me several times quickly then pulled me into him and wrapped his arms around me as he dove deeper into a long kiss that had me longing for something more.

We barely made it back to the hotel room where we tore at each other's clothes. He hauled me into the shower and angled the spray toward me as he leaned me against the shower wall. He tilted my chin back and smiled warmly into my eyes as my body heated.

"I'll do whatever it takes to keep you happy, Ivy. But I need you to promise me something."

"Sure."

"Promise me that if life here at Shadows gets to be too much, you'll tell me."

"I promise."

"I mean it." He brushed my wet hair back off my slick shoulder. "I've given more than enough of myself to my job, and you are what comes first now. I can't go through what Keith did." He swallowed hard, and I saw fear written all over his face.

"Hey," I slid my hands up his chest and then through his hair, "I don't want to end up like Lexi either. Luckily for you, I'm annoyingly in tune with myself." I smiled. I had to get him to see I was different than Lexi. "You have my word if I'm ever feeling unhappy, you'll be the first to know."

"Okay." He took a deep breath.

"Look at me, Ty." I waited until I knew he listened. "I'm like Sloane, not Lexi. She and I made a choice to be here, and like her, I want to stay here. You men aren't the only ones who love this mountain. I feel at peace here, too."

"Good." He slipped between my legs and entered me with such ease I knew I was made for him. "Because I want you here with me. I never want to let you go."

"No, you're not." I held up my hand and wiggled the ring. His eyes became hooded as he moved inside me. I lunged toward him and caught his mouth with mine and tried to take over the kiss, but classic Ty, he took over and I willingly gave in.

He dragged in a breath, stealing mine, then moaned as he started to move inside me. Painfully slowly, like he was savoring every moment of it.

I leaned my head back and concentrated on every spot he touched. The pleasure built in my stomach and spread to my chest, the warmth building hotter by the minute. I'd thought I was happy before, but this—my lips broke into a delirious smile as he dragged a hand up my side and cupped my breast—this was a whole new level of pure joy.

"I can't believe you're gonna be my wife," he whispered as he hiked my leg over his hip and inched his fingers down the back of my thigh. "You'll be mine to do this with for the rest of my life."

I sighed, as I could barely form a thought.

"Mine, to possess and devour." He grabbed my other leg and lifted me up the wall then wrapped both legs tight around him and held both my butt cheeks in his hands. He moved in a slow rhythm in and out. My breathing hitched as he increased the rhythm. "Make that noise again." He chuckled as he kissed my breasts. I felt weightless in his hands.

"Mmhm, yours," I murmured again as I grasped a handful of his hair and tugged, "all yours, Ty."

"That's right." He increased the pace even more as he continued to talk in my ear. He promised to love me forever, and he talked of all the things he wanted to do for me. His breath in my ear felt so erotic as I tried to concentrate on the words along with the physical sensations he created inside me.

He didn't need to promise me anything. I loved this man

with every part of me, and he loved me back, and that was all I could ever ask for. Well, that and…a rush shot through me, and I screamed, not caring who could hear me. My toes curled, my stomach seized, and my arms locked around his neck while I rode out one hell of an orgasm. I clawed at his back, wanting everything he could offer, then finally I sagged into him with a satisfied moan. My heart pounded against his, as he fought to hold off his own release. I loved that he made sure I was fully satisfied before he'd take his own.

He pushed me farther up the wall as his muscles flexed like steel. Every vein stood out on his face, chest, and arms. Then he buried his face in my neck and grunted as his fingers flexed against my back, pressing into me with such force, I hoped the shower wall wouldn't give. Finally, he took a deep breath then shook. The shakes came like aftershocks from a volcano as he found his release.

My heart burst with pure happiness to have had such an intimate act with someone I loved. Especially with someone who had professed his love for me the whole time and I knew it to be true.

"I never want to leave this moment," he panted as he looked up at me. "I want to stay suspended in time right here, right now."

"Well, that would be nice. But I was thinking…You up for round two?" I barely had the last word out when he threw open the shower door and tossed me onto the bed.

————

The next morning, we all gathered back at Zack's for a beautiful buffet breakfast. I flipped the ring around and attempted to hide it for as long as I could. Which turned out to be five seconds with Savi's radar.

"Did he?" I nodded as she grabbed my hand. "Oh, my God, let me see," she half screamed. I flipped the ring around, and she squealed.

"Good night last night, Ivy?" Mark winked and held up his room key. I saw he was indeed our neighbor at the Redstone lodge.

"Not complaining." I glared at him.

"No, I'd say you were agreeing." He jumped out of the way when I went to swat him.

"Abby!" Savi called to her.

"Marcus!" Abby answered in her best parent voice as she held up a finger toward Mark.

"Not cool, Sav." Mark frowned and whisked away as Mia circled in to see what the fuss was about.

Smart man.

"I'd ask what he did this time," Mia chuckled, "but I'm fresh out of caring, thanks to the twins this morning."

"In the barn again?" Savi asked.

"Worse, I found the little rugrats playing with Keith's toolbox up at the chopper hanger. Keith would have a fit if anything went missing."

"Boys," Savi sighed, "they never really grow up." Savi

nudged my arm then held up her own hand and wiggled her fingers at Mia. Mia immediately homed in on my finger.

"Oh, my God," she snagged my hand and beamed at me, "did we just gain another sister?" Mark chuckled again as he walked by, and Mia rolled her eyes. "You know what I mean."

"We did," Savannah yelled and drew me into a hug.

Ty appeared with his parents and Shelly and pulled me to his side. My uncle came over with my mother, and they stood beside us.

"What's going on?" Mom asked, and I took her hand and gave it a warm squeeze.

"Guys," Ty looked around at everyone, "I want you to know I asked Ivy to marry me." His family's faces lit up as I held out my hand and, I could feel their acceptance as they took in the news.

"Oh, honey! I'm so happy," my mother gasped.

A cheer erupted from Connie, and suddenly the entire room was cheering as word got around. People's faces started to blur as I was pulled into hug after hug. By the end of it all, my face hurt from smiling.

"Come on. Let's get something to eat." Sloane pulled me away as the gushing crowd began to disperse.

"Thanks. I was starting to eye Mike up at one point, I was so hungry."

"Mike, huh?" She smirked.

"He's colorful, like steak shish kebab." I shrugged as I eyed the wonderful spread of food in front of me. I looked up for a brief second and realized my uncle and Abby had begun to open their gifts. I liked that the attention was only partly on them as we all served ourselves. I looked back at the array of choices and decided to throw caution to the wind and heaped my plate with waffles and strawberries then topped it off with a heap of whipped cream.

Laughter broke out as Abby held up a pair of towels and my uncle's face turned beet red.

"I couldn't help myself," Daniel roared, and Sue covered her mouth. Obviously, there was a story there, and I made a mental note to ask about that inside joke later.

"So, there I was," Mark sat super straight and shook his shoulders like a happy little girl, "with this wig on and an overcoat, tryin' to be the best looking handcuffed and gagged female I could. You know, all helpless and stuff. I see one of Castillo's dipshits comin', holding his weapon, ready to shoot. I wait for him to get close, then at just the right moment, I slam my door open, and WHAM, right in his kneecaps. He went down, and I took him out." He looked super serious. "Do you know how hard that is with a bunch of fake hair in your face? I don't know how women do it." He pretended to fling back a piece of long hair from his eyes. Everyone died laughing. Even Keith was getting a kick out of Mark's story.

"And people wonder what these guys do for a living. I'm not really sure where to begin," Olivia joked, making her mother laugh harder.

"My question is," Cole pointed his fork at him, "where's the wig now?"

"What can I say? Mia is into some kinky shit." He ducked when Mia elbowed him, but he grabbed her and kissed her hard. "I know you can't resist my charm for long." He wiggled his eyebrows.

"I need therapy," Olivia muttered. She was becoming quite sarcastic for her age. I was intrigued with this girl, and I looked forward to being around to see what she'd be like when she was older. Good luck to any man who crossed her path.

I dove into my food as Ty arrived and pressed a kiss against my temple. He grinned at my full plate.

"Looks good." He eyed my waffles, and I saw he had pancakes. "You know, I should really try some of those for you. I mean, you never know. They could be laced with poison. I don't mind taking one for the team."

"Oh, yeah?" I took a big bite. "I think I'm good."

"So sexy." Mark chuckled as he reached over and wiped a bit of cream from my chin. He took a seat across from us. "I bet you're hungry," he muttered and grinned.

"You see Zack's plate?" I shot back, and his face twisted into a glare. Then his eyes went slitty as something devious crossed his mind.

"You know, Mia ate like that when she was pregnant with the twins." Ty choked on his pancakes.

"No, I think you had it right the first time." I chuckled. I knew I'd been careful in that department.

"Are you," Ty drew my attention to him, "could you be? Oh, my God, I should have—"

"No, no," I shook my head, "I'm on birth control." As much as I loved kids, I certainly wasn't ready for them yet. "You see me take it every morning. They're in that little round silver thing."

"Good to know," he said, deadpan.

"Ty Beckett," I stuck my fork out at him, "what the hell does that mean?"

"It means I want everything with you, Ivy." He cut his pancakes then glanced over at me. "A marriage, a family, a life. Raising kids with you is something I'm excited about. Not today, not tomorrow, but know I want that."

"I want that, too," I admitted. I realized I really did want all that and then some.

"Good," he popped a bite of pancake into his mouth, "because I want lots of babies with you."

"You say that now." Mia sighed so deeply it made the entire table break out in laughter.

I turned back to my breakfast, and as I chewed, I caught sight of Paul, who held out a hand to my uncle. They shook, then Paul leaned in and whispered something that made my uncle's eyes widen. He glared at Paul, who had a big smirk on his face. It changed to a full-out laugh as he turned on his heel and walked off with a bounce in his step.

What the hell was that?

TWENTY

PAUL

"Are you sure you're okay with this, Logan?" I tapped my phone against my knee as I glanced in my side mirror. Cole's eyes went to the rear-view mirror then his side mirror. We both kept an eye on the road behind us. Funny how we never lost old habits.

"We wouldn't be going if I wasn't sure," he muttered, but I knew his head was elsewhere. We'd heard chatter that morning that Talya's family had made a move to expand into Castillo's territory. There was also increased talk of retaliation against Blackstone. "Text Keith and let him know we're here."

"Roger that." I did what he asked and couldn't help but smile as we pulled into the drive to Camp Green. I forgot how much I loved this place. "It's strange, you know," I said my thoughts out loud as he parked. "I knew what I was giving up by leaving you guys. I knew what it meant to go undercover, and I think I did it well for a lot of years. But now," I opened the door to the Escalade and looked at Cole, "but if you asked me now, I'd never do it. It's not worth what I gave up." I waved a hand around. "I missed too much, even all this." We began to walk.

"Hey," Cole stopped, and I swung around to face him, "in case it doesn't get said in the future, I want to make sure it does."

"What?" I watched as his face tightened and the lines around his eyes deepened.

"It rocked Shadows when we thought you died. Losing a brother was something they warned us about, but that could never really prepare anyone for such a loss. You were mourned by every one of us, every damn day at the house. We dealt with it by including you in every one of our decisions when we went out that door. The fact that you were out there fighting right along with us is still something I can't bend my mind around. But I know I will, in time.

"But you," he rested a hand on my shoulder, "you gave up everything to be our brother on the other side, and I just can't thank you enough for that. I know my grandfather brought you to us for that very reason." He looked down briefly, then his expression changed as he glared at me. "That being said, so help me Lucifer, if you leave our family like that again, and I'm not in the know, I'll hunt you down and feed you to the Cartels myself." A cold chill ran through me but dissolved as his face broke into a smile.

"I appreciate the chat," I chuckled, "even if it took a bit of a dark turn there at the end."

"Yeah, well, don't leave us again and there'll be no dark needed."

"Nice to know you still have that scary as shit vibe going." We started walking toward the front doors. "I thought maybe Savi'd beat that out of you."

"Nah," he grinned, "she secretly loves it, and with all the kids, I still need it." He paused in his step and nodded at a pretty female just ahead of us. She chatted with Keith.

"Who's that?"

"That would be Liza." He let out a quiet chuckle, which piqued my curiosity. We watched as she covered her mouth as she laughed. It was subtle, but I knew there was something there.

"So?" I turned to him and raised an eyebrow.

"She's great, she's single, and I know there's a vibe there with Keith. She also knows what's happened with him."

"She knows?"

"Yeah, because I told her." His chin went up at that as if in defense. "Keith deserves more, when he's ready, anyway, and Liza just might be the one who can put a smile on his face. Besides he'd never tell her."

"Jesus, Savi really has softened you up." I dodged as I

expected him to throw a punch, but he did the exact opposite.

"It's the least I can do, for not being able to fix the situation," he confessed. I suddenly realized he carried the blame for Lexi's death on his shoulders.

My eyes went wide. "You know Lexi's death wasn't your fault. Truth is, Cole, if this is anyone's weight to bear, it's mine."

"It's none of ours, really." He sighed as he looked up. "It was hers. But in the process of it all, he and the kids were caught in the crosshairs."

We both nodded at Keith as he caught sight of us. He smiled at Liza and headed our way.

"Sorry to make you wait." The corners of his mouth pointed upward as he joined us, and Cole gently bumped my arm.

"Baby steps," he muttered. Cole was many things to many people, and right now he was healing a heart one smile at a time.

We chatted on our way toward the private airport that would take us to Idaho. Once we boarded the tan-colored jet and were in the air, I took a deep breath and thought how glad I was that the truth was out there. I could never have known just how much that decision would take from me. I shook my head clear and looked at Keith. He had his phone out and was flipping through some pictures Savi had sent of his kids. He smiled and held up a particularly cute one of Reagan sitting on her brother's shoulders. I grinned my appreciation.

"Brandon sure is good with her."

"He really is." He smiled.

"The girl you were talking to seems nice." I didn't care how pushy that sounded, I was determined to fight my way back into my brothers' lives even if it was obvious.

He nodded and turned his phone off. He slid it onto the table between us. "She is." He paused as he thought. "She's just a friend. It's feels nice to laugh sometimes."

"It's just what you need, Keith. Don't be afraid to let yourself enjoy life a little."

"She's a lot softer than I'm used to. It's different, you know?"

"Different can be nice." One thing about Keith, he was fiercely protective of those he loved, but also wore his heart on his sleeve. He'd quickly taken on the big brother role when Savannah first arrived, and from what I'd seen, Livi went to him for advice on lots of things.

"It is," he agreed and moved back as the flight attendant placed our drinks in front of us. "I'm not ready for anything, though. I just like to talk to her. Feels good." I noticed Cole was listening because his fingers went still on the keyboard of his laptop.

"Mm, it does." I had to push Talya's face from my head, and when I looked over, Keith's eyes were on me.

"What about you?"

"What about me?"

"All the time you were gone. You ever have anyone?"

"I did." I started to spin the glass around on the

napkin. "She was gorgeous, sexy, wild at the right times, sweet at others. She was perfect." I shrugged heavily.

"And?"

"And what?" Some of the pain seeped through the cracks of my memory. It wasn't a sharp pain, more of a slow burn. "There was an expiration date on the relationship." I could feel his eyes on me as he tried to read my body language. Normally, I'd hide it, but I was with family, and it felt good to show a little vulnerability.

"You were in love with her."

"Yeah," I let go of my glass and leaned back to take a deep breath, "but it gets complicated. She's from a Cartel family. Not Castillo's," I clarified. "She'd never forgive me if she knew the truth."

"I'm sorry, Paul." He cleared his throat. "We look for love our whole lives, then when we find it, we hold on tight, terrified to lose it, and it gets snatched away anyway. Life seems kinda fucked up, doesn't it?"

"Very." I held my glass up, and he tapped it with his.

We stayed mostly quiet after that, only making small talk here and there. Cole's fingers flew across his keyboard as he went back to work. He didn't stop until we landed.

I took the steps two at a time down from the plane and climbed into the SUV with the others. A few miles down the road, we pulled into a sketchy garage. The walls were covered in graffiti.

"Shit. If we weren't meeting friends," Keith joked, "I'd be worried."

"He'd never betray Mike," Cole assured me as we

made our way inside the bay. We passed a few guys who gave us a good once-over, but none of them made any attempt to stop us or speak to us.

Cole opened the door to what could only be described as a conference room and let me enter first. Grim Gates sat at the table, and his gaze flew to mine.

"It's all good." Trigger held up his hands as I swung a confused look toward him. "Sit, and I'll explain everything." My eyes widened when I spotted Vinni and his brother Niccola in the corner.

It was a like punch line for a joke. *A biker gang, a Cartel associate, two mafia brothers, and the three SMU operators walk into a bar...*

"Logan," Trigger nodded, "I have some intel."

"I appreciate you meeting us here." Cole seemed at ease, and I tried to follow suit.

"No trouble." Trigger shrugged as we all settled in.

I glanced at Rail. He sucked on a joint, his eyes in slits as the smoke stung his eyes then drifted toward the ceiling. The last time I'd seen him, he'd been drunk with killing. He was more composed this time as he sat next to Trigger.

Mike's lower whisper pulled my attention to the corner of the room, but I kept my gaze on Rail.

"My lead didn't go anywhere?" Mike asked Brick.

"Nope."

"So, what? He's just vanished?"

"Trail ran cold two years ago, and nothin' surfaced since."

"Shit, man, something's gotta show itself."

"Or he's dead."

"Gentlemen," Niccola greeted us. Vinni gave a polite nod, and all attention went to them. "We're all here for the same reason. For intel." He looked at me. "Elio sends his thanks for the information on Castillo last week. We now have a possible lead on one of the places Tieri has been staying."

"Happy to help." I pulled out a piece of paper. "I did some more digging and think you might want to check out a place in Eastern Canada. St. Patrick's Catholic Church in Halifax, Nova Scotia, on Brunswick Street."

"I know it." Niccola studied the address. "Been there a few times."

"So has Tieri," I added, which made his face jerk up to mine, "three days ago." I waited a beat. "I have some friends up there, and they just got back to me this morning."

Niccola stood and Vinni mirrored him. "I need to make some calls."

"Thank you, Paul." Vinni reached across the table for a shake. "This won't be forgotten."

"You know how to reach me if you need anything else." I watched as he hurried out to join his brother.

"Seems you're a good man to know." Trigger glanced at Grim, who sat relaxed with his leg up, his ankle crossed over his thigh as he studied me. His chin rested on his hand while his pointer finger swiped over his lips. His silver eyes burrowed into my head like a bullet. I knew

Grim well enough now to know he was trying to process my being here as someone other than who he'd thought I was. The Gates were incredibly wealthy, and anyone who ever crossed them was probably buried under their family-owned hotels and sidewalks in Vegas. I knew the fact that I'd fooled him all these years was a blow to his ego.

"I spent a lot of time with Castillo," was all I offered.

"Indeed, you did." Trigger pushed a lighter through his fingers and flipped it around repeatedly. "Did you know?" Trigger asked Cole and gestured at me.

"No," Cole answered honestly, "none of us did."

"Are there any more undercover agents who could potently meddle in my business over there?" Grim asked.

"No." Cole said in a firm voice. He wasn't lying. Chili and his operation would be shut down, at least until it was needed again. We had no interest in the drug trade. Our main interest was in people. Humans being trafficked was a no-go.

"Good to know." He broke eye contact with me, and I was sure he was happy to know Mike hadn't ever lied to him. "After some confusion over who got to kill Castillo," Trigger scratched his cheek and glanced at Grim, who still had his stare fixed on me, "the retaliation against your teams seems to be an empty threat."

"Oh?" Keith spoke up as the three of us leaned forward.

"The Canos were pleased as shit to see Castillo's Cartel fall and sure as hell aren't gonna hurt anyone who did their dirty work for 'em."

"You sure about that?" I directed my question at Grim, not willing to interrupt Trigger.

"Why would I lie?" Grim purred. "I'm not the one with something to hide." I rolled my eyes at his low blow. I certainly wasn't going to accept his word for it. "You asked for the truth, and I gave it." He studied one of his fancy gold rings. It bore so many chips and dents it told the real story of the way he fought. His hands might be scarred, but his rings carried the brunt of the damage.

"I trust him," Trigger interjected and pointed at Grim with his chin. "Me, him, and Elio all have history that dates way back. If Grim says there's nothing brewin', there's nothing brewin'."

When I didn't speak, Keith leaned over my shoulder. "If Trigger vouches for him, trust his word."

"Elva and Jerry Cano have no clue who you are, *Agent Paul*," Grim lit a joint and puffed on the tip a few times then hauled in the smoke like a backdraft, "nor will they." Again, his silvery cold eyes moved to mine. "As far as they know, I removed Castillo from his place at the top, and his men went AWOL."

"And what about that police unit that stopped us in the city?" Keith asked.

"What police unit?" Grim shrugged in a way that meant they had been either killed or bought off. I was going to guess they were killed. "No one needs to know you were there to wipe out their operation."

"We," I corrected.

"Yes, we." He pushed the smoke out the side of his

mouth. "We were in on it, all of us. But we're the only ones who know the truth. I'd like to keep it that way." I agreed but didn't speak. I wanted to know what else he had to say. "In exchange for my name never being associated with yours, I will forever keep your name away from my lips."

"We have no reason to involve you in anything, Grim," Cole said loudly. "We appreciate the information, and we'll be sure to be in contact if we hear anything that might be coming your way." He looked at Trigger. "You as well."

"What was in it for you, Grim?" I couldn't help but ask. "Did Castillo have something on you?"

"No," he tapped the joint and caught the ash with his hand as it fell, "I just hated that son of a bitch." He brushed the ash into a tin can on the table. I noticed Trigger glanced at him but didn't say anything. Instead, the lighter between his fingers spun faster.

"I have to know," I pressed my fist into the table, "that night when I saw you at the bar after Lexi'd been—" I shook my head, not able to finish the sentence. "Why'd you help me?"

Grim shook his head. "It's over now, anyway."

"Yeah, it is," Trigger grunted under his breath to him. "Tell him." Grim eyed Trigger for a moment. I could see the battle that went on behind those silver eyes, but Trigger held his stare, and it was Grim who looked away. He probably hated to explain himself to anyone.

"I was there to flush you out, drive a bullet into your

skull, and take the girl to Brick, who was waiting at the border."

"Fuck." I rubbed my head.

"You asked." Grim shrugged.

"This was before I knew who you were," Trigger clarified.

"I saw she was dead." He gave a quick glance to Keith then back at me. "But you still held her. You could have just dumped her—" He paused and cleared his throat. "Something about it was off. Let's just say I went with my gut." He ran his tongue along his teeth. "Anything else?"

"Okay, I think we're done here." Cole stood, and Keith and I followed his lead.

"Wait," something hit me, "do you know anyone in the FBI?" The corner of his mouth twitched ever so slightly.

"Not really. Why do you ask?" I shook off the fact that he might know Agent Collins, and I wasn't about to name drop anyone to these guys.

"Nothing." GG could be anyone. "All right, I'm done." I looked at Cole.

"Actually, I have a question, Paul." Grim fussed with the lapels of his expensive suit. "I know you loved Talya Cano. So, why'd you break her heart?"

Everything inside me twisted, and a painful heat shot up the back of my throat. It smothered me and made it hard to breathe. I wanted to ask if he knew how she was. The question was on the tip of my tongue and begged to be answered. It would give my heart something—

anything to ease the ache. But my mind kicked in and took over.

"Because she'd never forgive me," I whispered. "Because she'd never belong in my world." He seemed to consider my words. "It's better to be hated than constantly longed for."

"Understood." I was surprised by his answer. He seemed to get it. I inclined my head at him then turned and followed Cole, Mike, and Keith to the car. Once inside behind closed doors, I squeezed my eyes shut and tried to bring my heart back to a normal rhythm. The pain that came with thoughts of Talya was so raw. I hoped I never heard her name again. It was too hard to bear.

Keith's heavy hand fell on my forearm, but he didn't say anything. He didn't have to. He understood.

Cole checked in with his father on the ride back to the airport as we took off smoothly into the evening sky. The sunset and the few pink clouds that gave contrast to it was calming, and my head betrayed me as it brought up an image of Talya. I spent the next while purposefully tucking memories of Talya back in the box where she would have to stay.

"Are you going to miss this?" Keith asked from across the table.

"No," I kept my gaze out the window, "I think a desk job will do my body some good."

"Really?"

"No," I smirked, "but if I can do some damage from inside Shadows, then that's what my third act will be."

"I was thinking, we pretty much took out most of the guys who knew you, so maybe every so often you could join us." I heard the leather chair flex as he turned to look at Cole. "What do you think, Logan?"

"I'd say in time it could be an option."

"In time, yeah." I was unsure but pleased it was even being considered.

"Though Ray is looking to retire from Camp Green, Paul." Cole closed his laptop. "If you're interested in that, I'd gladly give you the position."

"Really?" I nodded a few times. "I'll give it some thought. I had pretty well decided I was done with this life, but I'm rethinking things a bit." I was surprised at how nice Cole's offer sounded. "Give me some time, and I might just take you up on that."

"Shit," Cole drew my attention back to him, "Liv found the doll I was working on to get the girls back." He turned his phone around and showed us a picture of Olivia holding the doll and the recorder from its back with Savi holding a sign saying "nice try."

"I hate to admit it," Keith chuckled, "but she's good."

"This isn't over." Cole tossed his phone with a proud smirk. Whether he'd admit it or not, he loved that it was *his* daughter who figured out what he was up to. One thing I knew for sure, this prank war was far from over.

I looked back out at the sky; it held a mere sliver of light. Life might not have turned out how I imagined it would, but maybe there was something still there for me after all.

TWENTY-ONE

TY

I stirred and yawned and reached out a hand to find her. As I slid my hand over the mattress, it bumped against something cold and hard and furry.

"Rise and shine, sexy!" a horrible little mechanical voice chirped at me. I jerked back with a shout.

What the hell?

I pulled out the note that was under it and glared at Ivy's handwriting.

"Found this in your drawer, thought I better play dirty. — xox can't get rid of me now!"

I laughed out loud and tossed the note on my nightstand. Then I tried to record me whistling but I couldn't crack the passcode. The wives were good! Instead, I placed the little robot monster inside her panty drawer and hoped she would at least jump at the sight of it. As I closed the drawer, something caught my eye and found my nose.

It was time to make things right, and not just with her.

I showered and dressed then, with my boots balanced under my arm, I awkwardly opened the bedroom door only to get nailed by three Nerf bullets. A wicked laugh from Liam rang out as he ran for his life.

"Friggin' little shit," I muttered. I fastened my watch as I made my way down the hall and cursed again as I stepped on a piece of Lego with my sock foot. "Seriously!" I picked it up and hopped to the wall to pull on my boots. As I stood, I found Reagan standing there with a nervous smile.

"That's mine, Uncle T." She gripped her stuffy and held out her little hand for the piece of bright pink Lego.

"I figured." I handed it to her and gave her a pat on the head and ruffled her hair to let her know I wasn't mad at her. "Next time, it's mine." I winked, and she giggled. I headed for the kitchen to find the one I was looking for. He sat at the counter with a bowl of Cheerios.

"I thought we left the war," I grunted at Moore. He scooped up a mouthful of cereal then pulled a bit of Silly String from his hair.

"I say we take 'em out," Moore agreed. "Just play them real dirty and scare the crap out of them once and for all. Dibs on putting Liam on the roof."

"No, that little shit's all mine." We both looked toward the door at the sound of running feet.

"Boys!" Mia called out from the other room. "Are you behaving?"

"Yes, Mom!" they called in unison as something crashed.

"Have kids, they said." Mia snickered at us as she walked in. "It'll be great, they said."

"It's all lies." Sloane grabbed a coffee as she whisked by. "You'd be best to remember that, Ivy. John and I live through all of them."

"Don't worry, Sloane, I plan to watch and learn." Sloane gave a wise nod as she left. "Good morning, sexy." Ivy kissed me on the cheek as she set her laptop down on the counter.

"Is it?" I glared. "I woke to a mechanical monster in my bed."

"I know you, Ty Beckett." She sighed dramatically. "If I didn't get to you first, you'd have been all over it and gotten me."

"You've been spending too much time with Savi." I snagged her by the waist and nuzzled her neck as I inhaled her perfume.

"Damn straight, she is." Savi grinned widely. "Us girls stick together in this house." She leaned forward and winked. "Because we always win." A shiver went up my spine as the girls clicked their coffee mugs.

"I don't even wanna know," Mark raised his hands in the air, "but speaking of winning at tag, who is *it*, anyway?"

We all looked around at each other, and I caught Ivy giving a slitty eyed look at Paul. He attempted to hide behind the paper, but I caught his smirk.

"What?" I asked the two of them.

"I stand corrected." Ivy removed her reading glasses from her hair. "You aren't the dirtiest player of them all. He is."

"Who, me?" Paul couldn't contain his smile.

"I saw you at the wedding. I saw what you did." She paused. "Which means…"

"Morning all." Doc came in, and Ivy suddenly bolted and the rest of us scattered. "Was it something I said?" he called out, and Paul's laughter filled the house.

Later that afternoon, our plan was in place, and when the snow stopped falling, Moore and I announced we had the ultimate game for the kids. They were all for it. We gathered all of them in the center of the yard and brought out the bungee cords.

"What's this called?" Liam crossed his arms as he watched us lay them out in straight lines over the snow.

"Wicked Webs." I held up one of the cords. "It takes, skill, concentration, and coordination to get out."

"Looks easy." He tried to sound cocky, but it wasn't working for him. Though the twins were troublemakers, they were good kids. They, just like their father, liked to have fun at all costs, all the time.

"We'll see, won't we?" I pointed over his head. "Grab your brother and stand over there."

"Come on, Ethan, let's show the old folks how it's done."

"Did he just call us old?" Moore looked up at me.

"Yeah," I grunted, "I think he did. Let's do this." We grabbed the cords and started to web them together, then we ran the cords in and out and around including more kids as we went. For Tabby, Gabriella, and Reagan, we made sure they would find a way to escape quickly, not because they were girls, but because they really needed a win against the twins. My mind went back to their ruined tea party that morning.

"See this," I showed Tabby, careful to be quiet, so her brothers didn't hear me. "When I give the signal to play, just pull it up over your head and you'll be able to get out. Okay? Show the other girls and you'll be free."

"Got it!" She nodded and gave me a thumbs up. She really was a little Mia. Smart and ready to fight.

"Now, this is badass." Brandon came up and grinned at the younger ones all webbed together. "That's cool." I nodded at him and surveyed our masterpiece. "You think you could teach me this, Ty?"

"Sure." I nodded for him to watch over my shoulder. I saw Olivia emerge from the porch and heard her call out to the others to come look.

It took us a few more minutes to rope in the little suckers, and when we were finished, we stood back with Brandon and Olivia and admired our work.

"That's impressive." Olivia laughed. "You do this to the Taliban?"

"No," I chuckled with Moore, "actually, this was something to screw with our bunkmates in training. While they were all tied up, we'd raid their bunks for booze and candy."

"You're quickly becoming my favorite, Uncle T." I grinned at her. I loved how all the guys here were quickly adopted as uncles. "All right, so now what?"

"Now we watch them struggle," I purred as we joined the others on the porch. After about three minutes, I gave Tabby the signal and she played her part well. She freed herself and went straight to work on the other girls.

"That's my girl," Mark called while the boys struggled hard and tried to figure out how she did it.

"Hey, Tabs," Ethan shouted, "how'd you do that?"

"Why should I help you? You ruined our tea party!"

"You serve air, for Pete's sake!"

"Good luck, boys." She stuck her tongue out, and the girls cheered as they ran off.

"Should I be concerned that you tie up children?" Ivy joked, coming up next to me.

"Yes, very." I wrapped my arm around her shoulders. "Do you have a moment? I want to show you something."

"Sure."

"I've got this." Moore waved us off as he rubbed his hands together. We left him to it, and I led her upstairs to the bedroom.

"If this is payback for this morning, I'm willing to take any punishment you deem fit for the crime." She gave me a sexy wink as I motioned for her to step into my room.

"We'll be discussing that one later," I promised her, "but for right now, I wanted to show you this." I brought her into the walk-in closet and rested my hip against the wall as she looked around.

"What am I looking at?" She wasn't getting it. I waited. Then she sucked in a sharp breath, and I knew it had hit her. "Where's your rucksack?"

"Put away." I smiled.

"Really?"

"Really," I repeated as I pulled her to me.

"That's growth, Ty."

"It is." She was right. "It's also my way of showing you I'm here with you. I'm not looking to leave. My place is here, my life is here. It's not me anymore, it's us."

"That means a lot, Ty. Thank you." She smiled and pushed up to give me a kiss. I pulled her in and gave my all to the kiss that sealed my promise to her.

———

After dinner, John built a fire in the firepit, and a few of us gathered around it. Others were off doing their own thing. It was peaceful, but I couldn't settle. I got up and walked down toward the frozen water. As the sun set over the lake, the orange and red colors lit up the fallen snow on the mountaintops. *What was it?* A strange feeling had come over me, and I couldn't shake it. I cleared my mind and took a couple of deep breaths as I tried to understand what my head was trying to tell me.

Then a warmth deep inside of me spread outward as I realized what I saw. It was different. It wasn't summer, and the loons weren't calling, but this was it. This was what I had imagined over the years. It was my dream, my vision, and it had come to be.

Some might have called it a premonition, but I didn't think it was that. I thought it was just a deep longing for something in this life. Something on a subconscious level I didn't realize I wanted. It was life saying you could have this happiness, but you need to work to make it happen. I manifested my own happiness, and along the way I found the love I sought. She was all I needed.

The scent of her fresh perfume came to me, carried by a soft breeze.

"It's beautiful, isn't it?" Ivy whispered. "We're so lucky."

"We really are." I wrapped a hand around her and took in the moment. I felt her shiver and urged her back toward the fire.

Cheers erupted from the house, and Mark raced out onto the deck. "Moore lost at tag!"

"Can I tell you a secret?" Ivy looked up at me with a guilty expression. "The girls and I messed with the scoreboard in the barn. You wanna know who actually lost?"

"Who?"

Her eyes darkened and her expression changed to a huge smile.

"Are you friggin' kidding me?" But just as I went to bolt for the house, she hit my arm and called out the words.

"Suck it, sucker. You lost!"

The End

ACKNOWLEDGMENTS

To my mother, my partner in crime.

To Elizabeth Clark and Jamie Johnson. Thank you for the
spins, the facetime calls, and for always being there
for me.

To my husband and kids for being my constant
cheerleaders.

To my beta and proofer family, Kim Kelchner, Kasey
Griffin, Veronica Nelson, Maggie Savarese, Rachel
Womack, Lyle Womack, Mandy Jones Freeman, Jamie
Johnson, Elizabeth Clark, Tara Marie, Tammy Fox-
Abercromby, and Deborah Lynn Peach. I appreciate you
all so much.

My career-long editor, Lori, thanks for sticking with me
and for always being a constant person I can rely on in
this industry.

Lyle Womack for all your invaluable help on the
Afghanistan research.

Thank you for your service.

My street team, ARC team, my reader group, and my fact-finding group, thanks for providing me a safe place to go to hang out, ask questions, and laugh!

And of course, to my readers. I wouldn't be here if it weren't for all of you.

Thank you.

J.L. Drake, born and raised in Nova Scotia, Canada, later moving to Southern California. Though she loves the weather in Cali, she would sell her left kidney for a good rainstorm. Jodi's love of the seasons back home in Canada definitely appear in her books.

When she's not writing, you can often find her sitting somewhere along the coast of Huntington Beach, reading, or at home curled up on a couch with her two children and husband, binge watching a good movie.

AUTHORJLDRAKE.COM

FOLLOW ME ON SOCIAL MEDIA

facebook.com/JLDrakeauthor

x.com/jodildrake_j

instagram.com/j.l.drake

tiktok.com/@authorjldrake

bookbub.com/profile/j-l-drake

<u>**BROKEN TRILOGY**</u>

Broken

Shattered

Mended

<u>**BLACKSTONE SERIES**</u>

Honor

Escape

Freedom

Courage

<u>**DEVIL'S REACH TRILOGY**</u>

Trigger

Demons

Unleashed

<u>**QUIET MAFIA SERIES**</u>

Quiet Wealth

Quiet Secrets

Quiet Power

Quiet Empire

<u>**DARK WATER SERIES**</u>

Shadows

Whiskey

Alpha

Tango

HAVOC OF SINS

Grim

Havoc

Sins

DARKNESS SERIES

Darkness Lurks

Darkness Follows

Darkness Falls

STANDALONE BOOKS

Behind My Words

Christmas At The Cabin

Omerta

For the suggested reading order, please scan the QR code:

www.ingramcontent.com/pod-product-compliance
Lightning Source LLC
Chambersburg PA
CBHW031514010826
48973CB00013B/1298